Blood Line: ~~Believe~~

"This debut thriller finds an entire family on the run from those who would sell bleeding-edge technology to the highest bidder. Ron and Valerie feel like true partners and parents, and Leecy is a believable teen ("...my life is on that phone!"). Clever scenes also have Ron playing with his legend as a one-man Native American kill squad who only used a knife and a tomahawk. Valerie's past as a Mossad assassin is more explicitly referenced; readers learn that she helped get Boris Yeltsin elected.

Davis sets a solid foundation for more adventures. Sharply written, starring characters readers will be happy to meet again." — *Kirkus Reviews*

"In this fast-paced new thriller, *Blood Line*, international enemies want a lovable family with a heroic past, dead, right now! Their teenage daughter knows nothing of her parents' work as professional spies, but quickly finds herself fleeing the comfort and safety of her world on an explosive flight for survival, with new dangers at every turn. She begins to learn the truth about her parents and joins them in discovering which among their international enemies wants them dead.

Blood Line is compelling, with accelerating pace, surprising twists and a spectacular ending—readers will be eager for the sequel, coming soon!" —*Alan Rinzler, Consulting Editor*

BLOOD LINE

A GRANGER SPY NOVEL

JOHN J. DAVIS

Be sure to visit www.johnjdavis.com for insider information, character bio's and author updates. Subscribe to *The Granger Report* for exclusive news and events.

Coming Spring 2015:

> BLOODY TRUTH
> A Granger Spy Novel

BLOOD LINE

A Granger Spy Novel

JOHN J. DAVIS

SIMON & WINTER INC. USA
www.simonandwinter.com

Copyright © 2014 by John J. Davis
All rights reserved, including the right to reproduce this book or portions thereof in any form whatsoever.

Library of Congress Control Number: 2014909579

For more information or to book an event or interview, contact Simon & Winter, Inc. at info@simonandwinter.com or visit our website at www.simonandwinter.com.

Printed in the United States of America

First Printing, 2014
ISBN 978-0-9903144-1-7
www.johnjdavis.com

ACKNOWLEDGEMENTS

Rebekah, you make all things seem possible.
Alan, you saw possibility and helped make it reality.
Thank you, Dr. Valencia.

CHAPTER
ONE

The sudden explosion of breaking glass and splintering wood reverberated inside the house like a clap of thunder. I was awake instantly, and the rush of adrenaline coursing through my veins propelled me out of the bed and into action.

"Valerie!" I yelled at my wife, who was already leaping out of the other side of the bed. "That should've set off the alarm."

She was rounding the end of our bed just as I flipped on the overhead lights and opened the door of our room. There was someone in the hallway, but the beam from a high-powered LED flashlight blinded my eyes before I could look away.

I heard a voice.

"Back the fuck up! Keep your hands where I can see them."

I felt the round end of a small pistol barrel poke me in the chest before I could blink my eyes and begin to see the revolver in one hand, the flashlight in the other.

"Both of you back up, hands in the air, and stay right where you are."

I raised my hands and backed up until I bumped against my bedside table. Then the guy swung the pistol and hit me in the face hard enough to get my attention, but not enough to hurt me.

He aimed his gun at Valerie again. "Not another step."

My vision had recovered, so I could see the intruder was wearing a black ski mask, t-shirt, jeans and boots. He was about five feet seven inches, and thin, about 160 pounds, so I had a distinct size advantage, being six feet and 200 pounds. But he had the gun, a revolver of some kind. That was actually another plus for me since the hammer wasn't cocked. Getting it ready to fire would take all the time I needed.

He started moving the gun in my direction again when I heard the scream.

"Daddy!"

It was Leecy.

"Valerie, there must be another one of them."

I grabbed the man's left wrist with such force the flashlight dropped to the floor and spun away. I knocked aside his right wrist with my left hand as he cocked the gun and fired, sending a bullet into the wall over my left shoulder. Letting go of his left wrist, I turned into him with my back, grabbed his weapon with both hands, and ripped it from his grip. I made a back left-handed throw of the gun to Valerie, who was leaping toward the door to Leecy's bedroom. She caught the gun in the air as I landed a back left elbow to the intruder's head, followed by a crushing right cross to his jaw, knocking him unconscious. I left the intruder falling to the floor and raced down the hall.

"Stop right there, lady," I heard.

"Let her go," she replied, very calmly and softly, "and I won't kill you."

I reached the end of the hall just as two shots slammed into the front door behind Valerie. I ducked back inside the cover of the hallway, but Valerie didn't move and she didn't return fire.

"Put the gun down and send my partner out here right now," I heard the man say, "or this will get messy."

I walked into the foyer with my hands raised in a sign of submission, but now he had two potential problems, and they weren't in the same place.

"Your partner is incapacitated," Val continued quietly, "and if you don't drop your weapon, you'll be dead."

"I'll shoot her if you don't put your hands up and send your man to bring my partner to me right now," he countered.

Streams of moonlight filtered through the dark room from the shattered doors the two men had broken through, but I could see the man hiding behind Leecy holding a gun to her head.

"Last chance to leave here alive."

He'd backed up as far as he could go, pulling Leecy with him to make his escape.

Valerie fired.

The bullet struck him in the center of his forehead, making a small black hole and propelling him up and back. The look on his face was that of a man realizing his mistake.

Leecy raced away from the dead man as Val dropped the weapon and stood next to me. The entire incident was over in minutes, but it didn't feel that way to me. I was drained. I was sweating profusely and my hands were shaking. Maybe it was my age; at forty-six, I wasn't as young a man as when I started in this business, even though I didn't think of myself as an old man. But that wasn't all of it. Now that I had a wife and daughter, I had something to lose.

I hugged Val and Leecy. I held my wife and felt her calming presence wash over me. As we both embraced our child, I thanked whatever gods there might be that my two girls were safe.

"What the heck just happened?" Leecy asked from the safety of the hug we had her sandwiched in.

"Home invasion," Valerie answered. "We need to call Lester and get him out here."

"I'll phone the station from the bedroom," I said, "and check on the guy back there while I'm at it."

"Yeah, okay, so you say it's a home invasion," Leecy went on, "but don't most invaders steal your stuff and not try to kidnap you?"

I was back in our bedroom, stepping over the limp body of the first guy, but could still hear Leecy's voice.

"And Mom....you...uh...just killed someone."

"I know, dear, but..."

"Dead."

"It was a lucky shot."

"Lucky shot?" Leecy wasn't satisfied, obviously. "That's not my point."

I was so relieved we were all okay that it hadn't occurred to me that Leecy's questions would have to be answered. And not just to her satisfaction: we'd have to answer similar questions by the police, and if this incident were classified as more than just a home invasion, we'd be in danger of generating a lot of unwanted attention.

I dialed our local police station and was relieved to hear the woman's voice on the other end.

"Elizabeth. This is Ron Granger."

"Hi, Ron. Why are you calling the police station at five minutes after four in the morning? Is everyone all right?"

Elizabeth Williams was the pregnant wife of Park City, Georgia's soon-to-be Chief of Police and current Captain, Lester Williams. Lester had been performing the job of Chief for the past two years. Everyone felt the current Chief's retirement was imminent this time, especially Elizabeth who ran the front desk and just about everything else at the station.

It was Val who first met Elizabeth and Lester when they both were working grunt jobs at her brothers' family business, INESCO. She'd encouraged them to go to the police academy in Atlanta and get the better jobs they now had on the local police force.

"Yes, we're all fine. We just had a little break-in here at the house and need Lester or whomever is on duty to come out and take a look," I said. "We've got one dead intruder and one that needs medical attention."

"Dead intruder? My goodness!" She said. "Sounds like those folks picked the wrong house to break into this morning. Are you sure everybody is okay?" She didn't wait for my response. "I'm going to tell the medics to take a look at all of you while they're there."

I thought about protesting but knew it would be useless, so I just said, "Thank you, Elizabeth," and added, "I hope you are feeling better. I know from talking with Lester last week the past few months have been difficult for you."

"I'm feeling just fine, thank you. Lester is on his way. I've got to call the coroner and the paramedics. Now hang up, Ron."

Elizabeth was a take-charge lady, no doubt about it.

I hung up the phone and laughed at my instinctive southern desire to be polite at a time like this. Val and Leecy were coming toward me down the hall.

"Get dressed, kiddo, and meet me in the kitchen."

"Okay, Dad. Hey Mom, I'm not finished with you."

I pulled off the unconscious man's belt and secured his arms behind his back to the foot of the four-post bed and then joined Val where she was in the bathroom stripping off her nightshirt and pulling on her jeans.

"Leecy has a million questions, and I don't have the answers for her."

"You've got the answers," I said. "You just don't want to tell her what they are, and neither do I, not yet. For one thing, we have to find out who these guys are and what they really wanted here."

"It could be something we did five or ten years ago that's finally catching up with us..."

"Right...for revenge, retaliation..." I agreed. "A lot of our enemies would definitely like to hurt us, but I'm betting they still don't know for sure who we really are. All they could possibly have is maybe our code names, or whispers, rumors, and vague, mixed-up descriptions that don't even match how we really look."

"And Ron," Val went on, "if our old enemies did know who and where we were, they'd come in greater numbers, more heavily armed and better prepared."

We stood silent for a moment, looking at each other.

"We've been out of action for many years now," I finally said, with a smile. "This could be exactly what it seems to be – just a couple of punks who broke into the wrong house."

"I doubt it," Val said. "Someone could even be thinking they could leverage taking Leecy to get us to work for them."

"What a terrible thought. Don't even go there."

"We have to consider everything."

"I don't know about that," I tried to reassure her, "but we've definitely reached the point where we have to tell our daughter a bit more about what we've done for a living."

"What if Lester and his boys don't treat this like a break-in, but handle it like an attempted kidnapping?" Val asked. "The FBI will roll into town with their usual resources, and they have the clearance to find out whatever they want to know."

"Well, honey," I pulled her towards me for a kind of sideways hug, awkward in the small space of the bathroom, "we've put off this conversation long enough. Leecy's not a little girl anymore."

"Don't say that, Ron," Val protested. "She's still my baby..."

"And," I continued, "maybe the one positive thing out of tonight's events is that we have to tell her now."

"What would my Grandma Leona do?"

"She'd say you need to tell Leecy about our past and your family's history the way she told you about her past and the legacy she created. I promise," I said, and I pulled her to me again and hugged her tight.

"You may be right, Ron, but it's not something you can do for me."

"I know."

"So let me figure out how to do it myself."

"Agreed."

I let her go and opened the bathroom door. The sound of approaching sirens hurried me along.

"The police are almost here everybody."

I turned toward the front door when I heard Leecy's voice coming from in front of me and not behind as I had expected. "Coffee's ready," she announced.

"I'm on my way," I said. Maybe we worried too much. Leecy really was a young woman now and she deserved to be treated like one.

The sirens got a lot closer, and I heard several cars entering our driveway. Red and blue police cruiser strobe lights danced across our front windows with the orange and red lights of the ambulance.

"I'm going outside to talk to Lester. You and mom stay in the house. Stay in the kitchen, okay?" I heard her say, "Okay, Dad," as I opened the front door and walked outside.

Captain Lester Williams climbed out of his patrol car, greeting me. "Hey, Ron; sorry to be here under these circumstances. You all okay?"

"Yes, we're just fine, all things considered." I shook his hand.

I could see other officers working at the trunks of their cruisers, and the paramedics were offloading a stretcher. The coroner wagon was just arriving.

"Tell me what happened."

I noticed one officer had a handful of clear plastic evidence bags, and another was carrying an empty cardboard box marked "Evidence, Granger House, Friday, June 21st, 2013."

"This won't be the official statement since that will come later; just give me the headlines," Lester said before I could start telling him what happened.

I told a sanitized version, with as few details as possible.

"These two robbers broke in and tried to rip us off. Real lunk-heads. It all happened so fast I really can't remember, but I got the upper hand on one, and Valerie was able to shoot the other. A miracle shot really. It's amazing we weren't hurt."

"What?" Lester interrupted.

"No joke. Kind of like the crazy shot that killed Kennedy. And when that happened I was able to jump on the other guy and tie him up. He's still unconscious inside, last I saw him."

"Okay...." Lester stood still without saying anything for a while.

"All right; good enough for now. Where are Leecy and Valerie?"

"Inside in the kitchen. Do you want to see them?"

"Not right now. I need to have my guys work the scene. We need to collect evidence, take pictures, remove the body, and get the other guy to the hospital in case he sustained any injuries when you jumped on him."

"Right."

"I can tell you right now, Ron, it seems to me this incident falls under the protections afforded a homeowner by Georgia's Castle Law, and that you've conducted yourselves in accordance with the law."

"Thanks for the reassurance, Lester. Of course, Val and

Leecy are real shook up about this."

"Let's go inside, then."

Lester and I started into the living room and made our way to the kitchen, where Leecy was huddled close to her mother. I could see the adrenaline was wearing off and she was beginning to feel the full weight of what happened to her. Lester noticed, too.

"Larry, Murphy," he said as he keyed his radio, "can you guys check out the Grangers while I work the crime scene?"

Two men pushed a stretcher into the room. One of them lifted a large orange medical kit off of the stretcher and placed it on the kitchen floor.

"I'm Larry," the tall, thin, blonde paramedic said.

"And I'm Murphy," the shorter, more muscular, black haired paramedic said.

"Looks like the young lady is up first," Larry said as he opened his medical kit, removing a blood pressure cuff and stethoscope. I watched and listened as he and Murphy checked Leecy's vitals.

"High, but within normal range, given the circumstances."

Lester came back into the room, brow furrowed. "Murphy, I need you to bring your stuff. The guy back in the bedroom is coming around. What did you hit him with, Ron, a baseball bat? I thought you said you jumped on the guy."

"Did you find one?" I regretted the words as they were coming out of my mouth and immediately said, "I'm sorry. I'm just a little rattled. No, I didn't hit him with anything like that. I may have gotten a punch or two in during the struggle. I don't know. It all happened so fast."

Lester disappeared back into the bedroom with Murphy in tow. Meanwhile, Larry confirmed what I'd known when he said, "You'll be fine, Miss. All your vitals are good. I'd recommend having something to eat and drink. Who's next?"

"I'm fine," Val said, "and I'm sure my husband is, too. Go do your job so we can all go back to bed."

Larry hesitated briefly. I could see he was thinking of challenging Valerie, but he decided not to. He retrieved his case and without another word, turned and walked away to find his partner. I followed him at a distance. Meanwhile, the coroner and his assistant were maneuvering the gurney with the body bag through the door and out to the driveway. In another moment, Murphy came butt first down the hallway, lifting the stretcher out of the bedroom with Larry at the head of the stretcher.

I could see the intruder's neck was wrapped in a brace and his body strapped to the stretcher. I stared into the open eyes of the now semi-conscious and unmasked man. He looked familiar. He tried to look away from me but couldn't turn his head.

"Valerie! Come take a look at this guy. I think I know him."

She got a good look at him as the two men carried him out of the house. The door closed and we were alone.

"I recognize him too, Ron," she said. "I think he works at INESCO. I'd have to check the personnel records, but I'm almost 100% certain I've seen him around the offices."

Lester came back through the room carrying a box filled with the plastic bags I'd seen earlier, which I assumed now contained crime scene evidence.

"Ron, Val, Leecy...I'm releasing the house as a crime scene and we're out of here. As I said before, this is clearly a case of home invasion and falls under the protections offered homeowners by the Castle Law. I'll need you all to come to the station later today to complete some paperwork. How does 1:00 p.m. work for you all?"

"We'll see you then, Lester, and thanks for your kindness," Valerie said.

Lester nodded at me and smiled. "You broke the guy's jaw. Murphy thinks you may have also fractured his neck at the C1 vertebrae. He said the guy's injuries are consistent with those of someone being in a minor car accident. If you don't mind me asking again, Ron, how the heck did you inflict so much damage on the poor sap?"

Valerie answered for me. "With his bare hands, Lester. See you at one." Lester walked out, and she locked the door behind him.

Just as we were starting to relax, the phone rang.

"Darn. I knew it would be only a short time before she called," Valerie said as she ran down the hall to pick up the kitchen receiver. I was right behind her. "Hi, Mom."

"Hello, Valerie." I could hear Catherine clearly, and I was still ten feet away. "When were you going to tell us? I had to hear about the police at your house from your neighbor, Mrs. Weatherington. You couldn't call your mother? And all of this bad stuff happening on the day before my baby's birthday! Tell me, what in Heaven's name is going on over there?"

I smiled at my wife and left the room in search of garbage bags and cleaning solution. I knew we had some quaternary ammonia in the garage that would take care of disinfecting the blood. I took my time finding the tools and other items, because I didn't want to get involved with Ma and Pa Simon right now.

When I came back into the kitchen about five minutes

later, Val was still on the phone, sputtering, trying to find the right words.

"I know, Mom.... no, Leecy is fine..." She looked at me as if to say, *help*, but I shook my head and mouthed *they're your parents, not mine.*

She fixed me with that look she gives me when she's pretending to be mad. I carefully made my way down the steps, avoiding the blood splatter and the mess that came with it, and put my hand out for the phone.

"Catherine, whoa, Catherine, no it's me, it's Ron. Catherine? Okay, just slow down a bit and listen to me. It's business as usual. Business, you know?" I couldn't say more on the phone, since there was always the danger of a tap. "I'm going to hang up now, and we'll come see you as soon as we can. Okay. Love you. Bye." I ended the call and tossed the portable phone on the couch, and turned to find Val staring at me.

"She's your kryptonite. Accept the fact that she is the one person in the known universe you cannot handle and let it go. There's no competition."

"Shut up and get to work," she said. "This place is a mess. Did you bring the quat?"

"It's on the deck along with everything else we need."

"First, I'll spray this room down with the ammonia and then we'll go check the bedroom. This stuff will kill any harmful pathogens in the guy's blood," she said, like I'd never heard that before.

Valerie and I tackled cleaning the den together. Time seemed to stand still when I was with Valerie. She had a way of making even the most mundane task enjoyable. And before I knew it, we were moving onto the sunroom and the broken French doors. The glass shards and splinters of wood were picked up and bagged, and the blue tarp halfway up when the phone started ringing again.

"You get it. I don't want to talk to my mother again."

I answered the phone on the third ring, saying, "Catherine, I promise we're coming over as soon as we can."

"This isn't Catherine; it's Lester, and I'm going to need all three of you to come to the station as soon as possible."

"What? Are you serious, Lester? What's the rush? I thought you didn't need us till one o'clock."

"Things have changed. Based on the evidence we collected, we had no choice but to call the FBI. Agents from the Atlanta field office have already arrived and started reviewing the evidence. They want to interview the guy you knocked out, but his jaw is wired shut and the doctors say it'll be some time before he is in any condition to communicate. Apparently he is under pretty heavy sedation from the surgery on his fractured neck vertebra. But the FBI agents want to talk to you three ASAP."

I looked at Valerie, who was coming down the stairs from the sunroom, and then at the clock on the mantle to her left and realized it was after 9:00 a.m. I was shocked at how much time had passed since we started cleaning the house.

"Lester, we can be there by 10:00 a.m. That's as soon as we can do it, unless you want us showing up there dirty and sweaty. We've been cleaning the house since you and the other officers left here three hours ago."

"Okay, I'll let them know."

"Lester?" I asked and then said, "Can you tell me what's changed? What's happening?"

There was a long pause before he spoke.

"The evidence we collected points to something more than

just a home invasion, and we were obligated to call in the FBI. That's really all I can say over the phone. But Agent Porter of the FBI will brief you and your family when you guys get here. Look, I've been overtime for the past sixteen hours, so I'm going off shift. Sorry, Ron, but I'll talk to you later."

And he just hung up the phone. I looked at Valerie and said, "Lester says he had to call in the FBI based on the evidence he collected."

"Just being a good cop."

"Right. Let's wrap up this cleaning. I want to shower and eat before we go."

"Leecy," she yelled as she walked down the hall. "Take a shower and get dressed. We have to go to the police station now instead of later."

"How come, Mom?"

"Don't ask; just meet us in the kitchen. There's something I need to tell you."

I stood there a moment thinking about what was happening. Valerie was facing her fears. She was telling our daughter, pulling the Band-Aid off a situation we'd been avoiding for too long, and that was a good thing for both of us. Now that they were drilling into these two kids breaking in, I couldn't stop the FBI from finding out I work for the CIA. Infrequently nowadays, but still employed nonetheless. I just hoped they didn't find out what I did at the CIA before I went quiet five years ago. But that was an irrational fear. No one at the FBI had the clearance level required to access mission-specific details in my file. My secrets were safe, just as Valerie's secrets were safe.

But hers were safe for other reasons.

I walked back into the kitchen, smelling Valerie's famous apple cider pancakes.

"The house is buttoned up for now. We'll have to order a new French door, and I put the rug from the bedroom and trash bags outside on the deck," I said, and then seeing Leecy sitting at the table, I continued, "Good morning, Sunshine. Are you feeling better?"

"Morning, Dad," Leecy said between bites of pancakes. "Yes, I'm feeling fine, but I think I could sleep all day."

"You can do that when we get back," Valerie said, "but right now I want you to eat up and take a quick shower, because we need to leave here in forty minutes."

"Leecy," I said, "we have to go to the police station to talk to the FBI about the evidence the cops found this morning. And there is a better than fair chance the FBI will bring up something about me you don't know yet."

Leecy stood up and carried her empty plate and water glass to the sink. "I know. Mom already told me."

"Really?" That was a surprise. "What did she tell you?"

"Just that you used your job at INESCO as a cover while working for the CIA. Oh, and this weekend the three of us would talk about it in more detail." Then she stopped and turned around, asking, "Is your time with the CIA the reason why you were able to knock that guy out?"

I thought a bit before I answered. "Sort of. But let's get through this interview with the FBI, and I'll answer that question more fully, okay?" I watched as Leecy nodded her answer in my direction. I thought I could see the wheels turning in her mind as she walked across the den toward the hallway and her bathroom.

I spoke with my back to Valerie. "Thanks dear and here I was thinking how proud I was that you'd told her about us both. Couldn't pull the trigger on your own story?"

"Don't be mad at me," she said, pausing for a moment and then continuing. "I told you I wanted to handle it my way."

"Okay. Come on, leave the dishes for later and let's go shower."

I reached out my hand for hers, and as she took hold of it, I was reminded of all that mattered to me.

CHAPTER
TWO

It was 10:15 a.m. by the time we arrived at the police station in downtown Park City, Georgia. Park City is a small town on the southern edge of the big city of Atlanta. Close enough to be a forty-five minute drive to downtown Atlanta, and far enough away not to have lost our small town charm. Though our downtown has its share of vacant buildings, it's not a ghost town yet.

I pulled the Jeep into the police station parking lot in front of the entry doors and next to a black SUV. I assumed it was the FBI's Suburban, which was confirmed by one glance at the front-end government tags. We were hurrying through the front door of the station when I heard an old familiar voice.

"It's about time you three showed up. Come on inside; these guys are waiting." I turned to see the Police Chief, Scott Rawlings.

Chief Rawlings was as round as he was tall. He was better suited for the role of Santa Claus - which he played every year in the Christmas parade - than that of Police Chief.

"Come on, Grangers," he called out. "Let's get this over with and get these Federals out of my town."

"Morning, Chief," Valerie said. "How are you today?"

"Morning, Valerie. Thank you for asking, but I'm not too good with all that happened at your place, and now the FBI.

I like it when things are quiet and peaceful like. This kind of stuff upsets my ulcers."

"Yeah," I said, "actual police work can do that."

"You got that right," the Chief said, and I heard Leecy giggle and then cover her laughing.

"Sorry for being late. I hope we didn't upset anyone?"

"No, I don't think anyone is upset young lady, but let's not keep them waiting any longer. Follow me."

"Is Lester gone already?"

"Shift changed at ten o'clock. Officers Brady and Carter are on patrol, and Johnson is manning the dispatcher's desk," Chief Rawlings answered as we passed the dispatcher's station, but I didn't see anyone at the desk.

The station was small and old. The water-stained ceiling, halogen lighting, three old computers, sign for the unisex bathroom, and terrazzo flooring screamed 1974, and were only marginally worse than the built-in dispatcher's desk that greeted us upon entering. Along the back wall was a row of three jail cells. Two had cots, and one only had a bench at its center. The entire office space couldn't have been more than eighty feet front to back, and the same side-to-side.

The Chief led us toward the last door on the left, the one closest to the jail cells. I saw Officer Johnson coming out of the very door we were walking toward. He saw the four of us approaching and hurried to meet us.

"Just in time; those three guys are getting antsy."

The Chief had no response, but ushered us inside, saying, "Here are the Grangers. I'll be in my office if you need me," and closed the door, not waiting for a response.

Valerie, Leecy, and I were left facing a folding table and three FBI agents seated on the opposite side. The agent seated in the middle was an African American who began speaking immediately.

"I'm Agent John Porter of the FBI. Please have a seat, and we'll get started." He indicated three metal folding chairs directly in front of us. We sat down without further ceremony.

"Thank you. To my right is Agent Travis Smith and to my left is Agent Briggs Smith. Thank you for coming in this morning. I know you all have already had quite the day and it's early yet. Let me say, this is an informal meeting, and not to be considered an interrogation. Honestly, I'm hoping you all can help me," Agent Porter said, smiling a tight-lipped smile that could only be practiced. Recognizing that smile for what it was, what he said seemed to be *fuck you, Grangers*. I was sure Val was having the same internal reaction.

"Now, first and for the record, today is Friday, June 21st, 2013, and the time is," he paused and checked the watch on his left wrist before he said, "the time is now 10:22 a.m."

I wondered where the record was being kept, because no one in the room was writing anything down. Then I saw the three cell phones - one in front of each of the FBI men. Innocuous, but obviously how we were being recorded.

Two of the three men, the ones with the last name of Smith, were young and lean. Agent Porter was softer at the edges, more like a banking executive than an operator like the Smith boys. They didn't look like analysts or office personnel of any kind.

I was beginning to see red flags everywhere.

Red flag number one: they were hard. I'm not talking about

gym hard from weight lifting, but the kind of hardness a man develops by being in battle – traditional or clandestine. If I had to guess, I'd peg them as Rangers or Navy Seals. Not too tall, but plenty lean.

Red flag number two: wrong hair. FBI agents have a dress code, but it doesn't include close-cropped hairstyles. Porter, being black, had a short curly afro, but the Smith boys' hair were old-fashioned crew cuts, extra short, almost a shaved head. Even if they were fresh from the service, most ex-military men let their hair grow. There was no sign of fresh growth, but there were signs of fresh haircuts.

Red flag number three: clothes that didn't fit properly. It was a mistake a sophisticated operator wouldn't have made. Agent Porter was nattily attired in a custom-fitted suit. His wingmen looked as if their suits had been plucked off the rack at J.C. Penney that morning. This level of preparation made me worry they were more like chained attack dogs than FBI agents.

Red flag number four: footwear. These Smith guys were wearing ankle boots with their ill-fitting suits. Seated next to a man wearing Prada loafers and a custom-fitted suit; I wasn't buying it.

Red flag number five: the Smith boys hadn't spoken yet. Agent Porter was doing all the talking. The longer they both went without speaking, the more I doubted they were actually who they said they were.

I knew Valerie was thinking the same thing I was thinking, because as she crossed her right leg over her left, she placed her right hand on her right thigh and extended all five fingers, which was our private signal for five red flags. And I was sure they were the same ones that I was thinking about.

To hide my smile I asked, "So, why are we here?"

"Well, like I said, I'm hoping you all can help me. See, the evidence in this case is interesting. It's the evidence collected at your home earlier this morning that brought us here to your town, and you three to the police station." He stopped talking and turned his attention to the brown file on the desk in front of him, and the room fell silent.

I sat there waiting for him to continue. I looked at Val and then at the other two agents. The Smiths were making themselves busy reading similar brown files.

Valerie said, "So, are you going to share the information or are we just going to sit here and watch you guys read?"

Porter continued reading without responding to Valerie's comment, and then said without looking up, "Mr. Granger, is there any reason you or your wife can think of that would precipitate the kidnapping of your daughter?"

"I thought this was about the evidence," I said, "but I'll answer your question. No, I cannot think of a reason."

"I can't think of one either," Valerie said, playing it straight.

Agent Porter snapped the file closed. He looked up from the desk, fixing us both with his deep-set dark eyes and smiling that fake smile again.

"Interesting. Given your background, Ron, can I call you Ron?" He didn't wait for an answer from me; he just plowed ahead. "I would think you might have a plethora of reasons at your disposal. And given your family business, Mrs. Granger," he turned his attention to Val and continued, "INESCO has been operating under government contracts since the late 1960s. I would think you, too, might have any number of reasons why your daughter might be the target of kidnappers."

He stopped talking for a moment. He laced his fingers together in front of him on top of the brown file folder and leaned forward on his forearms before he continued.

"Neither of you can think of any reason why Leecy, your sixteen-year-old daughter – and, I understand, soon to be a freshman at Yale; that's impressive – might be kidnapped. I find that more interesting than the so-called evidence we were called here to examine."

Agent Porter pushed himself away from the table and stood. As he did, Agent Travis Smith placed the cardboard file box removed from our house earlier on the desk.

Agent Porter pushed his chair under the desk and leaned against the wall behind him in a dismal effort of nonchalance.

"Here's the evidence we have so far," he said, and as he spoke, Agent Travis removed each item. "One smartphone, one pry bar, one piece of white paper with diagram, two .38 caliber revolvers with serial numbers filed off. That's your evidence Grangers, except the smartphone is a smartphone in appearance only and the diagram leads whoever is in possession of it directly to the bedroom of your daughter. We'll know more when we return the evidence to the crime lab in Atlanta, but the smartphone only performs one function as far as we can tell." He paused for effect and shifted his position against the wall before continuing.

"It deactivates alarm systems. Once the device is turned on, it searches for any alarm in its immediate vicinity. Its search radius is no more than forty feet. Once the device locks onto an alarm system, the user only has to press the deactivate button and the job is done. If not for this one piece of evidence,

I could dismiss all the others as just your standard home invasion tools and an attempted burglary gone wrong. The intruders just got the wrong room kind of thing." He stopped and retook his seat as the ever-ready Agent Travis replaced the evidence and removed the box from the table before Porter continued.

"Our preliminary research on all things, Granger, indicates the purchase of a home safe in 2009. I'll assume that the said safe is located in a room adjacent to your daughter's?"

"Yes it is," Val said, "but how do you know that?"

Porter continued to ignore her.

"If the crime was a home invasion and not an attempted kidnapping, then there must be something the two men were after. They just got bad information regarding the location of the safe. Simple, really. But if this is an attempt to kidnap your daughter, and I'm not convinced it is, there has to be a reason for that also." Agent Porter stared at each of us as though the weight of his statement would cause us to divulge the reason, but instead of spilling the beans as he expected, we just returned his stare.

"Okay," he said, "then let's look for a reason." He reopened the file he'd been reading when we entered the room.

"Ron Granger, no middle name or initial. Born May 1st, 1967, in Greenville, South Carolina. Ron, you were raised by your Irish grandfather and your grandfather's half-brother. The file reads that your great uncle was a full-blooded Apache Indian. Were you raised by these two men?"

"I was," I said.

"Was your great uncle an Apache Indian?"

"No, he was not."

"Really? The government got something wrong? That's been known to happen. I'll come back to that later. Let's see, the file also states that Ron Granger graduated from Valdosta High School in Valdosta, Georgia, in 1985, and enlisted in the Army under the GI bill," he paused, looking at me, and then said, "If I run across any other inaccuracies, please stop me so I can correct the file, okay?"

I said nothing.

"You were honorably discharged from the service at the rank of Sergeant in 1990. I'm reading from your Army file now," he offered. "I'm paraphrasing now. The US Army says that you were of unlimited potential. You performed off the charts on all physical and mental tests, and looking at you now, I can see that even at forty-six years old, you are in excellent physical condition. When you were discharged, your height and weight were listed at six feet and 200 pounds. I can see that hasn't changed much. A little gray in those sandy blonde locks of yours, and the green eyes to match. Yes, I'd say you're pretty much the same as your Army file described you upon discharge."

He turned a couple of pages in the file and began reading. "You enrolled at the University of Georgia and completed both your undergrad and graduate degree in Business by the Fall of 1996, at which time one of your former Army Commanding Officers – a Nicholas Hyder – recommended you for employment at the CIA. Tell me about your time with the CIA, Ron. Let's talk about the years between 1996 and 2003. What did you do before you went to work for the family business at INESCO?"

It was a bit unsettling to have my life laid out in front of me like that, just facts, devoid of all nuance and emotion. I looked from my wife to my daughter, and noticed both had downcast eyes. Valerie was looking at the floor in hopes her life wouldn't be laid bare in front of our daughter as mine had. Leecy was also looking at the floor, but the microprocessor that was her brain was working at the speed of light. I was hoping she wasn't mad at me for keeping secrets from her.

"You seem to have all the answers; why don't you tell me?" I said.

Porter closed my file and folded his hands together on top of it like a fourth grader when his test was completed. "First, tell me about your Great Uncle John. Is that right? I mean that's his name, right? The Indian?"

"He has nothing to do with the reason you're here."

"Oh, I know. I'm just curious. It's not every day I read a file of a man of half Irish, half Native American descent."

"There's nothing to tell that you can't read for yourself. My grandfather was Irish. My uncle was a full-blooded American Indian. They shared a father. That's it."

"Oh, come on, Ron. Where's the harm in telling me what tribe your uncle came from?"

There was no harm in telling him; I just didn't like nosey people. I thought about how the information could be used against me and decided it was okay to share.

"Great Uncle John wasn't Apache; he was Comanche."

"Thank you. I'll bet you have some great stories from your childhood. Must have been interesting being raised by half brothers that were so different from each other. That brings me to my next question: what happened to your parents?"

I was prepared for that question. I'd been asked that by

better interrogators than Agent Porter and had never revealed anything about my parents to anyone other than my wife. I wasn't about to answer Agent Porter's question, and judging from the look on his face, he knew it.

"No comment."

He continued by changing the subject. "Your time with the CIA is classified till 2035. If we want to figure out why an attempt was made to kidnap Leecy, I'm going to need you to share that classified information."

"As you well know, or should, I can't break the seal of confidentiality without fear of imprisonment. I'm allowed to say that I don't think anything I may or may not have been involved with between the years of 1996 and 2003 has anything to do with what happened at our home. You can always get on the phone and call someone at Langley with the proper clearance level to read the classified file for you," I said, and then added, "but the FBI has no clearance at Langley, so that won't work either. Sorry, I guess you'll just have to take my word for it."

"Since 2003, you've been part of your wife's family company. So, you two work together. What do you do at INESCO, Ron?"

"You already know from my file; it's sales."

"Come on now, Ron; you're being modest. You're an executive with the company, isn't that right?"

"A fancy title signifying nothing. I sell the products IN-ESCO makes in the rubber division."

Agent Porter smiled and then moved on by turning his attention elsewhere.

"Valerie Cathleen Granger, born June 22nd, 1969, right here in Park City, Georgia." He glanced at his watch before continuing and then smiled that smile again.

"Let me be the first to wish you an early happy forty-fifth birthday." He didn't stop for a reply; he just kept reading. "I see from your Georgia driver's license that you're listed as five feet, seven inches, with brown hair and brown eyes, and you weigh 127 pounds." He paused to verify the information. "You graduated from the local high school here in Park City in 1985. You went on to complete both your undergraduate degree from Yale and Masters Degree in Business from Wharton in four years." He paused as if this was his first time reading that sentence. "Like mother like daughter, academically and in almost every other way. Is Wharton in your future too?" he asked, looking at Leecy, but she didn't answer.

He continued. "I just have to say wow. I see where you get your brains, young lady. You graduated high school at sixteen, just like Mom, and now you're on your way to Yale, just like your mother. That's an impressive academic record, and it looks like you're well on your way to filling Mom's shoes." He turned back to Valerie. "You came back to Park City after you finished your education. You went to work for the family business, and by all accounts saved the then-struggling INESCO from financial ruin. You spearheaded the company's resurgence as a government-funded research giant while branching out into other fields, which have ensured the company's stability and continued growth." He stopped reading and looked at Valerie, smiling that bullshit smile of his. "You managed to do one hell of a lot since 1989, and I understand you've been part-time since the birth of your daughter in 1997?"

"Actually," Valerie said. "I've been part-time since 1996, but I didn't save the company by myself. My brothers, David and

Isaac, along with my father, Reuben, are responsible for IN-ESCO's resurgence and success."

"You're too modest, Valerie. We have files on everyone concerned with this case, and that includes your brothers and father. Unless we missed something, and I don't think we did, you, my dear, are the brains behind the company," Agent Porter said. "And you don't think that might have played a role in the attempt to kidnap your daughter?"

"No, I don't."

"Interesting. I say that because isn't it true that you're awaiting word on several proposals you've made to the Department of Defense and NASA?"

"Yes with regard to the DOD, and that could be said at any given time, but no, we haven't worked with NASA in thirty years. It's our job to make proposals. We're a research and development facility, Agent Porter. We currently have two dozen proposals in the pipeline at the DOD, and could have twice that number if they needed them. If we aren't innovating old technologies or inventing new ones, we aren't doing our job."

"I see," he said, and then followed up, "So you don't think there could be a connection?"

"No, I don't see how there could be a connection. Everything we do at INESCO with the DOD is done in secrecy. We submit our proposals under our alphanumeric prefix code, and then if the project goes, I assign our DOD numeric prefix code. A person would have to have both of those codes to identify an individual project. No, I don't see a connection between what we do at INESCO and what happened at our home."

"What if I were to tell you that the young man your husband injured was a former employee of your company?" Agent

Porter asked.

Valerie laughed and said, "I recognized his face, and if I'm not mistaken, he was employed in our rubber division as an entry-level compounder. I'd have to look at his employee file to be 100% certain about that, but he had nothing to do with, and therefore no knowledge of, anything going on in R&D."

Agent Porter stood up as his two silent cronies began packing up their files and other paperwork.

"One other thing I'd like to ask you, and that's, how does a woman with no history of firearms training that we could find make a shot like the one that killed the intruder? I mean, even on my best day, under perfect conditions at the range at Quantico, I can't hit the bull's eye. But you, Mrs. Valerie Granger, shot a man who was twenty-seven feet away in partial light between the eyes. How's that possible?"

"My dad taught me to shoot when I was a kid," Valerie said.

"That's your answer?" he asked. He stared down at Valerie for a little too long before going on.

"Okay. I see how it is. The conclusion we reached about thirty minutes after we arrived in Park City is that the unfortunate incident at your home was a home invasion by what turns out to be a couple of out of work ex-cons. The man that was killed was James Smotherman, recently paroled from the Federal Penitentiary in Atlanta. I'm sure with a few additional man-hours, the two men that entered your home illegally will be shown to have known each other in some capacity. Furthermore, I'm confident that the man in the hospital is Daniel Pickett, who targeted your home because of his having worked briefly as a low-level employee at INESCO. He most likely assumed there was cash or other valuables on hand. This incident was not an attempt to kidnap Leecy Granger, but they pay me to investigate, so I investigated. It was nice to meet you all, and I apologize if my line of questions ruffled any feathers. It's my job to find the answers, and that's not always a pleasant process to undertake."

The Smith boys, as if on cue, stood and filed out of the room, with Agent Porter lagging behind.

"I'll inform Chief Rawlings this case is closed and there's no need for any further concern. Good day, Grangers." He walked through the open door, but stopped as if something occurred to him, and turning, he came back into the room.

"One last thing," he began, "when I started with the FBI in 2002, there were stories – more like rumors really – floating through the agency. I never gave the stories much credence till I read your file this morning, Ron. Do you want to know why?"

"Not really," I said.

"Well, I'll tell you; I think you will find it interesting. See, the stories I heard were about a Native American CIA agent operating in the Middle East and Europe in the mid 90s. The rumor was, this operator was the CIA's best. He was so good, in fact, that he operated alone. I remember thinking that was ridiculous. I knew the CIA had kill teams, but no one believed there was this single guy out there somewhere. I didn't believe it. I dismissed the rumors. That's until I read your file and immediately began to wonder if this was the guy. I mean why wouldn't I think that? Now, add to the file what you did to Mr. Pickett with your bare hands and you know what I'm thinking? I'm thinking this is the guy. I'm thinking the rumors I'd heard all those years ago are actually true." Agent Porter leaned in real close to me and asked, "Just between us, are you the guy?"

I sat there looking at the now empty table, listening to Agent Porter and running down my list of things I didn't like about the Smith boys. Valerie was now standing, and I thought she might grab Leecy and leave, but she didn't move a muscle. I wondered what Leecy was thinking. And then I stood and faced Agent Porter.

"I heard those rumors, too. Did you hear that this guy used some Indian war chant or something like that before he killed his target? That he did all his wet work with a knife and tomahawk?"

I let that hang there in the air for a moment. Then I laughed. "Those stories have been floating around for a long time. Long before I even started at the agency." And then, leaning in close to Agent Porter's ear I said, "But if I was that guy, I would be a real dangerous man, wouldn't I?"

Agent Porter stopped himself from backing away from me. He covered his reaction well by shifting his weight from foot to foot, saying, "Yeah; it was just a crazy notion. You're right; those stories are ridiculous. Just rumors. CIA legends. I just thought with your heritage you would find it interesting, that's all. Good day again, Grangers."

He turned and left the room, closing the door behind him. I looked from Valerie to Leecy and saw no sign of concern or worry about what Agent Porter and I had said to each other. That was a good thing, because I didn't want to talk about it anymore, at least not in the police station.

"You guys ready to get out of here and get started with Val's big birthday plans?" I asked, changing the subject.

"Yeah, but first you need to know there's a problem with the FBI's take on this home invasion," Valerie said.

"What problem?" I asked.

"Tell your dad what you told me before we ate breakfast," Valerie said to Leecy.

"The guy that pulled me from my room called me by my name. He knew who I was and where to find me," she said, and then, "The FBI is wrong."

Valerie and I looked at each other and with a glance between us, decided to keep that information to ourselves.

Leecy continued. "I didn't say anything to Agent Porter because those other two guys, the ones with the same last name, made me uncomfortable. The one across from me kept checking me out as he pretended to read. What a weirdo! No, I think we need to find out what's going on, but first you two need to spill on the secrets because Dad, 'classified till 2035' isn't getting it done. And the rumors aren't rumors, are they? And as far as I'm concerned, Mom, Agent Porter is right about one thing."

"What's that?"

"Even a genius like you doesn't learn to shoot like you can shoot from her dad. So spill it. How did you learn to shoot like that?"

Valerie laughed and then continued in the whispered tone we'd been using as I walked toward the door. "Not here and not now, but I promise to tell you everything." She pushed Leecy toward the door. "We need to get out of here and go see your grandmother. The phone in my pocket hasn't stopped vibrating. I bet she's called twenty times."

"Okay, but I'm holding you to that. And Dad, you have some explaining to do. Don't think I will forget; you know I remember everything."

The three of us left the meeting room and were passing the bathroom door when Leecy informed us, "I need to make a pit stop."

"All right," I said, "I'll wait for you by the front doors."

"Look, guys, I'm going to call my mom and let her know we're on the way. I'll be outside," Valerie said as she walked toward the front door, and Leecy entered the unisex bathroom.

"Okay, meet you in a bit," I said to both of them.

I walked slowly to the front of the police station and sat on a bench against the wall opposite Officer Johnson at the dispatcher's desk. Suddenly, Chief Rawling's office door opened and out came the Chief, slamming the door behind him. I watched as he waddled up to the dispatcher's desk and spoke to Officer Johnson. Without a word to me at all, the Chief walked out the front door. Officer Johnson shrugged his shoulders at me and said in a whisper, the way southerners speak about things that are none of their business, "The FBI guy wanted to use the phone and file his report before returning to Atlanta, and asked the Chief to give them some privacy." He spoke with his hands as much as his mouth. "The Chief didn't like that, and suggested the FBI use the desk in our little bull pen here." He gestured wildly to the desk behind him. "But that didn't go over too well, so the Chief had to skedaddle. Looks like it made him pretty upset," he concluded.

"Oh, I see," I said, and nodded my head to signify I would keep our secret.

Officer Henry Johnson was the only other police officer I knew anything about besides Lester, and the only reason was because his hiring had been somewhat of a controversy in our little town. Officer Johnson was openly gay, and when the Chief hired him as the day shift dispatcher two years ago, there had been a bit of an uproar from some of Park City's citizenry.

The public debate and resulting national media attention was why the Chief hung on to his position for a few more years. It had been reported that the Chief had delayed his retirement to ensure that Officer Johnson got a fair chance to perform the duties of the job and not be dismissed by some new Chief that might have taken over at the time. The hiring had been a bold move, but some said it was a calculated strategy that garnered the Chief much respect and admiration. Park City's town council saw the bright side of all the attention. They thought the national exposure might lead to a financial windfall for the town by way of increased tourism, but that wasn't realized. No, the only two things realized were Officer Johnson was a fine police officer, and the town council named Lester the Chief of Police in waiting.

The Chief's office door opened again, and I watched the three-member FBI team emerge from its confines. The Smith boys led the way, followed at a distance by Agent Porter. The two Smiths passed me without a word or a glance. I watched them through the glass doors of the police station as the one named Travis climbed behind the wheel of the Suburban, and the one named Briggs took the seat directly behind him. I heard Agent Porter ease up next to me and turned my attention to him as he asked, "Were you waiting for me for some reason?"

I stood, and as I was about to answer him, the bathroom door opened, causing all three of us – me, Agent Porter and Officer Johnson – to look in the direction of the sound, only to see Leecy emerging from the bathroom. I noticed she was as pale as a ghost again. She looked like she had looked earlier this morning after the home invasion.

"No, I was waiting for Leecy."

He turned and exited the police station immediately. Leecy all but ran to meet me.

"We need to get out of here right now."

She was calm and steady, like her mother had been earlier this morning.

"Okay, let's go. What's wrong?"

I turned toward the front door of the police station with one arm wrapped around the shoulders of my daughter in time to see the big black SUV drive away.

I wished Officer Johnson a pleasant day, and I pushed open the glass door, hearing him say, "You, too, Grangers."

Leecy pulled away from me as soon as we were out of the station and raced toward the Jeep. She was already in the backseat before I even opened the door to the driver's side. Valerie was seated in the car, but I hadn't noticed her there because of the tinted windows.

"Agent Porter sure seemed upset," she said. "I could hear him speaking into his cell phone that he had big problems. I wonder what that's about. Anyway, we need to go to my mom's."

Val buckled her seat belt with a smile on her face that quickly faded as she turned to look at Leecy. "What's wrong? You're as white as sheet. Are you okay?"

I was putting the Jeep in reverse and looked in the rearview mirror to see the still ashen face of my daughter as she answered Valerie's question.

"No, I'm not okay."

I slowed down but then Leecy said, "No, Dad, go. Let's get out of here. You aren't going to believe what I heard."

I reversed the Jeep out of the parking space and turned left onto First Street. I was driving north out of downtown toward my in-laws' house, just a few blocks away from our house. Valerie unbuckled her seat belt and climbed between the front seats to sit next to Leecy.

"What are you talking about?"

"I was in the bathroom washing my hands when I heard a man's voice. I know eavesdropping isn't polite, but I couldn't help but hear everything being said through the walls. It was Agent Porter's voice. He was telling someone to leave the office or he would have one of his men throw him out. Then I heard a door open and slam closed."

"That's when they kicked Chief Rawlings out of his office," I said. "Keep going."

"I heard Porter having a one-way conversation; must have been on the phone. He said, 'Yeah, I'm in Park City looking into the situation. It's all under control.' And then another pause before he said, 'Yeah, well where did you find those two idiots?'. Then the pause was really long before he spoke again. And he said, 'We need the girl to make this work. There's definitely something to the father and possibly the mother. You say you didn't find anything on her, right?' There was another long pause, and then I heard Porter say, 'Well I guess that makes sense, but see if there's more you can dig up on Ron. I'll be in touch. I'm going to see what I can find out on my own. Nothing happens till Sunday afternoon, anyway. The beauty of that is they don't even know about the DOD decision yet.' There was another long pause," Leecy said, "and then Agent Porter said bye."

As Leecy finished telling us what she overheard, I realized I was speeding, but I didn't slow down. I sped up, because I saw the black SUV in my rearview mirror. It was about half a mile back. We were being followed; I had no doubt.

"Valerie," I said, "we'll have to stop by your mother's house later. I want to grab a few things from our house first, okay?"

Valerie's eyes found mine in the rearview mirror. "I agree. Home first, and then we get out of town for a few days. I'll deal with my mother later. Pass me your phones."

I handed her my iPhone and as she took it from me, Leecy very matter of factly said, "We're being followed," and handed Val her iPhone.

"I'm taking no chances with these phones," Val said, and turned them off before she rolled down the windows and threw them out of the car. "I don't want to give the guys behind us, or anyone else, a chance to track our location."

"Wait! Don't throw it away; my life's on that phone!" Leecy said.

"I know and I'm sorry, but the phones are just too tempting to keep around. They have to go."

I turned left off what had now become State Highway 64 and drove west on a dirt track about a hundred yards, where I turned right onto the power company's surveyor road. I kept my eyes on the rearview mirror. I thought they might have seen me make the first left turn, but there was no way they saw the second turn I'd made. I knew the surveyor road ran along the back edge of our property and would take us home and keep us off the main roads. There was a chance the guys following us might locate the road, so I sped up. We were in a race for our home. If Porter and his guys arrived before we did, they'd think they had a tactical advantage, and Porter would likely leave one of the Smiths behind to watch the place in case we returned. That Smith would have to be dealt with.

I needed to get the Go bags we kept packed and ready for a situation just like this, and nothing was going to stop me.

CHAPTER

THREE

We'd been awake since 4:00 a.m. It was now after 12:00 p.m., and I didn't see an opportunity for rest in our near future. The road we were driving on narrowed to little more than a trail. Large oak trees lined either side of the Jeep. The trees were so close I could smell the sap, and I was forced to slow down.

"We aren't going to get to the house before Porter and his guys," I said, as the Jeep lumbered through the water-filled ruts and holes in the trail.

"So...?" Leecy said. She started to say something else but stopped herself. She realized there was more to what I was saying and asked, "Why does that matter?"

I concentrated on the bumpy driving, and Val answered Leecy's question.

"It matters, because Porter will likely leave a man to watch the house. There are things we need from the house, and if there's an obstacle between us and those things we need..." She was interrupted by Leecy.

"Just stop with the ridiculous double talk and speak to me in a way that not only explains the situation but respects the fact that I'm part of what is happening here, okay?"

"She's right, Val. No more secrets," I said.

"Fine, you're right. You're both right, and I'm sorry. I just wanted to..." Her voice trailed off before she continued, "The truth is, your father isn't the only spy in the family. I was once a member of the Israeli group called the Mossad. I haven't been actively involved since before you were born, but there was a period of time where I was very active. I wasn't only a spy; I was more than that. I was an assassin. That's why I can shoot so well. There's more I need to tell you, but now is not the time because," she paused and pointed out the window over Leecy's shoulder as the Jeep slowed, "we're here. We're home."

I brought the Jeep to a full stop and killed the engine. I was parked at the edge of our two acre lot behind the wall of twenty-five foot tall evergreen trees that rimmed our property. Our breathing was the only sound inside the Jeep.

Leecy turned away from her mother to look in the direction Valerie was pointing and said, "Okay, so my parents are ex spies. I can get behind that. Mom was an assassin, and Dad used to kill targets for the CIA with a knife and a tomahawk. Okay, so that's my parents. What happens now? Be direct. I can handle it."

Val and I shared a glance and a shrug of the shoulders with each other through the rearview mirror before I unbuckled my seat belt. "We sit a few minutes and watch for signs of Porter and his two Smith boys. I want to know if they're here before we go get the stuff we need."

"What stuff?" Leecy asked.

"Weapon: guns, knives, telescoping metal batons. Three Go bags," I explained.

"Part of being a spy is being ready to move at a moment's notice. Go bags are essential to making that happen. Each bag is always packed and ready. Each one of the three bags contains false papers. Driver's licenses and passports for each of us, $25,000 cash divided into dollars, Euros, and Pounds, EuroRail passes, Metro cards for the NYC subway, and oyster cards for London's Tube system, because we have a safe house in New York and London we can access. There's a small amount of hair dye to effect a basic disguise, a change of clothes and a small amount of food. We can go anywhere at a moment's notice."

"Really? I've never seen that stuff. Where is it?"

Valerie answered this time. "The weapons and Go bags are inside the safe in the closet of the spare room. We've had a plan in place since you were born in case we ever needed to leave in a hurry. We kept the false papers and clothing updated and current as we aged. The food was thrown out and replaced as it expired, but the food's just a few energy bars for emergency rations."

"Okay," Leecy said. "What signs are we looking for?"

"Do you see anyone?" Val asked.

"No, I don't see anyone," Leecy said without looking away from the house.

"Next thing we look for is something out of place, but that takes some skill because you first have to remember how everything looked before you left the house to notice if something's been disturbed," I said.

I was turning in my seat so I could see Valerie and Leecy without having to use the rearview mirror when Leecy spoke.

"Do you mean something like a shutter out of place?"

I bent lower in my seat for a better view of the back of our house and found a perfect spot between two thin branches of the evergreen tree we were parked behind. I could see that the plantation shutter in one of the kitchen windows was flat and not angled like the others.

"Yes, exactly like that," I said. "Good catch."

"So, there's someone in our house?" Leecy asked.

"I think it's safe to say there's someone in our house," Valerie confirmed.

"Okay, well show me some of that super spy stuff. Let's see the rumors in action, like the old man goes and gets the bags and weapons without whoever's in there even knowing."

I looked at Valerie and laughed. "Okay, keep your eyes on the kitchen window. When you see my signal, drive the Jeep between the trees. Get it as close to the kitchen door as you can and help me load the stuff we need."

With that said, I opened and closed the door to the Jeep very softly, and began running along the line of evergreen trees. I ran the width of the property. Our lot is about two hundred feet wide. I jogged almost the entire distance before turning into the trees. I was now sprinting through the branches and across the grass to the rear of our detached garage. I ran on a line that kept the garage between the house and myself to avoid being seen by whoever was inside the house. I reached the rear of our detached garage and made my way around the right side. The front right corner of the garage gave me cover from the view of our kitchen windows and provided me with a clear line of sight down our driveway. No black SUV; good.

I watched the back of the house for any indication of where the man waiting inside might be hiding. Trusting my instincts, I bolted from my position and ran for the kitchen door. I was going for a shock and awe approach. My plan was to explode into the house with a straightforward brute force attack. Catching the man waiting for us off guard, I could gain the upper hand in the ensuing hand-to-hand combat. But I would have to disarm him first.

I turned the doorknob to the kitchen door with my left hand as I hit the door with my left shoulder, slamming it open. I ran into the kitchen and Agent Briggs Smith. He was walking up the stairs from the sunken den, talking on his cell phone when I exploded into the room.

I heard him say, "They're here," before he dropped his phone and ran toward me, drawing his weapon.

We collided in the space between our kitchen table and center kitchen island like two rams. My left hand stopped his right hand from pulling his weapon free from the holster on his right hip. I slammed a head butt into the bridge of his nose. I felt the cartilage of his nose compress fully underneath the weight of my forehead before I heard it snap and pop. I drove my right fist into his left side, punching his kidney with everything I had in me. I heard the air escape his lungs, carrying with it a groan of pain. With my left hand keeping his weapon pressed firmly to his stomach, I under hooked his left arm with my right arm. Grabbing a fistful of the back of his suit, I began steering him around the circular kitchen table. I pressed his back against the plantation shutters covering a kitchen window. I used the fingers of my right hand to move the shutter up and down, signaling Valerie and Leecy all was clear.

"Tell me everything, and I'll let you live. Tell me nothing, and I'll kill you where you stand."

He stammered as he coughed up the blood running down his throat from his shattered nose and said, "I was hired to work with Porter on a need-to-know basis. No details other than the need to apprehend you and your family ASAP."

"Were you talking to Porter on the phone just now?"

"Yes."

"Is Porter FBI, and how long do we have before he and Travis arrive?"

"Yeah, he's FBI; he's got the badge and everything. You don't have long. Maybe ten minutes."

"Okay, you're doing fine; just keep answering my questions," I said and then asked him, "What's your background?"

"I was a Ranger," Briggs Smith said.

I decided to step back from him and relieved him of his gun. I dropped the clip to his Glock 9mm to the floor and kicked it away while ejecting the round from the chamber before tossing the weapon in the opposite direction. I watched him carefully anticipating his next move. He wiped his face with the left sleeve of his suit coat. He was dropping his left arm, and I saw the right arm go for something behind his back. He pulled a knife with his right hand and pushed off the window, lunging at me knife first. That was a mistake.

I stepped back with my right foot and twisted my body to the right. My left hand shot out, clamping down on his right wrist like a vise. Pulling his right arm toward my body and relieving him of his knife with my right hand, I continued spinning to my left, slamming my right elbow into the back of his head. That's when I heard the approaching Jeep. I worried what Leecy would see when she entered the kitchen, and then realized this was exactly what she'd asked for.

Ranger Smith was pinned down on the kitchen table when Leecy and Valerie walked through the back door. I was pulling his right arm up and back, and the weight of my body pinned him to the tabletop. His legs were too far apart to use as leverage, and even with his left arm free he could do nothing.

"Wait," he gasped and groaned at me.

I held his knife in my left hand and pressed the tip against the base of his skull. "What?"

"There's more. Porter has a partner. I don't know who, but he's working with someone else."

"What do Porter and this mystery partner want?"

"I don't know. Like I said, I was hired on a need-to-know basis. All I know is they wanted your daughter at first. They wanted her held hostage till Sunday afternoon. They thought by kidnapping her it would get them whatever else they're after. I don't know why they think that or where they wanted to hold your daughter. I just know that was the original plan, because Travis Smith and I were hired to guard her. All that changed when Porter saw your daughter coming out of the bathroom at the police station. He now thinks she overheard him talking. Like I said before, he changed his plan from kidnapping her to taking all of you. He doesn't want you three free to use whatever your daughter might have heard him say. That's all I know, really; I swear."

I thought a moment and then said, "Good boy, Ranger Smith, but here's my problem. If I let you live, you'll just join up with Porter and keep pursuing your objectives. That's not good for the Grangers. But I'm a man of my word. I said you could live if you told me everything. I believe you've told me all that you know. So, I'll keep my word. But I need you to do something for me."

"Anything," Ranger Smith grunted.

"I need you to tell Porter and the other guy you're working with something for me. Will you do that for me?"

"Yes."

I looked directly at Leecy holding her gaze with mine.

"My CIA file reads I'm to be considered extremely dangerous," I paused and adjusted my feet a little, "and that I'm an expert in all forms of hand-to-hand combat. My file says I'm unsurpassed in tactical awareness, but the important part is how the file ends. It concludes with a note of caution."

Dropping my gaze from my daughter, I bent close to Ranger Smith's upturned right ear. I threw his knife across the room sticking it in the doorjamb twenty feet away.

I finished saying, "The note in my file simply reads: 'You've been warned.'"

With that said, I pulled his right arm back, lifting his torso off the table, and held him there momentarily. I said, "Tell Agent Porter one other thing for me. Those rumors he talked about? Tell him those rumors are true. Tell him he's correct; the rumors are about me."

I slammed his head into the table top with enough force to knock him unconscious.

I looked at Val and Leecy and said, "Let's get the stuff we need and get out of here. He was on the phone with Porter when I came in the back door. We don't have much time."

I left the Ranger where he lay on the floor beneath the table and headed for the back of the house, followed by Valerie and Leecy.

"I'll get the safe open," Valerie said. "Ron, why don't you wash the Ranger's blood off your face and hands?"

I was already headed for our master bathroom before she finished the sentence. I lathered my face and hands with the liquid soap Valerie kept in the dispenser on our sink, and rinsed off with warm water. I was drying my face as I thought about what the Ranger had said. Porter was working with someone. Did he mean the two guys that broke into our house, or someone else? Could that person also be FBI?

"Time to move. Let's go, Ron," the call came from Valerie. I dropped the towel in the sink.

I caught up to my wife and child at the end of the hallway.

"Dad?" Leecy said, pointing at the unconscious man beneath the kitchen table as we walked through the back door. "Why didn't you just kill that guy? Won't he do exactly what you said and just hook back up with Porter and the other Smith?"

"Yeah," I said, "he will. But I need him to deliver the message for me. And I gave him my word. If he talked, he got to live. I don't want whatever we're involved in to come to killing. I don't want to be that guy again."

"If you two are finished, we have everything we need from the house. The other items we need, we'll have to buy," Valerie called.

Thirty seconds later, we were in the Jeep. Valerie was driving, Leecy was riding shotgun, and I was in the back seat. We heard the sound of an approaching vehicle. I couldn't see it because we were on the backside of the house. The sound was getting louder. The vehicle was heading up our driveway. I was digging through one of the Go bags for a weapon when Val spoke.

"Hold on; this is going to be close," she warned us as she jammed the accelerator to the floor.

The Jeep shot across the backyard. She steered in the direction of the large evergreen trees she'd driven between earlier. I looked out the slanted rear window of the Jeep's fastback top in time to see the nose of the black Suburban. It was about two car lengths behind us. I could see Travis Smith behind the wheel and Agent Porter in the passenger seat.

I was facing the rear when the sound of branches rubbing against the sides of the Jeep caused me to face forward. The Jeep was awash in green, like being inside a car wash, and then we were through the trees. Valerie hit the brakes and turned the steering wheel hard to the left. We were on the narrow trail behind our house, but Valerie wasn't slowing down like I had earlier. She was speeding faster and faster between the trunks of the trees. The trees were dangerously close to the sides of the Jeep and, unlike moments before, these weren't small leafy green branches, but the hundred-year-old trunks of oak trees.

I turned in my seat again and looked out the rear window in time to see the nose of the Suburban break through the evergreen trees. I watched it stop, back up, and then complete the left turn Valerie had made with much less effort.

"They can't follow us; the Suburban is too wide," I said as I watched the chase vehicle slam its front right bumper into one of the oak trees. The doors of the Suburban flew open and I was yelling, "Gun! Leecy, get down!"

We were driving a long, straight, narrow, rut-filled track lined with mighty oaks. The Jeep was a big silver moving target that Porter and the other Smith could disable with one well-placed shot. I was reaching for Leecy. I yelled for her to take cover. I wanted to push her down into the floorboard of the front seat. As the Jeep dipped and rose through the ruts, a 9mm bullet ripped through the vinyl rear window and punctured the roof.

"Oh my god they're shooting at us!" Leecy cried.

Valerie turned sharply to the right, using the Jeep's emergency brake momentarily to rapidly decelerate. She drove expertly between two large oaks and then swerved back to the left again. She was now driving on a parallel track to the one she'd turned off of.

"I can't see them anymore, so they can't see us. You can slow down now," I said to Valerie from my twisted position in the back seat. "We're clear."

I felt the Jeep slow a tiny bit and asked, "How'd you know you could turn back there?"

"I used to take Leecy hiking back here when she was a baby. You were out of town back then; we had to have something to do. I'm glad I knew it was there; that one shot was enough."

"Well that was ...uh...fun," Leecy said, peeking around the side of her seat. "I can now check attempted kidnapping, high-speed car chase, and being shot at off of my bucket list. All I need to do now is learn how to fight. Can you teach me how to fight like you?" she asked me. Turning to her mother, she said, "And can you teach me how to drive and shoot like you?"

"I can teach you what I know," I said, "but if you want to learn from the best, you should learn from your mother."

Leecy adjusted herself in her seat. She was now sitting all the way up, giving me a view of her profile. Her eyes were fixed on her mother. Leecy said, "Really, Mom? Is that true? The man whose CIA career was so epic that it evolved into legend and rumor says you're better at this stuff than he is."

I could see part of the smile creeping across my wife's face from my position in the back seat when Valerie answered. "The truth is, your father and I both possess specific skill sets. I'll be happy to teach you everything I know."

"Okay, I like the sound of that, but what about your spy

days, Mom? Dad's secrets are out on the table. Well, most of them, I think. When do I get to hear your secrets?"

"I promised to tell all and I will, but first we need supplies." Changing the subject, Val then asked, "What else did Briggs Smith tell you, Ron?"

"You heard everything. The part where he told me Porter was working with someone is what has me the most concerned. He didn't know who, and I believed him."

"Any ideas?"

I'd already given that question some consideration and said, "Two thoughts on that subject. First one is that Ranger Smith could've been referring to the two men that broke into our house this morning. And second thought is that we haven't met the person yet, and won't know they're with Porter till it's too late to do anything about it."

"That sounds scary. Why only those two options?" Leecy asked.

"I can't think of any others at the moment, but give me time."

"No, your Dad's right," Valerie said as she turned left between two trees and found the original trail again. "We need to devise a plan, part of which is to trust no one."

Valerie was in full flight mode now. She thought we couldn't trust anyone, but I wondered if there wasn't someone. Lester came to mind, and I thought of another person, but I had to be careful mentioning her. Valerie wouldn't like the idea forming in my head.

I unbuckled my seat belt and sat with my back to the passenger side door, stretching my legs across the seat in an effort to find a comfortable position. The Jeep shot across State

Highway 64 and continued on the dirt road in the direction of the next asphalt-covered road, which was State Road 16.

Valerie saw me fidgeting in the back seat and said, "It's just a few more miles before we reach the intersection at State Road 16, and then you can drive."

"Oh, it's not that bad," I said, and then asked, "Is Stubbs's Store still open? It's been years since we've been out this way."

"I have no idea, but we're going to find out."

Stubbs's was an old country store named after its owner, Charlie Stubbs. The store was located in what most people would call the middle of nowhere, but for others the remote area was home. The store sold everything a person might need if that person were a local, and nothing a tourist would be interested in except gasoline. I looked through the windshield of the Jeep and saw the side of the old cinderblock building coming into view. The soft glow of lights emanating from the glass front doors could be seen in the overcast grey skies. We were in luck.

Valerie crossed State Road 16 and turned right into the dirt parking lot, stopping on the concrete pad next to the one and only gas pump.

"If you pump, I'll pay and pick up the other items we need. If he has both fuel and prepaid mobile phones that is," Valerie said as she climbed down from the driver's seat.

"I'm going with Mom," Leecy announced.

"Leave me the keys so I can move the Jeep," I said.

"On the seat," Valerie called over her shoulder.

The pump on my left dinged as it came to life. I looked toward the glass doors of the store and saw Val giving me the thumbs up sign to go ahead and start filling the gas tank. With the tank topped off, I drove to the far side of the building, out of sight of Highway 16, and waited. I was beginning to wonder what was taking the girls so long when they rounded the corner of the building carrying a grocery bag apiece.

We ate a picnic of sorts in the parking lot of Stubbs's. Ham sandwiches, corn chips and bottled water, with a candy bar split between the three of us for dessert. Val called her family on one of the three prepaid mobile phones. She kept her calls under 2 minutes, which wasn't easy when it came to her mother, but it was a necessary precaution in case Porter was tapping her family's phones.

"All right, I think that'll hold her for a day or two, but no longer than that," Valerie said as she ended the call.

"That bad?" I asked.

"She's extremely distraught and the only thing that'll calm her down is seeing that we're all okay with her own eyes and hugging her grandbaby. Her words, not mine."

"So, what now?" Leecy asked.

"First of all," Val went on before I could get a word in, "we stay away from the police because all Porter would have to do is flash his badge and any local or state cop would do whatever he said." Apparently reading my mind, she added, "Yes; for now that includes Lester. We have to be very careful about who we trust. That's if there's anyone we can trust."

"Maybe we have someone we can call that can help us figure out what Porter is after, and maybe even who he is working with," I said.

"You think she's still around the agency?" Val asked, reading my thoughts again.

"Who's still around the agency? What agency? The CIA? What are you talking about?" Leecy asked.

"I'm talking about my handler."

"What's a handler?" Leecy asked.

"When a CIA recruit becomes an operator and enters the field, he or she is assigned a handler. As a spy, this is your one and only contact person. They work directly with you and monitor your behaviors. The handler is to make certain a spy stays on mission and doesn't become lost in his cover identity. The handler helps a spy stay grounded. They act as boss and therapist to some degree. If the relationship is solid between the spy and the handler, they form a very deep personal bond. If my old handler is still with the agency, she'll move heaven and earth to help us," I answered.

"There's always a price to be paid when you call in a favor with these people," Val added.

Leecy was perched on the hood of the Jeep with her back to me. She slid off the hood and turned to face me and asked, "If your old handler is still with the CIA, how would you contact her? And what price would she want for helping you? I mean what would you have to do in return?"

"I'd contact her like I did before I moved to non-operator status with the agency a few years ago. The agency recorded one set of active operator dates for my official file. My active dates are officially 1996-2003, as you heard Agent Porter read, but I've used my position with INESCO and the international travel that comes with it as an unofficial cover. Sporadically at first, and now seldom if at all. My objectives changed, of course. I mainly gathered information for the agency when tasked. Anyway, what's important here is I can still contact my former handler. We worked together for seven years. If she's around the CIA in any capacity, she'll help us. My contact codes and passwords from my operator days will still be active, even if they're unmonitored. All I need to do is make a call and enter in a coded ID tag, a coded message and a call back number. I'd need a payphone to do that. As far as the price I'd pay for asking for help, I don't know what they'd want from me, but it's worth any price, because she'll help us. I know she will."

"Your handler was a woman?" Leecy asked.

"CIA agent and Special Officer Tammy Daniel Wakefield," I said, and then added, "She was in charge of my training class and later became my handler. She was a top-notch agent. The only person other than you and your mom I would trust completely."

"Well, I don't know what other choice we have. There's a pay phone inside the store mounted on the wall between the ladies' and men's rooms. Make your call. We'll clean up and be ready to roll when you come back," Valerie said.

"On it," I said as I turned and jogged toward the store.

I found the pay phone and dialed a number I'd memorized on the day I graduated from training. I punched in my identification code, followed by the distress code and the number of the phone in my pocket, and pressed the pound key. I replaced the receiver and headed for the waiting Jeep. I could see it parked directly in front of the glass doors as I walked from the back of the store to the front. I was about to push the door open when I heard the cashier say something. I stopped.

The cashier called to me saying, "Look, I don't want no trouble from you folks, but the TV lady just said there's an all points bulletin out for a silver Jeep, and three people by the last name of Granger. They got your faces plastered all over the TV, mister. They just did one of those breaking news things and it's all about you folks. They say the FBI is looking for you. Says they want ya'll for questioning about an assault on a federal agent. As far as I'm concerned, I haven't seen you, if you know what I mean. Just do me a favor and don't come back."

"Yes, I understand, and thank you very much," I answered, and ran for the Jeep.

"There is an APB out for us. We're on the news. Best stick to the back roads. We need to ditch the Jeep and soon."

Valerie pressed the gas pedal down. The Jeep shot forward and veered right for the same dirt track that had brought us here. The four-wheel drive hugged the dirt road. Stubbs's store fell away from the rear window of the Jeep and was soon completely out of sight. We were heading Northeast and deeper into the woods, far away from any paved roads. I didn't worry about getting lost. Valerie grew up in this area and knew these roads as well as anyone from around here could. I did worry we would lose cell phone reception. I checked the reception bars on the prepaid mobile and saw only one bar visible. That bar faded out and back in with every passing mile.

"We can drive this dirt road all the way to East Park and find another car there," Valerie said. "From East Park, we can head to the Atlanta Airport. We can get lost in one of those cheap motels around the airport. Maybe you'll get the call by then, and we'll have some help."

"Great," Leecy said, "so we have plenty of time to talk. And Mom, you promised to tell me everything. So start talking."

I saw Valerie looking at me in the rear view mirror. I knew this wasn't the way she wanted to tell Leecy about her past, but we didn't have the luxury of choice any longer. A rogue

FBI agent, if Porter was in fact FBI, had an APB out on us. We were wanted for questioning.

"Might as well tell her now, Val. This may be the only chance you get."

Valerie began by asking, "Do you remember your great grandmother Leona?"

"Sure I do. I'm named after her, and the wife of Dad's great Uncle John. I used to call Leona Granny Granny. She was Grandpa Reuben's mother, right?" Leecy said.

"That's right. Do you remember her talking about being in the USO during WWII while she was attending Julliard in New York City?"

"Yes, I do. She showed me the section of cloth wall map she used to chronicle all her travels on during the war. Didn't her sister attend Juilliard, too?"

"Her sister, Edith, had a beautiful singing voice and was eventually a singer at the Metropolitan Opera. Leona was the dancer and actress of the family. Okay, that's good; we're on the same page and that's important."

"Really, what does you being in the Mossad have to do with Granny Granny Leona in the USO?"

"Everything. It's because of what she did during the war that I came to be a Mossad agent. You see, she was part of a group that was the precursor to the Mossad."

"Get out!" Leecy exclaimed. "You're joking. I've never heard of the existence of any such group during WWII. They didn't talk about it in my history classes. Dad, is she telling me the truth?"

"It's the truth. Just listen to what she has to say. I promise it's all true."

Valerie continued. "I wouldn't lie about this stuff. I've been waiting sixteen years to tell you this story. I wanted to tell you the same way that Leona told me, but that's not going to happen now. Just sit back and listen, okay?"

"Okay," Leecy said.

"The USO was formed in 1941 by President Franklin Roosevelt. When it became clear the United States was headed into the war, FDR combined the resources of several different organizations working to support the troops and called that newly created entity the USO. Your Great Aunt Edith and Great Grandmother Leona joined the USO, along with many other young women. Not long after the two sisters joined the USO, they were approached about joining another group. Leona told me that she and her sister were visited in the apartment they shared by two men. These two men explained how the sisters' involvement with the USO provided the perfect cover for what they wanted them to be a part of. The two men, and the organization they represented, were recruiting Jewish men and women to be part of a secret group that would work to help German Jews escape from Europe."

"Wait," Leecy interrupted, "so, Granny Granny and Great Aunt Edith were both part of this secret organization?"

"Yes and no. The men represented a group of wealthy Jewish businessmen with connections in Europe and Israel who didn't think enough was being done to help the German Jews escape the atrocities being reported from Europe. Both Leona and Edith agreed to join the group, but Edith was badly injured during the training and had to drop out. Leona went on alone and trained near their home somewhere in the city of New York. She went to a warehouse somewhere in the old meatpacking district everyday for the grueling training. Do you remember the steak place we ate at a few years ago? I think it was somewhere down there. Leona said the training was often brutal work, but admitted to having a preternatural ability for the job."

"Granny Granny was a badass?"

I could see the smile on Valerie's face.

"Yes, Leona was a badass. When her USO tour left the port of New York in early 1942, she was a very qualified singer and dancer, and also a trained killer who could hit the bull's-eye of a target from sixty to one hundred fifty yards away with a number of weapons of the day, choke a man twice her size unconscious, throw a knife with deadly accuracy, and break an arm or leg or hand. She knew how to disable a car, plane or boat, send Morse code, build small efficient incendiary devices, and also perform basic field emergency medicine."

"Really? Little Granny Granny the ballerina could do all of that? That's so cool. Oh my god, why haven't you told me about this before? Man, I could've had the best show-and-tells in school."

"Well, it all seems so silly now, but I didn't want you to be afraid of me. Because like Leona, I can do all those things and more."

"Holy crap, Mom, are you kidding me? That's nothing to be afraid of; that's awesome," Leecy said. "Tell me more about Granny Granny."

"Okay, the two men that represented this much larger organization followed along with Leona's USO troop and arranged for her to be in certain places at certain times to help with the smuggling of Jews across borders, and when needed, spy on the enemy and collect intelligence. Neither was easily accomplished. When she was helping smuggle Jews to safety, she herself was in constant danger. The spying wasn't easy, either. The sophisticated spy equipment that exists today wasn't available back then. Leona was often sent on missions to collect intelligence about prisoner transports with nothing more than paper and pencil. This was long before cell phones or computer encryptions. She used hand passes to transfer the information through a chain of spies, which were mostly women.

"Leona always preferred a very public place like an alehouse or club for passing information. She'd conceal her messages in the lining of her handbag and switch bags with another female operative at a specific location and time. All of that was planned to the last detail prior to any mission."

"She was the female James Bond!" Leecy said.

"Yes, in a way, I guess she was," Val said thoughtfully. "She told me it was the greatest time of her life. She used all her skills as an actress to cross checkpoints with false papers. That reminds me of her map. I wish we had the map she made with us, because it shows all the USO stops and some of her mission locations. Leona didn't talk about all her missions with me, but I do remember the details on two of them."

"Tell me," Leecy said.

I noticed Valerie was reducing speed and looking to her left like she was searching for something very specific. I only saw woods dense with foliage. Valerie turned left and drove between the branches of pine trees and found what looked like a long abandoned road now covered with weeds and small saplings.

"This road used to be the main road to Atlanta. My great grandmother on my mother's side of the family told me how she once traveled it on horse and buggy. It looks like local hunters have maintained it over the years. Maybe we'll be able to navigate it for a few more miles," Valerie said, as she slowly accelerated over the first of what appeared to be hundreds of small trees growing in the middle of the old wagon trail.

"Tell me about the missions," Leecy said again.

"Okay, okay," Valerie said, smiling at Leecy's enthusiasm. "It was 1943, and Leona was in a group of two women and four men sent into Frankfurt posing as a medical team to extract twenty Jewish men and women being held for transport to Auschwitz.

"Their plane took off from a small airfield in Sicily, which was already in Allied hands, and they received their briefing about the mission during the flight. The flight was terrifying because the pilots flew very low over the war-torn fields and landed in a field with lanterns marking the area. Other members of the organization met the plane. She and the other women on the plane dressed as nurses. Two of the men dressed as doctors and the other two as German soldiers. They were loaded onto trucks marked as medical transport and driven into Frankfurt."

"This is crazy. They could've been shot down or captured, and all for twenty prisoners!" Leecy interrupted.

"Well maybe, but sometimes one's life is worth the risk. Anyway, at that time the city of Frankfurt had been bombed, but not to the point of complete destruction. The heavy bombing of Frankfurt didn't occur until 1944. Leona told me she was most afraid at the first checkpoint, but the medically marked vehicle was waved through with minimal inspection. This was two years before Patton and his Third Army arrived in Frankfurt, so the German army held the city, okay?"

"I'm with you."

"Leona said she and her group were targeting a prisoner

holding facility in the heart of the city. Once the truck they were traveling in cleared the first checkpoint, the truck stopped, and the second phase of the plan went into action. The drivers removed the medical Red Cross insignias from the doors of the truck, revealing the swastikas that had been painted underneath. The truck was now displaying the proper markings for military transport. The men inside the rear of the truck tore off their medical insignias and armbands and became officers of the SS. The women remained disguised as nurses. It was common practice for the Nazis to bring in medical teams to calm and reassure prisoners. Leona's group used that to their advantage. They drove into Frankfurt and back out with twenty rescued Jews. They made it back to the plane and flew home to Sicily. Not only that, Leona's first husband was among the men she helped escape that night."

"What? Great Grandpa Ernst was among that group of people? I mean, that's pretty amazing. Did she marry him right away? She must've been scared the entire time."

"Yeah, I think she was scared, but Leona was tough. She wanted to help. She didn't marry Ernst till after the war. She said they exchanged names on the trip out of Frankfurt. But he, along with the other rescued Jews, was put on a ship bound for the US. When he arrived in the States, he promptly enlisted in the army. He was sent back to fight in the war a year later. Ernst found her after the war by tracing her through the USO."

"What's the other mission she told you about?" Leecy asked.

"There were dozens of missions, I knew, but the only other one she told me about in any detail was in the winter of 1944.

By then, the Free French and Allied troops had invaded France and taken back Paris. Leona's USO group was stationed somewhere outside of Paris. The mission she volunteered for was the rescue of two OSS officers who were trapped in Frankfurt. Two men had been forward scouts for the pending military action by Allied forces that would eventually lead to Patton's Third Army rolling into Frankfurt, and these two OSS officers had been pinned down in the city, unable to effect escape. The city had been ravaged by bombings, and what was once a beautiful medieval city was left in ruins.

"For this mission, Leona posed as a German citizen. She carried false papers hidden in her purse saying that one of the men was her husband and the other her brother. She had to walk into the city this time, but with the proper papers, she said she could go anywhere. Leona told me how people, families, just seemed to wander in and out of what was left of the city seeking shelter, food, clothing, anything. She'd never seen such destruction and hopelessness before, but she had a mission to complete and that helped her maintain focus. To find the OSS men, she used the description they'd given of the area where they were hiding that had come from the last radio transmission the two men made. She searched the entire first day for the two men, finding them just before the curfew siren. This mission was one of the times she used her combat training."

"Wait. What does the OSS stand for, and what do you mean she used her combat training?" Leecy asked.

"The OSS was the Office of Strategic Service, an American secret intelligence agency that was the predecessor of the CIA. By combat skills, I mean she had to kill a man."

"What? Just stop, okay? I'm having a hard time believing

my Granny Granny killed anyone. And I thought her group was there to help the German Jews, not American intelligence officers." Leecy said.

"Well, first of all, she did kill a man in Frankfurt, and several others in other missions. Secondly, the OSS officers were part of the effort to end the war and stop Hitler. Her group had heard about the situation and wanted to rescue the two OSS men. Whatever the reasons for taking action, the point is she took action. In a war, not everything is cut and dry or black and white. Lines are blurred and hard choices are made, because they have to be made."

"I get it. I think. It's just not the Granny Granny I knew," Leecy said.

"This is why I worried about telling you my secrets for so many years."

"No, Mom; it's not like I'm upset or anything. It's just hard reconciling my memory of her with these stories. Back to the story."

"Okay. When Leona found the two Americans, they were both injured. She used her medic training to bandage the wounds and gave them food and water to build their strength. Leona told me that on the evening of the third day, they'd planned to make their way south out of Frankfurt to the airfield she'd used in the other mission. But a German civilian found her out."

"What? How?"

"The German Military knew they were somewhere in this neighborhood and made daily announcements of a reward if they were turned in. So when this local man stumbled into the ruins of the building where they were hiding, she knew they were in trouble. She saw the look of recognition come over his face. She spoke German fluently and tried to convince the man that her cover story was true, but she could sense he didn't believe her and was just waiting to get away and turn them in. So she offered herself to the man. She seduced him," Valerie said.

"Oh my god!" Leecy exclaimed. "How terrible!"

At that moment the Jeep came to a full stop in front of a downed tree. Valerie turned off the Jeep.

"Leona told me she let the man embrace her and take her down on the floor, and as he removed his pants she stabbed him between his ribs, puncturing his heart with a dagger she kept hidden in her clothes. The two Americans used some of the dead man's clothing to complete their disguises, and the three of them left the building. With their false papers in hand, the three of them walked through the remains of the city for miles before they were picked up by some locals and given a lift on the back of a horse-drawn wagon. And speaking of walking, it looks like that's what we're going to be doing," Valerie said as she pushed open the driver side door and got out of the Jeep.

I was still in my semi-reclined position against the back door of the Jeep when Leecy turned to face me, asking, "Is she serious?"

"About what?" I answered.

"About Granny Granny killing a guy like that?"

"Oh, yeah; she's quite serious. Wait till she tells you about her years with the Mossad."

"Who are you people and what have you done with my parents?"

I was pushing open the rear door when I answered her, saying, "I love you too, sweetheart."

CHAPTER
FOUR

Leecy and I joined her mother at the front of the Jeep to stare at the fallen tree blocking the road.

"Well, it's too big to move out of our way, so we'll have to walk. I figure we have about five miles before the woods give way to East Park. We'll need a car and somewhere to stay the night," Valerie said as she glanced at her watch. "It's 3:15 p.m. The sun won't set till after eight o'clock. Let's grab our Go bags and stuff them with the extra supplies we bought and move out."

I checked the reception on my mobile phone and saw there were no bars. There was nothing I could do about that. I could only hope if there still was an Agent Wakefield she would leave a message.

"Here, come get your backpacks." I said. "I've packed them as full as they're going to get. What do we do about the Jeep?"

"The Jeep will be fine," Val said. "No one is coming out here till the fall when deer-hunting season begins. We can come back for it later."

"Quick question. You did say each bag has $25,000 in it? I get to keep that money, right?" Leecy asked.

"Not a chance," I said.

"Okay, worth a shot. So tell me about after the war, and

what does all that have to do with you, Mom?"

Val shouldered her pack and climbed over the downed tree before she answered. "Right, so after the war, your Granny Granny continued to tour with the USO for a while. According to that cloth map she made as a keepsake, they went to places like Nuremburg, Munich and Stuttgart, and a bunch of smaller towns throughout Germany."

Valerie wasn't waiting for us to climb over the tree. She had one speed and that was full speed. Leecy and I jogged to catch up to her. I took up my usual spot when we were hiking as a family: at the rear of the line of Grangers.

"When the USO disbanded in 1947, Leona had been back in the States living and working in New York since 1946. She wouldn't marry Ernst for another two years. She was busy pursuing her career as an actress when the same two men that had recruited her years before paid her another visit in September of 1947."

"Oh no, what did they want her to do this time?" Leecy asked.

"This time they had good news. Good news, that is, with a caveat. They laid out plans for a new secret organization that would be in what we now know as Israel."

"But there was no Israel in June of 1947. I studied that in history. The UN General Assembly passed the partition of Palestine resolution in August."

"Right, A-plus for your studious efforts. But Jews had been living in Palestine for years before the UN vote. There were several underground outlaw groups fighting the British, before they finally left, and the Palestinians, who had been living there for generations. You've heard of the Irgun, who were responsible for the famous King David Hotel bombing in 1946?"

"Right!" said Leecy. "That was awful."

"Yes, but it had a big impact on popular opinion both for and against. But these men who recruited your Granny Granny Leona weren't from the Irgun, but another group still in the planning stage within the Labor Party government formed by David Ben Gurian. A group that started out as the Central Institute of Coordination, and eventually became known as Mossad. They offered her a job in the new organization, but she declined. Then they upped the ante and said they'd provide financial assistance of any kind to any member of her future family, assuming she would have one of course, as long as they agreed to become part of the Mossad. She asked them why such interest in her future family. Why sign up her children or her children's children when they'd have all of Israel to select candidates?"

"Yes, that's weird, Mom. What did they say?" Leecy asked.

I smiled at the questions. Not because I knew the answer, but because I understood the reasoning behind the approach the then fledgling Mossad was taking.

"They said it was Leona's bloodline."

"Bloodline?"

"And they were right," I chimed in.

"Yes, dear. They wanted to recruit the best and brightest; to pursue the future generations of those bloodlines deemed to be extraordinary to protect Jews and Jewish interests around the world. The men told her the new organization wouldn't forget what she had done during the war and would be waiting to answer her call. They left her with contact information. She never saw them in person again."

"So the Mossad paid for your education and you worked for them?"

"Yes, that's correct. I was sixteen, same age as you are, when Leona told me the stories I've just told you. She took me to the Ritz-Carlton in Buckhead, Atlanta. We had tea. She said she hadn't thought twice about the offer when her sons were born, or when my brothers were born. No, she said it never entered her mind to act on the offer till she held me in her arms. She said she knew in an instant what my future would be."

"So, spill it. What happened? What did you do?"

"I jumped at the chance. Not because I wanted to be a spy. No, I wanted to go to college, and Dad's business was struggling. There was no way he could afford to pay tuition. So, I told Leona 'let's do it.' The next thing I know, I was an early enrollee at Yale, and there was only one request made of me while I was there."

"What was that?" Leecy asked.

"I had to learn Russian."

"Russian? Why Russian?"

"All in due course," Valerie said and then continued. "So, I was at Yale and it's the fall of 1985. I loved school and, like you, I never seemed to have enough to do. But the great thing about college is you can take on as much work as you can handle. I was racing through my classes with a double load each semester. The only wrinkle was that during holiday breaks in the schedule I didn't get to come home; I was sent to Mossad training camps. My first camp was in upstate New York near Lake Placid."

"Sounds like you just studied all the time and never had any fun," Leecy said.

"I had fun. Plenty of fun. For me it was exhilarating. I was with other girls like me. We all shared similar backgrounds and did everything together. I was learning a fighting style called Krav Maga. I learned how to shoot everything from a pistol to a sniper rifle. Actually, I learned how to fire several different sniper rifles, like the Russian Mosin-Nagant, the US Army XM21, and the Israeli Imi Galtaz. I also learned basic pharmacology: drug interactions, drug contraindications and side effects, which in most cases resulted in death. I was doing what I loved to do, which was learning. I soaked it all up like a sponge. About midway through my first training session, I was given a dossier."

"You mean a file on somebody?" Leecy asked.

"Yes, a file on a target to be precise."

"That didn't take long."

"Well, I wasn't there to learn to bake a cake. Anyway, the first assignment was easy. See, the dossier wasn't just given to me. All of my fellow students also received a copy."

"Why?"

"We were told to memorize the contents of the dossier and develop a strategy for eliminating the target in a way that wouldn't attract the attention of the police, or arouse any suspicion of foul play."

"Why would the Mossad care about police attention? They're known for high profile public assassinations. It's how they send the message to their enemies."

"You're right, of course, but that's not always the case. This target, as well as the next three I was eventually given, were to be handled in a much more discrete fashion. The death was what was important, not taking credit for the death."

"Okay, so give me the details."

"Like I said, every girl was given the same task, and we had to present our solutions forty-eight hours after receiving the dossier. My solution was chosen. I'd made use of the extensive background information on the target's daily habits and routines, as well as the target's medical history. In January of 1986, I traveled to Buenos Aries and dispatched a Nazi war criminal that had escaped detection for almost forty years.

"Waiel Hiemlich, the Nazi in our dossier, had been tried in absentia at the Nuremberg Trials and found guilty of murdering Latvian Jews. He'd been sentenced to death, but escaped Europe and lived in seclusion in Argentina. The Mossad found Hiemlich by spreading lots of money around the region. I arrived on a Monday evening and made my way through the city to a hotel near the café the target frequented every morning. He would drink two cups of coffee and smoke two cigarettes to start his day. My plan was simple. I knew from the medical portion of his dossier he suffered from hypertension and refused to take medication for the condition. That fact coupled with his smoking was a deadly combination, and one I could use to my advantage.

"I arrived at the café early Tuesday morning before the target. I wore a loose fitting blouse and bikini top underneath, and short shorts and sandals. The pictures I'd seen of the target showed a thin, older man, very reminiscent of his younger self. I hoped my attire would help provide the distraction I needed. I didn't have to wait long before I saw the target approaching the café. He took a seat at the outdoor table next to mine and even greeted me. The information in his file proved accurate, and as a waitress appeared as if on cue with his first cup of coffee, I leaned over towards him, letting my breast caress his shoulder, and asked him for a light. As I held my cigarette, I slipped a tiny capsule of colorless, odorless epinephrine into his coffee as he produced his lighter. He lit my cigarette and one of his own, and we chatted in Spanish and sipped our coffees. When he ordered a second cup, I leaned over again and dropped in another dose of epinephrine. Then I got up slowly and said goodbye with a smile and a light kiss on his cheek.

"As I walked away from the café, I heard the screams from the waitress. I was back at school before the Buenos Aires newspaper reported the death of the local man as a heart attack. A copy of the article was slipped under the door of my dorm room at Yale."

"Did you feel bad killing an old man?"

"Not a bit. This man was responsible for the deaths of tens of thousands of Latvian men, women and children. All Jews. Not a soldier among them. And he was free, living a comfortable life without a drop of guilt or remorse. He'd already lived longer than he should've."

"You mentioned three other missions. Can you tell me about those?"

"I didn't have another mission for a while. My training continued and by the middle of my second year at Yale, I knew I would have enough credits to graduate early. Like I said, I hadn't had much contact with the family back home, because the schedule I was keeping was intense, but I knew the family business was struggling. So, I called Leona and asked her to ask her contacts about my attending graduate school. Whoever they were, they were all too happy to pay once again and like before, there was only one caveat: I had to get an MBA, a Master's Degree in Business Administration, with a specialty in international economy. I agreed and they paid, so off to Wharton I went. My plan was two-fold. One part of the plan was to save the family business by growing sales overseas, and the other was fulfilling my obligation to the Mossad. I owed them one year of service for every year of education I received. That was the deal I agreed to."

"By the start of my first year at Wharton, I'd been able to pitch my new plan for INESCO's future to your Uncles David and Isaac. Then the three of us convinced our father. I was on schedule to graduate in the spring of 1989. I was on cloud nine. I was a graduate from Yale and a soon-to-be graduate of the Wharton Business School, and all in four years. INESCO was moving in the right direction, and I was working with the Mossad fulfilling my four-year commitment.

"My second assignment was a little more complicated. I was sent to Beirut to assassinate a Lebanese scientist working to help Palestine develop a long-range missile program. It was the summer of 1987, and the Lebanese Civil War had been ongoing since 1982. My pre-mission briefing took place in a hotel near the Wharton campus. I met with half a dozen members of the Mossad over a two-day period. The importance of drawing little or no attention at all to my mission's objective was reinforced repeatedly. Two assassinations in Athens in 1986 had garnered too much press. I was directed to take out the target without any blowback on Israel.

"The target was Fakald Juli. The report said he had a personal security guard of five to six men at all times, except when he slept or was visited by prostitutes, but even then he wasn't really alone, just out of sight of the guards. It seemed that Fakald had a bad habit of liking sex outdoors, so he'd take these women out on the balcony.

"Big mistake.

"I was flown into the Israeli-controlled security zone and my contact drove me to an empty, bombed-out building in the heart of the Syrian section, directly across from the target. The two buildings were separated by a one square block park. Really just a few trees and shrubs, but no grass to speak of, just dirt.

"I was left alone in the third floor apartment with a twelve hour window to do the job. The sun had set and it was dark outside. It was six p.m. local time. War was sporadic by 1987, but it was still very dangerous. I was scared of being found. I knew what opposition forces would do to me. So, I busied myself setting up my Sardius sniper rifle with suppressor and night vision scope. I knew from my intelligence report that he took a lover about every three days. If the pattern held true, he would be at it again that night. All I had to do was wait."

"You're in war torn Beirut in 1987 trying to assassinate someone in the dead of night from how far away?" Leecy asked.

"300 meters, give or take."

"Jesus Mom, if you'd been captured they would've tortured you or worse."

"Well, I wasn't captured. As a matter of fact, I was never even seen. Fakald appeared naked on his balcony with his back to my position at two a.m. He was dead a second later."

"What about the prostitute? He wasn't out on the balcony alone, was he?"

"No, she was there. She was just out of my line of sight, and ran back into the room screaming for his bodyguards. I took the rifle with me when I left the room, after signaling my contact to pick me up. We were back inside the Israeli safe zone in minutes, and I was on a plane within the hour. The killing was treated as an accident, because of all the regular shooting and street fighting in that area. There was no blowback on Israel. We were in the clear."

"Tell me something: how far can you shoot and hit the target?" Leecy asked.

"800 meters was my longest shot in practice, but I've never had to shoot that far for real. I thought my next mission was going to be a long distance shot, because of all the training they were putting me through, but it turned out to be something quite different. I was sent back to South America in the fall of 1988 to assassinate another Nazi war criminal named Mikhail Klein.

"Klein lived in the central region of Argentina, near Lake Laguna Mar Chiquita. He had this cabin near the abandoned Gran Hotel Vienna. I arrived in Cordoba, Argentina and was met by my local contact and driven to a location northeast of the city.

"The target was known to be an avid fisherman, taking a small boat out on Lake Laguna Mar twice a day. I thought about how to do this job, and decided that drowning would be the best way. Actually, all I had to do was separate him from his boat and let fatigue do the work for me."

"What do you mean?"

"Well, the lake isn't very deep, but it is large. I swam behind him at a discrete distance until he reached the deepest part of the lake and began fishing. I eased up very quietly behind his little boat that was no bigger than a kayak, really, and tipped it over. He never saw me, and by the time I'd swum to shore he'd drowned. The locals treated it as it was: a drowning. No fuss. Just an accident."

"Crap, Mom, that's cold blooded."

"Maybe so. All I knew at the time was it was the end of a very bad man. As all the assignments to that point had been. But that all changed, when I got a very unusual call."

"Oh no, why do I sense danger of some kind?" Leecy asked.

"Couldn't it just be bad news? Why do you think something dangerous is about to happen?" Valerie asked.

"I was just thinking about that time in history. Reagan was the President till January of 1989. He'd given his famous 'tear down this wall' speech imploring the Soviet leader Gorbachev to tear down the Berlin wall in 1987. When the wall started to come down two years later on November 9, 1989, there was unrest throughout Europe, but never more so in Russia. The tide was turning away from Communism in the Soviet Union. The world waited for the Soviet Union's collapse, and though it took another two years, the Soviet Union did collapse in 1991. Gorbachev resigned and was replaced by Yeltsin and the Democratic Russian Movement had taken hold."

"Like mother, like daughter," I said.

"What?" Leecy asked.

"Nothing. I just bet there aren't fifty people that can recite the geo-political history of the late 1980s and early 1990s without using Google, but you and your mother have it memorized," I said.

"So what, I remember everything I read," Leecy said.

"Why do you think I said like mother, like daughter? You're both geniuses."

"Oh, I thought you were poking fun."

"I would never do that. Never," I said.

"Are you two finished or do we all need to kiss and hug for another ten minutes?" Valerie asked.

"Enough said." I shut up.

"Leecy, you're spot on with your history lesson. The geo-political climate was very unstable. Not everyone involved was ready for the change that was coming. That's part of the reason why the Soviet Union held on two years after the wall came down. The dominos eventually fell, but it took a little help to get them all down, and that's why my phone rang in the winter of 1989."

"Wait, you were involved in all this?" Leecy asked.

"Yes, I was. But before I get into that you need to know something. You need to understand the Mossad had become far more than just assassins. Sure, there are assassins in the agency. That's true. There were also some of the world's brightest minds and forward thinkers working to predict world events. And they get more than their fair share of predictions right." Valerie paused and stepped across another downed tree. Then said, "So, I get a call instructing me to report to a local hotel for a meeting. That was standard operating procedure, like I told you already. I had done it so many times, but from the moment I walked into that hotel room I knew this meeting was different. There was only one person there, not the usual half dozen, and I'd never seen her before. She introduced herself only as my mission liaison. I remember asking at the time what was meant by mission liaison. The woman never gave me her name, nor did she ever answer my question, at least not directly."

"So, what did she say, Mom?"

"She said I'd been chosen because of my marksmanship. I'd scored as expert with the soviet Dragunov SVDSN sniper rifle and, coupled with my Russian language skills, I was the perfect candidate." Valerie stopped talking.

Leecy didn't say a word. I assumed she was running

through the many possible scenarios that her mother might've been involved with. I could almost see her putting together the bits and pieces of data like the sniper rifle, the language skills, and the training to piece together the puzzle. That's why it didn't shock me when Leecy arrived at the correct assumption.

"So, Mom...you're responsible for the rumored assassination of Victor Wilhelm Volodarsky, the old Soviet hardliner leader back in 1989? The death had been covered up and the only reason I'm aware of it is that one of my assignments in AP History involved a lot of research on the U.S.S.R., and I found a website dedicated to the conspiracy theory about his death. His own people were said to have carried it out, because they feared he was turning moderate in his views. There was even a story about ex-KGB officers conspiring to kill him, which is why the Soviet government swept the whole thing under the rug. He'd been a man of the Party, so to speak, but his growing popularity had put him at odds with some other hardliners and they killed him. But now you're telling me you did it and helped pave the way for Boris Yeltsin to be elected to the Congress of People's Deputies of Russia. That assassination helped the Democratic movement in Russia to take a firm grip on the region. Holy crap, are you kidding me?" Leecy said.

Valerie stopped walking and turned to face her daughter. This was the moment Valerie had worried about for so many years and now it was upon her. My fears got the better of me and in an effort to take the heat off Valerie I made an assumption.

"Don't be too hard on your mom," I started to say, but was cut off by Leecy.

"Be too hard on her for killing a man that wanted to continue oppressing his own people? Not likely, Dad. No, I want to hear all the details. Every single one of them, and don't leave anything out. Okay?"

We were very close to the end of the trail. I checked the time and the bars on the cell phone. It was after 5:00 p.m., and I had one reception bar.

"Where do you think we are?" I asked.

"We're on the southern end of East Park. We'll need a car from here. We have about fifteen more miles to cover before we reach the hotels that ring the Atlanta airport. I can use some of our cash and my fake ID to buy a cheap car from one of the used car lots in East Park, or we can wait here till the sun sets and borrow a car for a little while," Valerie said.

"Steal a car? Now you tell me you can steal a car. Okay, I vote steal a car." Leecy said.

"No stealing unless necessary," I said. "We'll buy a cheap car. We don't need any more attention than we already have. Don't forget there is an APB out for us, and the FBI is looking for us."

"I know, but stealing a car sounds like more fun. Did the Mossad teach you to steal cars, Mom?" Leecy asked.

"Among other things," Valerie answered, and she started walking again.

"Really," Leecy said thoughtfully, and then rushing to catch up to Valerie, asked, "What else happened in the hotel room with the liaison lady?"

"I was briefed on the mission. I was given my code name, travel documents and my liaison's code number, and told how to contact her. And to be ready in one hour."

"That's great and all, but break it down for me," Leecy said.

"My mission, as you already surmised, was to assassinate Mr. Volodarsky. He was the leader of a group that wanted to restore the pre-Gorbachev, pre-Perestroika status quos in the Soviet Union, so he had to be eliminated. My code name was Scorpion. Any communication that didn't contain my code name wasn't to be trusted. My travel documents for that mission were under the name Beth Bradley. I was traveling on a student visa studying international business administration. All of the papers were false, but the fact that my cover was based on my actual studies made it very easy for me to be believable if questioned. My liaison's code number was 31261714. I contacted her using a similar method to the one your dad used earlier at the store to contact the CIA. It was the early days of cell phone technology. Pay phones were more reliable."

Valerie walked through the last of the woods and stepped onto the dead end of a dirt road. I stopped behind Val and Leecy. I could see over their shoulders to the back of an abandoned warehouse, but nothing else. "Where to now?" I asked.

"If nothing has changed since the last time I was here," Valerie began, "we follow this dirt road for about a mile. Then we hang a left and walk about a half-mile. We'll find the southern end of the main drag that runs through East Park. That's where the used car dealers traditionally set up shop, but like I said, it's been a while."

"How long is a while, exactly?" Leecy asked as she followed her mother out of the woods and onto the dirt road.

"Twenty years or more," Valerie said.

"Wait a minute," Leecy called, but Valerie just kept on walking.

"We're basing our decisions on twenty year old information? Since when has that ever been a good idea?"

"It's all we have," I said and placed a hand on Leecy's back-pack to move her along. "We don't have our smart phones anymore, because we don't want to risk being tracked or traced. So, we walk and see what we can find. I know standing here talking doesn't accomplish anything."

"What if we walk all this way and there's no car dealer? No hotels. What then?" Leecy asked.

"We figure it out," I said. "This is what it was like back be-fore smart phones, iPads and the Internet. This is what it was like when I was an operator with the CIA. The information I received wasn't always accurate. I had to improvise. I had to adapt to the situation. I was forced to think for myself and solve problems and find solutions that weren't always appar-ent. Same thing with your mom and her time with the Mossad," I said.

We caught up to Valerie at the intersection of the dirt road and the asphalt of the main drag and turned left. I could see the edge of the expanded East Park no more than a block away.

"The town has expanded. Looks like a car lot dead ahead. We'll be driving in less than thirty minutes."

"What? You're just going to walk onto the lot and buy a car?" Leecy asked. "Won't we look weird wearing these packs? Won't that draw unwanted attention?"

"In any other town maybe, but not here," Valerie answered.

"Why is that?"

"I read an article one time detailing Georgia's hiking trails. There was a section about the trails around East Park. The article mentioned how common it was for hikers to be seen crossing the streets of the small town and eating at the local diners. So, I don't think we'll stand out at all. And as far as buying a car is concerned, all the dealer will care about is the cash in my hand."

"Well okay, then," Leecy said. "When do I get to hear the rest of the story?"

Checking her watch, Val said, "It's almost 6:00 p.m. Let's get the car and some food. When we find a hotel we can talk some more."

I was checking my cell phone reception. I had three bars, but no calls. I looked up to see Valerie watching me and shook my head. She turned and walked the last hundred yards to the first used car dealer on the block and as she did she said, "Wait here. I'll be right back."

I dropped my pack on the grass and sat down next to it. Leecy joined me, and together we watched Valerie enter the small office of the used car dealer. My eyes drifted from the building, looking further down the road. I could see fast food joints, mini-marts, and gas stations.

The sound of an approaching car caught my attention. I looked up to see a brown 1990's Oldsmobile Delta 88 sedan roll to a stop in front of us. I grabbed my pack and climbed in the backseat, because Leecy was already opening the door for the front passenger seat.

"How much?"

"Twelve hundred dollars. I figure the car will last a month," Valerie answered and then said, "Now, we eat. After dinner, we drive to the Atlanta Airport and find a hotel."

Dinner was from Chick-fil-A, not because we loved fast food chicken sandwiches, but because it was the best among a lot of bad choices. We ate grilled chicken sandwiches with whole-wheat buns and drank bottles of water. We shared a protein bar, and each of us ate a banana. The bananas were purchased from a fruit stand next to the gas station where we filled the tank of the Oldsmobile.

The drive to the Atlanta Airport took longer than expected because of traffic. Leecy was asleep in the front seat by the time we stopped at the Motel 6 south of the airport. Valerie got us a room through the Plexiglas-enclosed check-in window, and then drove us around the hotel to park near, but not in front of, room 121. I grabbed Leecy's pack from the front seat and carried it along with mine into the room, following Valerie through the door. I returned to the car to carry my sleeping daughter to the room. I placed her on one of the double beds, and Valerie covered her with a blanket. I motioned for Valerie to join me outside the room and she followed me out the door.

"No word from Wakefield?"

"Not yet, but it's early. The CIA is actively checking my operator's communication designations. But it may take longer than I hoped. We need to talk about what we are going to do if the cavalry doesn't come."

"I don't see that our plan of action is any different with or without the CIA. We need to piece the puzzle together. We know five of the players. The two from this morning, Smotherman and Pickett, Agent Porter, Travis Smith and Briggs Smith, but we don't know if Porter is really FBI or not. Ranger Smith told us Porter was working with someone else, but we don't know who it is," Valerie said.

"Right, and he told us whatever Porter and his partner want, they thought they could get it by kidnapping Leecy. So what does that tell us?"

"Whatever Porter and his partner are after involves IN-ESCO."

"Yep, no other reason to go after Leecy. Smart if you think about it. Your brothers and father would give away the company to save Leecy," I said.

"They wouldn't hesitate. But that doesn't tell us what Porter and his mystery partner are after. I'd need to access the computers at INESCO to figure that one out."

"Okay, so if we hear from Wakefield, maybe she can help us figure out who the mystery partner is and what they want. With all the cell phone and email data being collected and analyzed by government agencies, I wouldn't be surprised if there's some chatter about this somewhere. With a few keyword searches, I bet Wakefield could tell us the answers to our questions."

Valerie looked at her watch. "It's after 8 o'clock, let's try and sleep. We've been up since four this morning. I'll sleep till midnight if you'll take the first watch."

"Happy to do it," I said and then added, "I'm sorry your birthday plans didn't work out the way we wanted them to."

Val turned and kissed me full on the lips.

"I love you. Don't apologize for something that's not your fault. We can always celebrate my birthday later. I just want to keep Leecy safe."

I held her and kissed her again.

"I love you, too. We'll keep her safe. There's nowhere she could be safer than with us. Now get some sleep."

Valerie gently closed the door to room 121. I walked over to the Oldsmobile and climbed inside. The car was backed into a parking space at the end of the row of motel rooms. I had an unobstructed view of the parking lot and entrance to the motel. In the distance I could see the interstate, and beyond that, the glow of the busiest airport in the world. I settled in behind the wheel and remembered my CIA training for situations just like this. The trick wasn't just to stay awake, but to remain alert. I was taught the best way to do that was to focus on the details.

I started the process by counting the cars in the parking lot. I moved from doing that to the windows of the adjacent motels and counted the number of rooms with lights shining behind pulled curtains. From there, I moved to cars exiting the interstate and then planes taking off from and landing at the airport. I would circle back to the cars in the parking lot eventually and begin the process all over again.

I was on the third round of my mind game when the phone in my pocket began to vibrate. I pulled the phone from my pocket. I was confident it could only be one person, because only one person had the number for the phone, and without taking my eyes off the black SUV exiting the interstate I said, "Granger. ID number 63682416, code Robert Earl Davenport."

"Well, I'll be damned," the voice of Agent Tammy Daniel Wakefield said, "I never thought I'd hear from you again as long as I lived, and here you are calling in a code RED, operator in distress. What in the hell are you into?"

"It's nice to hear your voice, Tammy, but I've got a little problem down here in Georgia," I said.

The SUV I was watching turned left after exiting the interstate and drove along the highway access road toward the row of the three motels, one of which was ours. I could see it making a right turn into the parking lot of the first one, where it disappeared from view.

I relaxed a little and said to Agent Wakefield, "I was hoping to enlist the help of my old agency."

"If you mean you want me to help you with the All Points Bulletin you and your wife and daughter have on your heads, that's a big ask, Ron. I don't know what you think I can do about that."

"If you'll hear me out, I think you'll find that the situation is not what it seems to be. There's more to the story."

"There always was where you were concerned. At least that hasn't changed. Before you enlighten me, answer this one question."

"Go ahead."

"What's in it for me?" Agent Wakefield asked.

I can't say I was shocked by the question, but I was surprised. The quid pro quo usually came after the favor had been granted, but I couldn't argue the point. I didn't have much to offer in return, but I had an idea of what she wanted.

"Dealer's choice."

"Well, all right then. Let's hear your tale, but be forewarned that this conversation is being recorded."

I smiled. This felt all too familiar.

I started at the beginning and told her everything that happened since the morning's break-in and attempted kidnapping. She listened only. She never spoke, never asked a question. I knew from prior experience that this kind of attention was a good sign. Her silence meant she believed me.

I was ending the story when the black SUV I'd seen earlier came into sight. I watched it cruise through the parking lot of the motel next door. The SUV moved directly across from my position in the car, so I could see clearly that it had a damaged front right quarter panel. I slid down in my seat in an effort to hide behind the steering wheel. I was able to kick my legs over the center hump into the passenger side footwell and get my head below the steering wheel height. I knew without question the SUV was looking for us, but what I didn't know was how anyone could've found us.

I had finished the story and hadn't spoken for a minute, watching the SUV, when Agent Wakefield responded.

"The Westin downtown. Be here tomorrow at 10:00 a.m. I'm in suite 2211." She paused a minute and then added, "It'll be good to see you again."

"One more thing," I asked, "have you been tracking the number I gave you?"

"No. Why?"

"Is it possible to trace a prepaid cell phone?"

"Better pull the battery from your phone now," she said quickly, and hung up.

I flipped the phone over, popped the battery out and removed the SIM card. I returned the dismantled phone to my pocket and was about to open the driver's side door but stopped, because the black SUV had also stopped. If I opened the door, the interior dome light would come on and most certainly be noticed by whoever was watching.

I had to turn off the dome light. I had to get to the room where Valerie and Leecy were sleeping. It was only a matter of time before they made their way to the Motel 6 parking lot. I had to act.

I peered over the steering wheel. The width of the Motel 6

parking lot and a thin grass divider was all that lay between them and the Oldsmobile. The distance was about two hundred feet. I couldn't risk opening the door. I couldn't risk reaching for the dome light. I had to assume the occupants had night vision gear and were actively using it. All I could do was wait.

I heard an engine revving and peered over the steering wheel in time to see the black SUV moving again. I watched it drive the length of the parking lot next door before turning toward the parking lot's exit. I popped the plastic cap off of the interior dome light and removed the light bulb with my right hand, opening the door with my left. I checked the SUV's position as I silently closed the car door, and saw its taillights illuminated as it stopped briefly before continuing to turn right. I'd be out of sight of the van for a few seconds. I ran to the room. Inserting the old fashioned key into the lock, I turned the doorknob and stepped inside to find the girls awake and staring out the window.

"We saw you talking on the phone. Agent Wakefield called. She's going to meet with us, but we owe her, right?" Valerie said, still looking out the window with Leecy.

"That's right, my dear. We meet tomorrow morning at the Westin in downtown Atlanta in suite 2211, but right now we need to decide what we're going to do about the SUV," I said, and then because it just occurred to me, I asked, "How long have you two been watching me through the window?"

"Ten minutes," Leecy said. "Mom spotted the SUV when it exited the highway. I don't think we have anything to worry about just yet. We need to sit tight. You did remove the battery from your phone, right Dad?"

"Yes," I answered, "Better late than never."

"They can't pinpoint our location without the phones. There are hundreds of rooms on this street. I wonder if they were listening to the call as well?"

"I didn't think prepaid cellphones could be traced." I said, "But now I do, and that makes me wonder if they heard everything."

"Don't you read the papers, Dad, or watch the news?" Leecy asked. "The secrets are out. The NSA scandal blew the lid off the government's cellphone, smartphone tracking and data collection techniques months ago. The old-fashioned trace-and-track gave agencies a location based on cellphone towers, but with smartphone technology the trace-and-track is more exact. Most of the applications on the iPhone generate a location pulse. This constant location signal sent by a smartphone, or map or application to the satellite, pinpoints the exact location of the user, but the cellphones we have don't have that feature."

"Forgive me, I've been out of the spy game for a while. The last time I was tasked with a mission was 2007. You're a lot more up on this than I am, honey."

"You're forgiven. The guys in the SUV are tracing us the old-fashioned way and have a general location for our phones, but not an exact location. That's why they're driving around. They're trying to pinpoint our location. Now that our phones are powered off they might as well be looking for a needle in a haystack. There's only one way to track a prepaid cellphone like the ones we have. The person or agency doing the tracking must have the phone numbers. That means your contact at the CIA gave you up, the number was obtained from her without her knowledge, or, most likely, the store where we got the phones gave Agent Porter a list of the ones we bought."

I was standing near the door to the room peering through the curtains. I listened to my daughter explain the situation and was just about to ask her another question when the SUV entered my field of vision. I froze. They were driving straight for us. I brought my finger to my mouth signaling for quiet. The big black SUV rolled by our room and kept moving. I shifted my feet and turned my body to allow my eyes to follow it. I watched as it stopped in front of the Oldsmobile, which was parked at the end of the parking lot ten doors away from our room.

I looked down at Valerie. She was seated with her back to me in a chair at the small table in front of the window. I saw the 9mm Glock in Valerie's right hand, and bent down to Leecy's ear.

"Move as quietly as you can to the bathroom and close the door." Leecy did as I asked. I moved from the door to the wall behind Valerie. I had a better view from that angle. I watched the doors open from over Valerie's shoulders. I flinched the slightest bit as two familiar faces and frames exited the vehicle and walked to either side of the Oldsmobile. The white bandages on the face of Agent Briggs Smith gave him away, and I wondered if I'd made a terrible mistake allowing him to live.

Agent Travis Smith opened the front passenger side of the Oldsmobile, and we watched as he did a double take. Must be reacting to the dome light not working. Then they took out their flashlights and inspected the vehicle and the dome light.

I tapped Valerie on the shoulder and motioned her toward the bathroom. We grabbed the Go bags and moved as quietly as we could through the small dark room. We didn't talk till we were inside the bathroom behind the closed door.

"It's safe to assume," I started saying, "they now know we're here. I screwed up on the dome light. I should've replaced the plastic cover. They'll more than likely use their FBI credentials to get a look at the guest registry."

"Yep," Valerie said, "and as soon as they realize the car is parked in front of a vacant room they'll know where we are. We have about fifteen minutes before they come for us."

"I'm sorry. I screwed up. I guess I'm a little rusty."

"No need for apologies."

"Okay, so now what?" Leecy asked and then said, "we can't stay in this bathroom forever."

"We run," I said.

"Let's go," Valerie said.

I followed Leecy and Valerie out of the bathroom and we all shouldered our packs before reaching the door. Valerie looked through the peephole and then the curtains before opening the door to the room. She had her Glock in her right hand, and she opened the door with her left.

"All clear. Stay close to me," she said before she opened the door all the way and sprinted across the parking lot toward the adjacent hotel.

I closed the door to the room and ran to catch up to the girls, who were already crossing the thin grass divider, when the sound of a car's engine roaring to life caused me to hesitate. I looked toward the sound and then in the direction of the girls, who dropped down and were crouching behind a Ford pickup truck parked in a spot close to the motel building next door. I removed my pack, shoved it under a car, and was crawling after it as the black SUV came into view.

From my hiding place beneath the car, I watched Travis and Briggs walk toward the room we'd vacated moments before. Using a key they must've gotten from the night manager, they walked right into the room. The lights came on for about fifteen seconds and then off again. I watched the Smith boys come out and close the door. Agent Briggs Smith pulled a phone from his pocket. He was walking toward me as he dialed. I could hear his half of the conversation.

"We found them, but they aren't here. We've got the car, but we lost the cellphone signal.

"No, I mean we found where they were, but they've moved on.

"How could they have made us?

"Yes sir.

"He wants us to report back and wait for further instructions," Agent Briggs Smith said to Travis Smith, and then he added, "If I ever get my hands on the old man again, I'm going to kill him. Porter keeps riding my ass about what happened at the Granger house."

"Well, you did let a forty-six-year-old kick your ass," Travis said with a laugh, and turned for the driver side of the SUV.

"Yeah, well, Porter's partner is looking into the dude's file. What do you wanna bet that everything I told you the old man said turns out to be true?" Briggs Smith asked.

"Whatever. He's forty-six years old," Travis said, and closed his door before driving away.

I pressed myself into the asphalt as the big SUV made a U-turn. Its headlights washed over my position for a split second. I waited to move from my hiding place till I could no longer hear the SUV's engine. I crawled out from under the car and was reaching back for my pack when I heard Leecy's voice.

"Do you need a lift?"

I stood to see my daughter smiling at me from the front

passenger seat of the four-door Ford pickup truck she and Valerie had been hiding behind.

"I don't want to know," I said.

"Dad, it only took Mom three minutes and forty-five seconds to steal this truck. And we switched the license plates with the car parked next to it," Leecy said, and then asked, "How cool is that?"

"It's not cool. It's just necessary," I heard Valerie say from behind the wheel. "Let's not make this more dramatic than we have to. You coming, Ron?"

"I'm coming," I said. I opened the rear door and climbed in the back seat.

CHAPTER
FIVE

"Why is Wakefield in Atlanta? Did you ask her that? What do you think she wants from you in return for her help?" Valerie asked as she accelerated slowly through the parking lot like nothing had happened at all.

"I don't know," I replied, "and I never got a chance to ask her. That's the least of our concerns right now. I think we should be more concerned with the fact that the Smiths and Porter got on to us so easily. How'd they do that?"

"You know my theory, Dad; either your contact at the CIA gave you up or they got the number without her knowing."

"Tammy would never give us up, Leecy," I said. "It's more likely they got the numbers from the store where we bought the phones."

"You're right, Dad. They probably looked at a map and made an educated guess as to where we might go. They checked the store and bingo," Leecy said. "Why would the lady you say you trust so much and that knows you so well betray you? That doesn't make any sense to me."

I was already thinking ahead.

"How are we supposed to drive into a big city like Atlanta, enter a hotel and meet with Wakefield with an APB out for us? I don't see how we can do that. Maybe one of us, but not all three of us."

"We'll be fine," Valerie said.

I listened with my customary amazement as my wife rattled off the plan, and her extreme confidence in what she was saying was contagious. I believed we had nothing to worry about.

"Here's what we'll do," she continued. "First we drive into the city and park the truck close to the hotel. Then we walk the short distance from the car to the hotel lobby and into the elevators like we're guests at the hotel."

I hoped it would be that simple. She thought it would be that simple, and if history was any indicator, she was right. I trusted her, and that's all that mattered.

I settled into the seat as we left the airport lights behind us. I could see the clock on the dashboard. It was almost 2:00 a.m., only 24 hours since the break-in.

Leecy broke the short-lived silence, asking her mother, "Will you tell me about the mission to Russia in the winter of 1989?"

"Sure, we have a little time now," Valerie said, and then began, "I told you about meeting with my liaison and being told to be ready to go in one hour."

"Yes, I remember all of that. What happened next?"

"It was snowing and freezing cold when I arrived in Leningrad. I was met at the airport and driven to a safe house in the heart of the city. There was a briefing on the latest intelligence report, and after the meeting I slept for about three hours, and then ate dinner with the others before walking to the Rinaldi Hotel a few blocks away. A room had been reserved for me using my false credentials and my team had given me a key. Once I was in the room, I checked the closet and found a red wig and a KGB officer's uniform. I changed into the uniform, put on the wig and left the hotel through the rear entrance. I walked two blocks and entered the front door of 31 Blokhina Street at exactly 2045 hours. I remember there was a group of young men gathered in the vestibule. They were smoking and passing a bottle of Vodka around. I told them in Russian not to loiter and move along. Part of the plan was to make certain I was seen. That group of guys was perfect. I figured they'd surely remember the red-haired female KGB officer entering the building. They grumbled at me in Russian, but moved along.

"Once the men were gone, I climbed the stairs two at a time. They were metal stairs, and I thought the echo would wake the dead before I reached the roof access door, which I found open just like I was told it would be. I stepped out onto the roof and the wind cut through the heavy wool overcoat. I could see the glass onion dome in the center of building thirty-one's roof. The dome was in direct line of sight with the front of the Yubileiny Concert Hall. I crossed the roof and entered the dome to find the Dragunov SVDSN sniper rifle and backpack in place.

"The rifle was mounted on a bench rest and aimed in the direction of the front of the concert hall through the one glassless pane in the dome. I checked the contents of the pack and removed my change of clothes. The plan was for me to leave an insignia button from the uniform and blame the KGB for the assassination. That piece of evidence along with the gang of guys as eyewitnesses in the lobby would be all that was needed."

"Very clever," Leecy said.

"So, I removed the wool coat and pulled a button free, dropping it on the floor. Then I folded the coat as a kneepad before placing it on the floor. I checked the weapon thoroughly, making sure it wasn't loaded and the barrel wasn't obstructed. Three hundred meters isn't a difficult distance, but it's challenging, and was the exact distance I'd been training at for months. But I also had to find something through the scope to help me gauge the wind. I watched the flags atop the concert hall billowing for a few seconds. The wind was minimal, so I only corrected for it by turning one click on my scope. That click recalibrates the scope's bull's-eye, accounting for the wind's effect on the bullet. Now I was ready to load up with the 7N1 Russian sniper round, and the weapon was ready to fire."

Valerie paused. We were exiting Interstate 75 at Techwood Avenue. She took Tenth Street and turned right again on Spring Street. Spring ran south for four blocks before intersecting with North Avenue, where she turned right and drove over the interstate below, making a left into the parking lot of a Comfort Inn.

"I'll be right back," she said, parking in front of the hotel check-in window.

I watched her from the backseat. She walked up to the Plexiglas window and booked the second hotel room of the night for us, paying cash in advance.

She opened the door to the truck, tossing me a key card and saying, "Come on. The room is close by. We can walk from here."

She wasn't exaggerating. The room was on the first floor directly behind the office. I was unlocking the door to the room and about to ask if we needed to set up for watch detail when Leecy spoke first.

"Finish the story, Mom?"

I dropped my pack and lay down on one of the small double beds.

Valerie dropped her pack on the small desk and walked to the bathroom to wash her hands and face. I watched her reach for a towel and simultaneously check her watch.

"Look, it's after three in the morning. We have to be up and moving in six hours. Let's get some sleep."

"Who knows what will happen tomorrow? Just tell the rest of the story and then bed time."

"Okay," Valerie agreed, and picked up where she'd left off. "At that point, it was a waiting game. I changed out of the KGB uniform and into the American student outfit from the backpack: Guess jeans, sweatshirt, Reeboks and heavy jean jacket. The last thing I removed from the backpack was the detonator I'd requested. In our meeting earlier that day, I was worried the single shot would give away my position and not give me enough time to escape. So I'd asked for a car rigged with light explosives to be placed next to the concert hall, 150 meters from the sniper's nest, slightly north of my line-of-sight, which meant I'd have to shoot with my right hand and activate the remote detonator with my left.

I finished my exit prep work by packing the uniform in the backpack along with the wig just as my watch alarm chimed. I took up my position behind the rifle and watched through the scope for Volodarsky to exit the building. And then he did. There he was, his big profile in the scope."

I heard Leecy gasp to herself, but say nothing.

"I had a clean shot. I remember saying to myself *breathe,*

and then triggering the car bomb while simultaneously squeezing the pistol grip and the trigger. I watched the target's head explode, sending a plume of red mist into the air."

"Oh my god!" Leecy cried out, plain and clear this time.

"He was dead. I left the rooftop the same way I'd arrived, but I used the back door this time. I was wearing the backpack, and I walked across the inner courtyard behind the Blokhina Street building to the rear door of number 5 Zverinskaya. I walked through that empty building and out the front door unobserved. I crossed the street to the Rinaldi Hotel and took the stairs to the third floor. I found the trash chute for the incinerator room and dropped the backpack and its contents inside the chute. I was assured the chute connected directly to the incinerator. I was worried about that because I hadn't been able to verify that fact for myself, but I had to trust the intelligence report. I walked to my room and retrieved the small travel bag from the closet and packed the clothes I was wearing. I washed my face and hands and dressed in the clothes I'd been wearing before I put on the KGB uniform. All I had to do was wait for my flight to leave Leningrad. I would fly to Moscow the next morning, then Berlin, and in two days I was back in the USA."

"Holy crap," Leecy exclaimed, "you did all that? Man, you've got ice water in your veins. What were you, twenty years old back then? That's just nuts," Leecy continued as she walked across the room closing the door to the bathroom behind her.

"Well, that one will hold her for a while," I said.

Leecy was back in two minutes, ready for bed.

"Are you okay?" Val asked.

"I'm fine. I'm just really tired and excited and scared all at the same time. It's confusing. It's the kind of thing I want to do, but...I don't know. Let's talk about it tomorrow," Leecy said and added sweetly, "Goodnight, Mom and Dad."

It was 8:30 a.m. Saturday morning, the 22nd of June – my wife's birthday. I'd left her and my daughter sleeping in the hotel room and wandered back across the interstate overpass using the pedestrian walkway to the corner of North Avenue and Spring Street. The gas station there served double duty as a Dunkin Donuts. I planned to buy Valerie a birthday donut and return to the room to surprise her with it. But I hadn't slept much, if at all, so first I sank onto a counter stool and into a large cup of black coffee.

My seat at the counter faced the parking lot. I watched the locals filling their cars with gas and their bellies with donuts for ten or twenty minutes, waiting for the caffeine in the coffee to kick me into gear.

I picked out a traffic camera at the stoplight and two more mounted on opposite corners of the Varsity restaurant across the street. There was no escaping the eye in the sky. I wondered if cameras somewhere had caught my family and me, and that's how Porter got onto us. I seemed to recall a camera at the Chick-fil-A yesterday, and several red light cameras along our route. If Porter and his team were searching all the cameras in the Atlanta area, they would find us. There was nowhere for us to hide.

At 9:00 a.m. I ordered another cup of coffee and bought bottles of water, some fruit and yogurt, and one donut with sprinkles. With a bag full of food in one hand and a drink carrier in the other, I made my way back to the hotel and my girls. I was struggling with the key card when the door to our room opened.

Leecy said, "Yummy, breakfast. I'm starving," and grabbed the bag I was holding between my teeth.

"The donut is for Mom's birthday; don't eat it," I called after her, and closing the door behind me, said, "I hope you both slept well, 'cause it's going to be a long day."

Leecy was holding the donut facing the bathroom door and I took the hint, grabbed Val's coffee and stood next to Leecy and waited. We sang, "Happy birthday to you," as the bathroom door opened.

Valerie took her cup of coffee from me and said with a sleepy smile "Thank you, I appreciate the donut...and the sprinkles especially."

"You're welcome. We need to think about heading to the meeting. I noticed the traffic was standing still as I crossed over the interstate."

"On a Saturday?" Leecy asked.

"Yep, the traffic was at a standstill in the four southbound lanes."

"I'm sorry, guys," Val said as she ate her donut, "but this isn't exactly how I wanted to celebrate my birthday. Can I just have a do over later?"

"That's a great idea," Leecy said. "A party when this stuff is behind us."

"Deal," I said, "but what about the traffic issue?"

"Not a problem. I know how to get to the Westin without using the interstate. It's why I picked this hotel," Valerie said. "Ron, you drive, and I'll tell you where to go."

I was first out of the room and into the truck. The girls were moving slower than normal, but that would soon change.

All Leecy needed was food, and Valerie needed a little caffeine. I connected the ignition wires, and the truck roared to life.

"Which way, birthday girl?"

"Make a left out of the parking lot."

We arrived at the Westin fifteen minutes early, or on time, according to Valerie. I couldn't ask anyone else to hot-wire the truck, so I drove past the hotel valet stand and away from the hotel for a block, finding a self-parking lot on Williams street.

"Okay, this is as close as we can get," I said. "Are you guys ready?"

"Ready," Valerie and Leecy said together. It sounded like music to my ears.

We grabbed our packs and covered the one block distance to the hotel at a leisurely pace. I watched the faces of the people we passed on the sidewalk and none of them paid us any attention. They were all busy with handheld devices just like Val said they would be. The doorman at the hotel was the only person to make eye contact with me, but he showed no signs of recognition. We crossed the lobby to the bank of house phones located near the reception desk. I picked up one of the receivers and pressed 2-2-1-1 on the keypad. The phone rang once, and I heard an unfamiliar female voice.

"We have you on camera. Walk to the elevators and take the next available one. We'll activate it for you," the woman instructed and ended the call.

I replaced the receiver. "Follow me, ladies."

I led the girls across the lobby, finding the elevator bank for the hotel guests. There was an open elevator door waiting for us. The door closed as soon as we were inside. I watched as the number '22' illuminated on the panel of buttons, and we were moving.

"They have us on camera and also took control of the elevators," I said. "Tammy has embraced the technological age."

"It's kind of cool, isn't it?" Leecy asked.

"Yeah, I guess it is," I said.

"I'll reserve judgment till I hear what it is she wants in return for helping us," Valerie said as the elevator stopped and the doors opened on the 22nd floor.

An attractive, young blonde woman dressed in a black pants suit and bright white shirt with a gold chain around her neck was waiting for us at the elevator doors. Unless CIA regulations had changed, jewelry was forbidden. The reason for the ban was that jewelry is too personal. No field agent would ever wear a necklace, and unless I missed my guess, a small medallion of some sort was dangling from the gold chain around the blonde girl's neck. Either the regulations had changed since my time with the agency or she wasn't a field agent.

"Please follow me."

She led us on a short walk to room 2211, opening the door but not following us inside.

Room 2211 wasn't a bedroom, but more like a den, and so far, it was empty of anyone but us. Couches, tables and chairs were arranged into several sitting areas, and the connecting doors on each end of the room were cracked. I walked to the windows and saw Centennial Olympic Park, Phillips Arena and the Georgia Dome below.

I turned when I saw the connecting door on my right open.

It was Wakefield. She hadn't changed much ~ still very slim, her long, blonde hair straight with gray highlights. She was wearing flats, but remained tall at six feet without heels.

"Hello, Ron," she said as she entered the room, touching a finger to her right ear as she walked toward us. "Hello, Valerie...Leecy...I'm Special Agent Tammy Daniel Wakefield. Please call me Wakefield. It's nice to finally meet the woman that tore Ron away from active duty with the CIA, and his beautiful daughter," she said, extending her hand to each of them.

"It's nice to meet you, too," Leecy said, and then she asked, "What can you tell me about my dad? I want to know all about his time as an operator with the CIA."

Valerie offered her hand, saying, "For now, we'd just like to know what it's going to cost if you help us."

I could see Wakefield breaking into her familiar smile before she answered my girls' questions.

"Young lady," Wakefield addressed Leecy first, "I can only tell you what I'm allowed to talk about, but it's probably stuff you already know." Wakefield then said to Valerie, "Direct and to the point. I like that. You live up to the reputation." And then addressing Valerie and Leecy together, she said, "If you two will allow me, I'll answer both your questions later. Right now, I'd like to address your current situation by first explaining why I'm here in Atlanta. I'm sure that's another question you have for me."

"It is." Valerie said, as she took a seat on one of the couches.

Leecy joined her mother on the couch, but I remained standing. Wakefield paid me no attention and sat on the couch opposite Valerie and Leecy. She touched her right ear again before going on.

"I'm in Atlanta with a small contingent of agents. There are three tech agents working computers in the room behind me," she gestured to the door she'd entered through and then pointed at the other connecting door, "and three tactical agents or investigators on standby in the other room. But that doesn't explain why I'm here. I'm here because of your company, Valerie. I'm here because of INESCO."

"Why does INESCO merit the attention of the CIA? I thought the CIA was prohibited from conducting missions on US soil," Valerie asked calmly.

"You know your company's business. You know what you're into down there. Whenever the government is involved in a relationship like the one with INESCO, there's always the possibility of espionage. We've picked up some chatter about a pending project your company has undertaken for our government. And given the security protocols put in place by you, your company, and the DOD, no one should be aware the project even exists. But there is chatter, nonetheless. You're correct; the CIA is prohibited from actively pursuing interests in the US, but in this case, that line has been blurred into non-existence."

"What do you mean by chatter?" Leecy asked.

Wakefield allowed a slight smile to cross her lips before answering. "I'm sure you all are aware of our ability to collect and disseminate cell phone data, calls and texts, as well as email," Wakefield said.

"I thought that was the NSA," Leecy responded.

Wakefield laughed a small, secretive laugh. "The NSA collects metadata that consists of numbers called by one phone and how long each call lasts. We saw this Snowden thing coming. We knew our data collection techniques were about to be exposed. The NSA was chosen to be the fall guy for the rest of the intelligence community collecting data. The NSA makes the news and gets the attention while the rest of us continue doing the very thing, and more, that the NSA is being accused of. After this meeting, you'll never use a cellphone again."

Wakefield paused as the door behind her opened on cue. Another agent entered the room, a man about 5'10" tall and 180 pounds, with dark red hair, wearing a dark suit and bright, white shirt.

"This is Senior Field Agent Thomas Moore. He just came over from behavioral analytics. Before that he was part of multi-agency task force working to stop the human trafficking problem around the world. He's become a vital part of our efforts here in Atlanta, and what he's giving each of you now is a National Secrecy Agreement. Sorry, but it's required."

Agent Moore handed each of us a one-page sheet of paper. He had a slight smile on his face that I hadn't figured out yet, so I reserved judgment about this guy.

"This agreement says that if any of you divulge to anyone outside of this room what's discussed here you'll disappear from the face of the earth. You'll spend the rest of your days held in a CIA black site, never to see the light of day again. Please sign the documents or this meeting is over."

Wakefield said this with a smile on her face a politician could envy.

Agent Moore spoke for the first time.

"You can call me Tom. Here are some pens. Just leave the documents on the table when you've finished signing them."

Then he turned and left the room the way he'd entered.

I crossed the floor and signed the document without reading it. I needed to know what Wakefield knew, and that was the only way she was going to tell us. I watched as Valerie and Leecy both sped-read through the document, reading the entire page in seconds before signing it.

"Great," Wakefield said, and gathered the papers. "Thanks for your indulgence; now we can continue. Where was I?"

"You were talking about how every agency, not just the NSA, has the capability to access cellphone and email data," Leecy reminded her.

"Thank you, Leecy. That's right. When INESCO popped up in their data mining last month, Valerie, the following keywords were connected to your company's name: sale, bidder, and millions."

Wakefield stood and walked toward the mini bar. She opened the small fridge and removed a bottle of water. Twisting the cap off, she took a sip, and then returned to her seat before continuing.

"Help yourself," she said. "Don't be shy. See," she paused again, taking another sip of water before replacing the bottle's cap and placing it on the table, saying, "What the public doesn't understand is that the data doesn't come streaming to us in conversation form, at least, not yet, anyway. No, that only happens if we have a specific email address or phone number to track. Take my call with Ron last night. I assumed, because of the APB on your heads, that any phone number he used was compromised. So to protect the contents of the phone call, I scrambled the transmission. If anyone was listening to our call, all they heard was static. We don't get static when we are searching the data, but we get all the calls jumbled together, or linked end-to-end like one long run-on sentence. Do you follow?" Wakefield asked.

I answered, "Yes; continue, please," before Leecy could speak. I could see Leecy had a lot on her mind and wanted to ask Wakefield a thousand questions.

"Now, in this INESCO case," Wakefield began again, "it's not working as effectively as we'd envisioned. We can't determine what every one of the conversations is about. We're pretty sure, however, that there's going to be an attempt to sell an INESCO product before Sunday at noon."

I could feel Val gasp, though she hadn't made a sound anyone else could hear.

Wakefield stood up and motioned for us to follow her.

We trailed behind her into one of the connecting rooms. There were three Agents seated at computer terminals. The female Agent that had met us at the elevator, Agent Moore, and what looked like a teenage boy were working keyboards at lightning speed.

"You've met Agent Moore. He's not only one of my top technical analysts, but also a supremely qualified field agent. This young lad," Wakefield gestured toward the teenage boy, "is new to the team and a recent graduate of MIT. His name is Zachary Taylor. Yes, he looks young, but all that matters is he's highly skilled." Wakefield now pointed to the woman in the bright, white shirt that had greeted us at the elevators. She was clutching at the object attached to her necklace - another bad habit, I thought. Wakefield said, "And this is Senior Technical Advisor Julia Sands. She's Team Leader. These three have been here in Atlanta with me since we got the call on Monday."

Wakefield turned and left the room. We followed her, and I closed the door behind me. She crossed the den and headed for the other set of connecting doors.

"Why CIA involvement?" Leecy asked as we walked across the room. "Why didn't the DIA handle it?"

"That's a good question," Wakefield acknowledged, and stopped walking. She turned to face us as she answered Leecy's question. "As one can imagine, the enormous amounts of data to be analyzed can pose a substantial burden for any one agency. Recognizing this fact was the first step in a multi-step process eventually leading to the development of A.D.D.T. or Actionable Data Deployment Teams. The people in this suite with me are all part of my team," Wakefield said, continuing across the room and opening the door to show us her second, three-man team.

"These three men are my field investigators. Whenever Julia's team comes across information that necessitates further investigation, these guys hit the bricks. Team leader is Ryan," Wakefield said.

A short, stocky man with close-cropped, blonde hair, wearing a bright white shirt and black suit, waved a finger in our direction.

Wakefield continued the introductions by saying, "The man on the phone is Franks, and the other guy is Hodges. When these boys hit the streets, they use FBI as their cover."

Wakefield finished and closed the door.

"Those three guys represent the 'Action' part of the Actionable Data Team. And before you ask me, yes, I do think what happened at your home yesterday is directly related to whatever is going on with these data hits about INESCO," Wakefield said, and leaned back on the couch.

"I assume you and your team have connected the two events, and that's not just a speculative statement on your part," Valerie said.

With that question, the doors to Julia's room opened. Advisor Julia Sands appeared in the doorway carrying a large whiteboard. She propped the board up against the floor to ceiling windows near where I was standing, and stood next to the board like she was waiting further instruction.

"How do they keep doing that? How do they know when to walk into the room with whatever it is you need, Agent Wakefield?" Leecy asked.

Wakefield touched her right ear with her right forefinger and said, "Ear pieces. They're listening to everything we say."

"Oh," Leecy said. "That's so cool."

"Yes, it is cool, isn't it?" Wakefield agreed. "Now, here's how we have connected the dots, Valerie. Explain what you've been doing, Julia."

Julia cleared her throat and began.

"The top of the board has the names of the two men that broke into your home ~ James Smotherman and Daniel Pickett. Beneath their names, I've listed their histories. The first item listed under Smotherman is his release from Atlanta's Federal Prison one month ago. I next connected the two men," Julia said, pointing to a lime green circle and line connecting Smotherman with Pickett, "to a stay at the Fulton County Prison two years ago. As you can see, they were cellmates for sixteen months."

I stopped listening as Julia continued walking us through the facts we had already figured out on our own, without databanks of eavesdropping. What I was noticing was that the further she progressed down the board, the more the medallion on that gold chain worked itself free from the confines of her shirt.

"What's that hanging from your neck?" I asked.

"What?" Julia said confused by my off-topic question, as were Leecy and Wakefield, but I could see that Valerie had also noticed the oddly-shaped pendant hanging freely from Julia's neck.

"Oh," Julia recovered, realizing what I was asking her and returning the pendant inside her blouse. "It's the symbol on the command key of my Apple keyboard."

"Very interesting," I commented. "It looks like a pretzel."

Julia smiled as she grasped the pendant beneath her blouse with her left forefinger and thumb and said, "That's actually one of the many names the symbol has. It's also known as the Meta key, special key, and shortcut key. It kind of represents the work that I do."

I was about to say something else when Leecy's sudden outburst filled the room.

"Oh my god, you guys think there is a mole at INESCO!"

I looked at the board, scanning the information until I read what had elicited such a reaction from my daughter. There it was, near the bottom of the five-foot tall whiteboard.

INESCO has a mole.

"Yes, we do," Wakefield said.

"But you don't know who?" Valerie said, as she finished reading the board.

"No, we don't know the identity of the mole, but it makes sense that there is one." Wakefield stood and walked to the whiteboard, dismissing Julia before saying, "Let's start with what we do know. We know the identity of the two men that attempted to kidnap your daughter. Fact one, they shared a jail cell for sixteen months. Fact two, they were in possession of sophisticated burglary tools. Fact three, they had weapons with filed-off serial numbers. Fact four, they had a detailed map of your home marking your daughter's room location, and fact five, one of them had previously worked at IN-ESCO."

I watched as Wakefield crossed the floor and retook her seat before speaking.

"That prior relationship, coupled with what I told you Leecy overheard Agent Porter say, plus what I got out of Briggs Smith – it all confirms your data mining hits on INESCO."

Leecy interrupted me. "If the two guys that broke into our home didn't know us personally, then someone else told them about us. I see now. Individually, the pieces of data collected point nowhere, but taken collectively, they mean whoever is behind this knows about us. Knows about our family. There has to be an insider."

"And those two guys, Smotherman and Pickett," Valerie said, "they don't know us or anything about us. During our interview in Park City, I told FBI Agent Porter that Pickett worked at INESCO, but as a low-level compounder in the rubber division. Pickett wouldn't have had any knowledge of what INESCO's doing in R&D, or of our family's products, new or old. So your conclusion, Agent Wakefield, is there has to be someone else at INESCO involved. But who?" Valerie turned to face me. "Is the mole the mystery partner Briggs Smith told you about, Ron? Or someone else?"

"Before we start down the mystery partner road," Wakefield broke in, "let's talk about the FBI agents you met in Park City:

Porter, Briggs Smith, and Travis Smith. There's no record of FBI agents by any of those names."

"I'm not surprised the Smiths are fake, but I was convinced Porter was the real deal," Valerie said.

"So was I," I said. "I pegged them as ex-Army Rangers. But I thought Porter was legit FBI."

"Neither Travis nor Briggs Smith is FBI," Wakefield said, "but working off of Ron's intuition about the men, we found something. Briggs Smith is a former Army Ranger. He was honorably discharged last May. We found no record of him after May 2012, though. Nor any record of the one calling himself Travis. Like Porter, the one called Travis doesn't exist in any database anywhere. Agent Moore took personal charge of the search after my conversation with Ron last night and hasn't turned up anything," Wakefield said.

We were all silent for a few moments; then Tammy gave us one of her million dollar smiles.

"We need a little break, and I'll bet you're all pretty hungry. I'll order up some lunch and while we eat I can answer some of your questions about your father, Leecy."

Then turning as she stood to leave the room, she spoke directly to Valerie.

"And I haven't forgotten about you, dear. I'll have an answer for you before our meeting is over."

Lunch consisted of room service sandwiches and salads. It was food, and we were hungry, so we ate. I was thinking about the intention behind Wakefield's performance this morning. The little mind game dance she'd danced with my daughter. A long time ago, I'd been the one eagerly answering her questions, connecting the dots for her and reminding her where she left off in a conversation, only to discover later it was how Wakefield judged people. To what end now, I wondered. I hoped she wasn't about to tell Valerie the price for helping us was our first born, because Valerie might kill her.

Leecy was the first to break the silence. "Okay, what can you tell me about my dad and his time with the CIA?"

Wakefield didn't suppress the smile that crept across her face this time. I could tell my old friend liked what she saw in Leecy. That made me nervous, but I tried to remain calm.

"Well, let me think a moment. There are things, regardless of the agreement you signed earlier, that I cannot discuss." The connecting door opened behind Wakefield, and she turned to see who was entering the room unexpectedly.

"Yes, Tom?"

Agent Moore said, "Oh, I heard talking and assumed the meeting was starting up again, and you had indicated you wanted my input this afternoon."

"No, no, we're just chatting. But come join us," Wakefield said. "You might appreciate this."

Agent Moore sat in one of the chairs positioned at the end of the couch occupied by Wakefield. He tried to mask his eye movements by ducking his head as he sat, but I could see he was checking each of us closely. I was finished eating and decided to stand and retake my position at the windows. I was more comfortable where I could see the entirety of the room. I made eye contact with Valerie and we spoke to each other through the glance. She looked briefly in Moore's direction and then back at me with a slight turn of her head, indicating that she didn't think he was the mystery man. I'd reached the opposite conclusion shortly after I met him, simply because my gut told me to believe it. I had no evidence to support my feeling, but it was there nonetheless.

"Why are you guys in a hotel?" Leecy suddenly asked. "Why aren't you set up in some old vacant building or CIA black site somewhere in the city?"

Wakefield laughed.

"Because this isn't a movie and we aren't on TV. We need power for our equipment. We need to be able to access the Internet and the data storage facilities. We can't do that from a vacant building that doesn't have electricity. The CIA doesn't maintain operational black sites around the country like office space or underground bunkers. When we're in the field, the idea is to blend in and become part of our surroundings. This hotel serves our needs in the most efficient and cost-effective way. We use their electricity; we access the information we need over their phone and cable lines - after running basic encryption software and maybe boosting the signal a bit. We're just another small business group in one of the hotel's medium-sized suites."

"Okay, that makes sense, but what about the maid service? You know, the housekeeping staff?"

"We're registered as foreign dignitaries. We explained that our country's customs do not allow strangers to access our rooms while we're occupying them."

"That's it? That's all you had to say to be left alone?"

"Yes. Requests like that are made daily all over the world; it's very common."

I listened to the conversation and heard what was being said, but watched Agent Moore very carefully. I thought he might give himself away but I had to admit, he wasn't registering any of my red flags. Maybe my gut was wrong. I let it go and looked out the window, and saw something very interesting: I saw him staring at my back. He had avoided all eye contact with me while I faced the room. Maybe I wasn't crazy.

"Satisfied, dear?" I heard Wakefield ask Leecy.

"Hey, it is what it is, right? So tell me about my dad."

I could see Wakefield in the reflection of the window. She turned her head in my direction and said, "I was against the recruitment of your father into the agency."

"What? I mean why?" Leecy asked.

"I was in charge of training new recruits at the CIA Farm in 1996. 'The Farm' is what we call our training facility in Williamsburg, Virginia. People often think it's in Langley, but it's not. I know I look older than your father, but he and I are the same age. When he was recruited into the agency, I thought he was just too old. Most of our recruits come to us in their mid-to early twenties; your father was almost thirty. So in my infinite wisdom, I tried to make him resign his offer of employment. In other words, I wanted to make him quit."

"I take it that didn't go as planned," Leecy said.

"No," Wakefield said, "it didn't."

"What happened?"

"I told your father I was going to prove he was too old."

I watched as Wakefield paused in her telling of the story. I knew the next few minutes would be hard on her, but she didn't hesitate long before continuing.

"Your father was recommended to the CIA by his Commanding Officer from the Army. Granger's CO said he was of 'unlimited potential.' He came to the agency, as most recruits do, with multiple college degrees in business and international finance, as you may be aware. He was the eldest of the class of 1996 by six years. I was in my new position in charge of all recruits at the Farm, and rather full of myself. I didn't want any recruit making me look bad. So with my intentions clearly stated, and your father aware of them, training began.

"Granger shot well enough to qualify at the range, but he wasn't the best with a gun in his hands. He passed all the physical and mental testing with - and I remember how much I hated seeing it at the time - way above average scores. In fact, his scores on those tests were leading the class. Looking back, I should've accepted your father fully at that time. He was outperforming all other recruits overall, but I didn't accept him. I was determined to prove I was right."

I turned to face the room.

"She's leaving out that I had a chip on my shoulder. I had something to prove. And, well, Wakefield gave me someone to prove it to other than myself. I remember when she told me she thought I was too old to be there. Do you remember what I said to you?"

"Certainly I do. You said, and I quote, 'I'm the best candidate in the room. You'll see.' And you were right. It became very clear how right your father was once combat training started. Your father doesn't need a gun or a weapon of any kind, because what he is, or was, spectacular at is hand-to-hand combat."

"It's true, then," Leecy interrupted. "What you said to Ranger Smith in our kitchen about your CIA file?"

"Just listen to Tammy," I answered.

"I don't know what he's told you or what you've heard, but I can assure you there hasn't been an agent since your father's time capable of doing what your father did back then."

"Times change," I said. "It's all computers and smart-phones now, with databases and keyword searches. The world is a different place. Your agents need to be a different breed of agents than I was."

"Did you finally give up, and accept Dad was the best in your class?"

"Not exactly. No, what I did was ask Granger to teach his fighting style to the class and the teachers. I told him to share his talents so the CIA could incorporate the new technique into future training class's combat sessions."

"What did he do?"

"Your father refused. He just said no. And no explanation. This infuriated and embarrassed me. So, I decided to teach Granger a lesson and break him."

"Break him?" Leecy said. "Good luck with that."

"True enough. I brought men in from every special military force under the guise of guest combat technique trainer. Force Recon Marines, Navy SEALS, Delta Force operators, and Rangers. Big, small, fast, strong, young, old - it didn't matter. Then I watched as he waded into each opponent individually, and then two, three, even four opponents at once attacked him and were all soundly defeated. Granger put seven men in the hospital during a two-week span. He would have killed them all had it been a real combat situation. I finally realized the only thing that could stop your father was a bullet."

"Wow, Dad was a badass just like," Leecy stopped herself from saying something she shouldn't. "What happened next?"

I could see that both Wakefield and Moore had caught Leecy's almost slip of the tongue about her mother's past.

Sure, Wakefield knew about Val, but Tom Moore didn't, and we didn't know Agent Moore. Leecy was astute enough to realize that. But neither pressed her for more information.

"Your father was made that class's NOC, or the agent to assume the non-official cover. He was sent around the world for the next six years to do what it seemed he was born to do. The CIA hasn't had an operative like your father since he assumed inactive status in 2003. Your father was without question the agency's most effective operator at that time, and he probably could still be."

I was about to object, but Moore surprised the room by speaking for the first time since he took his seat.

"This is the guy all recruits are required to study in initial training. I don't mean to sound surprised, but it's safe to say your reputation creates a larger than life image. I thought you would be bigger, and look more like an Indian," Agent Moore said.

I laughed.

"I think that was the plan from the beginning, Agent Moore. The reputation is what others think you are, and it's sometimes just as important as the man it represents. I think the CIA worked very hard to cultivate that reputation for me." Then addressing Wakefield, I said, "I didn't know my mission file was classroom fodder."

"Not exactly. Your wild Indian persona and its cultivation are course study requirements as an example of the lengths taken to create effective covers for our spies," Wakefield said. "'The Art of Building a Legend' is the name of the class."

I noticed Valerie was watching Moore now. I saw her left index finger extended on her left thigh. She saw me looking at her, and tapped her finger once, indicating one red flag.

But which one, I wondered. I ran through my checklist and couldn't come up with an answer. Valerie's intuition was a finely-tuned instrument unlike any I'd ever seen. I trusted her implicitly. Maybe she didn't like the way he said what he said. Whatever the reason was, my gut and her intuition were now on the same page.

Wakefield was talking again. "After your father's training class graduated and he had left the Farm, I got curious about his background and put several agents to work on his family tree. I wanted to know everything there was to know about him. And with the resources of the federal government behind me, do you know what they uncovered?"

"What?" Leecy asked.

"A Native American bloodline stretching back to the late 1700's. This was before the Comanche moved east to Kansas and Texas. Before they broke away from the Shoshone Indians."

"Yeah, I know all that stuff. What's the big deal?" Leecy asked.

"Really? Did you know the CIA determined which tribe's blood flows through your and your father's veins?"

"If you say it's Apache that will be another thing you got wrong about my dad."

Wakefield appeared stunned and looked at me.

"Geronimo, Cochise and Parker all rolled up into one. That's what we've thought for decades. And your kid is telling me we got it wrong."

"You got it half right. My great uncle was Comanche," I said.

"So, the rumors floating around the agency since the mid-1990's about the guy that used the Indian war chants before killing his targets are true!" Moore blurted. "You're that guy?"

I saw Valerie extend a second finger on her thigh as I answered. "I was an operator, but that other stuff was all part of a legend created by the agency, that's all. Come on, Tom; you know the first rule of the CIA is 'nothing is as it seems.'"

"So when did you become my dad's handler?" Leecy asked Wakefield.

"After your father became the NOC, I requested a change of post. I asked to be his handler. I was doing that job for another agent before coming to the Farm as trainer. I was better at being a handler than being a trainer."

Tammy shifted gears again. "But let's get back to the reason we're here and the task at hand. We have three things we need to address. First, who's the mole? Second, who's the mystery partner Ranger Smith and Porter are working with? Third, what is it they are after?"

"If I may," Agent Moore offered, "I'd like to address the mystery partner now so I can return to my computer."

"I asked Agent Moore to join us to share his findings and thoughts on this mystery partner," Wakefield said. "Please go ahead, Tom."

"We learned of this mystery partner only last night, because Ron...may I call you Ron?" Moore asked and I nodded yes. "Ron told Wakefield about him when they spoke to each other on the phone. What we can't do is confirm it. We can speculate that the partner was one of the two men that broke into your home, but I discount that notion only because Ranger Smith revealed the existence of the partner after the break-in, in which one man was killed and the other hospitalized," Moore said.

He stared at Valerie and then at me. He was clearly suspicious about Val's role in all of this.

"This leads me to believe the mystery man is still out there somewhere. I believe the mole and this mystery partner are one and the same. The mole would possess the intelligence needed to obtain a high-level job at INESCO, a job that would find him in a position of access to classified information. His level of intelligence would also make him uniquely qualified to organize and implement a plan to gain control of said product or information or research – whatever it is. He could hire Porter and the Smith boys using the Internet to access the thousands of paramilitary sites and chat rooms."

Moore was churning through his theories so fast that he had to stop for a sip of water before starting up again.

"Julia has had the team searching those very sites for days. Obviously, this mystery partner possesses the computer skills needed to clean his virtual trail, or we would have him in custody by now. Anyway, everything he would need he could find online or make himself: the fake FBI badges, diagram of your house, and the alarm device. A simple keyword search reveals the Internet site of the architect firm you employed to design your home. From there, he hacked their system and found your design plans. The alarm device is something he probably made, given his obvious skill set. So I say again, the mole and the mystery guy are one and the same."

"Let's assume you're correct. How do we find him?" Valerie asked.

"That would require a search of INESCO's personnel files. The search would have to be done at INESCO, as your company's system is not online. Rather antiquated, isn't it?" he asked, with a smirk that made me want to punch him in the face. "Anyway, you'll have to search the files and find a connection somewhere to something. The problem is, that kind of search could take days. We don't have days." Looking at his watch, he said, "No, we have less than twenty hours."

"Well, what do you think?" Wakefield asked.

I was about to offer my opinion when Leecy said, "I'm not buying it. There has to be another guy, and he has to be in law enforcement. Maybe he's with the CIA or the FBI, or how about the NSA? For all we know, he could be you, Agent Moore. The reason I believe he is part of one of these agencies is: how else do you explain the APB?"

Moore looked embarrassed. "We considered that, and came to the conclusion that the report had been planted by the man posing as FBI Agent Porter."

"Maybe, I guess, but how did he do that? Doesn't a department of the FBI, like a PR department or something, handle that sort of announcement? And wouldn't the news stations that ran the APB verify the request before airing it?" Leecy challenged.

"Right, and we determined that the newscast ran only in the Park City market, transmitting from Columbus, Georgia. No one outside of that broadcast area heard it. Secondly, our team of investigators discovered that the local station ran the APB solely on the fake Agent Porter's authority. After all, he did fool you three and the Park City Police Department," Moore said.

"But, how do you explain..." Leecy started to challenge Agent Moore again, but was cut off by Wakefield.

"Thank you, Tom," Wakefield said, "that'll be all."

CHAPTER
SIX

Moore closed the connecting door behind him and the room was silent for a moment. Then Wakefield took charge.

"Leecy," Wakefield said, "you were about to say something, please continue."

Leecy didn't hesitate. She jumped right in with, "Okay, what I was going to suppose was there's a mystery partner. We know about Porter and the Smiths. Let's assume there's a mole, and let's also assume there's this other person."

I interrupted my daughter, saying, "and just for the sake of giving this mystery person a name, let's call him 'Moore.'"

"Yes," Valerie agreed, "let's pretend the mystery man is Agent Moore, because a guy like Agent Moore would have access to the data, and the skill set to manipulate it."

"Okay, for the sake of the story, let's use Moore as the mystery guy. You three lay it out for me," Wakefield said.

"First, I need a little background on Agent Moore to make the story as plausible as possible. Tell me what you can," I said.

Wakefield thought about it and then said, "Okay, I'll play along. Agent Moore is listening," she gestured to her right ear, "he'll get a kick out of this. Now, I don't have my agents' files memorized," she said as she considered Moore's past, "but I believe he was recruited from the military, and if I'm not mistaken, he was a member of a Special Forces-type group, but I don't recall which one."

"That's good enough," Valerie said. "For our purposes, let's just say he served in the Army and was a member of their elite Ranger group."

Walking toward the whiteboard, Leecy said, "Agent Moore is connected to Briggs Smith, because they were both Rangers. Let's also assume that Travis and Porter are also part of that elite group. So, they all know each other directly or indirectly, but they share a common background. Porter, Travis, Briggs and Agent Moore are now connected."

"Now," Valerie offered, "let's assume Porter, because he had the demeanor of middle management, worked somewhere that put him in contact with ex-cons. Maybe he was a parole officer, prison warden or guard, or maybe he was at one time an actual FBI agent."

"We would know about that, all of that. That would've turned up in our search," Wakefield said.

"Not if the guy doing the searching was also part of the team trying to steal whatever it is they're after," I said.

"I see," Wakefield said, "so what Leecy was suggesting was there are actually two moles, then."

"Yes, because as my dad said yesterday, there's nowhere to hide anymore, and I believe that. So, how did those three guys, Porter, Travis and Briggs, just disappear? Someone had to make them ghosts, and who better to do that than the guy in charge of looking for them?

"There's another thing. When Porter interrogated us, how is it he came to have files on all of us? If he was an actual FBI agent, that might explain it, but he isn't, at least not now. He got that information somewhere, and oddly enough, his file read almost exactly like the story you told," Leecy said.

Wakefield stood and said, "This isn't a game or supposition. You three really believe my agent is behind all of this. Why?"

"For all the reasons we've stated, and the fact that his reaction to Granger's CIA history wasn't shock or surprise, but confirmation," Valerie said.

"How the hell can you read that on a person?"

"The same way I can tell that you believe everything we've laid out for you, and you're only pretending to be indignant," Valerie answered.

"I only believe that what you're saying makes sense. It's logical to a point, but what you haven't explained is the connection to INESCO."

She was right. We hadn't tied that together, and I wasn't sure how we could. But leave it to my daughter to do just that; make a connection even if it was a stretch.

"Look at the board," Leecy said, "INESCO has an ex-con in Pickett on the payroll. What if that's the connection?"

"Explain," Wakefield said.

"I don't know," Leecy said with her eyes closed. I could see her searching her memory like a Rolodex. "Umm, I seem to recall an article about a state-run program that incentivized Georgia's businesses to hire ex-cons. I want to say that the state paid the business part of the new hires' wages for six months." Her eyes opened and she pointed at the board. "So, INESCO hires the ex-con Pickett through this program. If there's one hire through the program, maybe there's another, and maybe Porter heads the program. That connects Porter to the break-in, and to the mole at INESCO. That is, if the mole turns out to be part of the program. That would connect it all, right?"

"It would be a very tenuous connection at best, and it's all supposition at this point," Wakefield answered. Then she said as she stared at the board, "but if Porter is in a position to track his newly employed ex-cons, then he knows one of them is working at a company that supplies the DOD and NASA. Porter keeps a close eye on the man. Maybe Porter threatens to have the man sent back to prison by framing him for something. I don't know how, but Porter has leverage over the guy. The guy is either directly involved with or has knowledge of an INESCO product that may pay off on the black market. Desperate to get out from under Porter's control, he tells Porter all about it. Porter enlists the help of his old Army buddies. He's smart enough to know that he needs help if he's going to try for whatever the hell it is. A person in a position like Agent Moore's is a perfect accomplice," Wakefield said, looking toward the connecting doors Agent Moore had pulled closed earlier. She turned back toward the board, saying, "Yes, I can see how all of that would fit together very nicely. The only problem is: we looked under all of those rocks and found nothing."

"I'm not surprised. The first rule of espionage is 'nothing is as it seems to be,'" I said, and then offered, "I think this situation is much simpler. I think Porter purposely placed ex-cons with INESCO. I think this has been in the works for a long time. Porter, Moore, and the rest have just been either waiting for the mole to reach a position with INESCO that afforded him access to the right technologies, or they were just waiting for the right project to come through the IN-ESCO pipeline."

"Conspiracy, now, is it?" Wakefield asked.

"No. Well, maybe. Or it's just real smart people figuring out a way to make a huge pile of money on someone else's work. The one thing I know for certain is the motives never change. This was to be a good old-fashioned theft with a hostage kicker. Why do they need leverage? Why try and kidnap Leecy? Answer: They can't get to what they want at INESCO. The mole knows it's there, but needs someone else to get it for him."

Valerie jumped in, saying, "We've got to get back to the office and search the personnel files. If Leecy is correct, then all we have to do is find the employees that are part of this state program. Once we have the names, we question all of them until we find the one that's involved. We make him tell us what they're after and then we keep it safe. Game over."

"Or we call Lester," Leecy said, "and have him question Mr. Pickett. Daniel is probably still in the hospital. I'll bet for a lighter prison sentence, he will spill the beans on the guys at INESCO that are part of the program. He might even know the one we're after."

Wakefield was walking toward the connecting doors and pulling them open as Leecy finished her thought. I was following Wakefield at a distance when she started barking orders to the operatives on the other side of the suite through her earpiece.

"Ryan, be advised we have hostile on site. I have two Agents unconscious. I need you and your team in tech-ops."

I reached the open doors to the room and looked over Agent Wakefield's shoulder. Julia and Zachary were both unconscious in their seats, probably knocked out by one of the invisible gases I knew the CIA used to incapacitate their enemies without killing them, or maybe tazered. The odor of burnt plastic also filled the air, and I noticed the computers were smoking. Agent Moore was nowhere to be found.

I was moved out of the way by the other three members of Wakefield's unit as they rushed into the room. Hodges and Franks bent over Julia and Zachary, assessing the situation and reporting the two victims had been tazed, while Ryan conferred with Wakefield.

"We can use our laptops to access the hotel cameras and search for Moore," Ryan said. "He couldn't have gone far. Maybe we can locate him with his cell or earpiece transmission signal."

Wakefield ordered, "Get to work on the cameras in and around the hotel. Go back thirty minutes, and search forward. Forget tracking him. He's too smart to have his cellphone or earpiece on him anymore. Our best hope is to search the cameras."

I walked away from the room toward Leecy and Valerie.

"Moore is the third man. He is our mystery man. He's gone. Better make that call to Lester now," I said.

Valerie removed the prepaid cellphone from her Go bag and dialed 411. I heard her ask for the Park City, Georgia police department before I turned my attention back to Wakefield.

"How can we get in touch with you if we need you later?" I asked her. I was thinking it was time for my family and me to go.

She looked around the room at all the destroyed equipment and said, "He poured acid on everything we were using, but," she reached for a small black case on the floor next to Julia, "he missed the backup earpieces we keep for emergencies. Do you remember how these things work?"

"No, I've never used one."

"That's right. You refused to wear the old ones with the wire and the battery pack. You'll like these new ones a lot better. No wires. The battery is built in, and they are rechargeable. The earpiece sends and receives communications between all those wearing one. These are all tuned to the same frequency. You talk, and I hear what you say, and vice versa. I guess Tom didn't get a kick out of the conversation after all. He has the upper hand for now." She moved to place the earpiece in my ear, but I took the device from her hand. "Just slip it inside your ear and give the outer edge a light tap with your finger to activate it. No one will know you're wearing it, and after a while, you'll forget it's there yourself. There is one drawback."

"What's that?" I asked slipping the tiny thing inside my left ear canal.

"The range is less than twenty miles."

I was starting to remove it when Wakefield placed her hand on my hand, stopping me. "No, leave it. I'll get this place cleaned up, and we'll head to Park City. If you need us, we'll be ready." She let her hand fall to her side, continuing. "You three need to get to work on those files. Maybe together we can still salvage something out of the mess Moore made of this case. Find out what they're after. Let's use it to catch those bastards," she said. She looked from me to the men busy cleaning up the communications room and reviving the injured agents.

I realized how close we were standing to each other and moved back a step before saying, "I owe you something for asking for your help. Let us take care of Moore and his gang for you. We can minimize your exposure that way. Keep the CIA and your team out of it, if possible."

"But that's not what I want. That's never been what I wanted, and you've known that since we met."

I felt my face blush and shook it off. I'd been very close with Wakefield during my years at the CIA, and I was always aware of her as a woman with powerful feelings that leaked out whenever we worked together, either close-up or at a distance. There had always been an unspoken chemistry that nearly, but never explicitly, overwhelmed our professional relationship. We'd both worked hard to keep it at bay. That wasn't always easy to do. Seeing Tammy again reminded me just how difficult it had been.

Wakefield changed directions, saying, "No, this time I want to recruit your daughter. I can tell she's as sharp, if not more so, as you. Add to that her mother's influence and bloodline; that kid is a can't-miss prospect."

I looked over my shoulder at Valerie and Leecy. Val was still using the phone. I wondered what she could be talking to Lester about for this long. Leecy was busy checking her Go bag contents. Something was off with those two.

"I think Valerie has other plans, but Leecy is going to make her own decisions about her future. She has a mind of her own, Tammy. We all know that," I said softly. "So, you can try to recruit her, but there's no predicting what direction she might choose at this point. So let me clean this up for you. I owe you from long ago. It'll make us even."

"Okay...okay for now...but I'll be listening if you need me. All you have to do is ask for help, and we'll come running."

I saw Ryan, Franks and Hodges give me a quick glance and nod. I realized they were listening to everything Wakefield and I had said.

"Earpieces," Wakefield reminded me.

Valerie came over with Leecy, looking grim.

"Bad news. Talked to Lester. Daniel Pickett died less than forty-five minutes ago," Valerie informed the group. "Lester says there's an investigation into the death, but I'm sure that Porter and Moore found a way to get into the hospital and tie up their loose ends."

"They won't kill the man they have in place at INESCO, will they?" Leecy asked.

"Moore would've heard everything you three said even if he wasn't in the building at the time," Wakefield said. "I've offered an earpiece to Granger. Would you two like one?"

"Absolutely!" Leecy said.

"Agent Wakefield," Ryan said, "the computers are completely fried. The acid ate through the motherboards. But we spotted Moore on the surveillance cameras exiting the building twenty minutes ago and entering a black SUV. We were able to track both his cellphone and earpiece signals south out of the city, then lost them both. We extended our camera search and located the SUV again south of the airport, but we need to go mobile."

"All right, that squares it. Wrap up this HQ and be prepared to evacuate in fifteen minutes," Wakefield said. Then facing me and my family, she asked, "Do you need a lift? Or do you wanna use the stolen truck you arrived here in?"

How did she know about the truck? I didn't really care at this point. Nothing fazed me anymore. I was beginning to accept this new world of high-tech surveillance.

"Can you drop us in East Park near the old tobacco warehouse?" Valerie asked.

"I'm happy to take you anywhere. Earpiece?" Wakefield asked.

"Yes, thank you," Valerie said.

"Don't be surprised by our silence. Once my team puts in earpieces, we only speak when spoken to. No idle chatter. The boys, as you saw, will speak to me directly rather than use the earpiece technology."

There was a buzz of activity in the suite. Julia and Zachary had been revived with no apparent long-term damage, and were assisting Hodges in Tech-ops. Ryan and Franks had disappeared behind the connecting door on the far end of the room. I assumed they were wrapping things up as the entire team prepared to vacate the suite. It looked like we would all go mobile together.

"Five minutes. Let's go."

We followed Wakefield down the hall and into a waiting elevator. Wakefield inserted a key card and pressed the B3 button. When the doors opened, we were in the subbasement of the hotel, near the incinerator room. Valerie, Leecy and I followed Wakefield through the labyrinth, ending at the rear of one of two black SUVs parked there.

As we climbed into the SUV to wait for Wakefield's team to arrive, Leecy asked, "Is there a way that I can do both, Mom? I mean, can I be both a CIA agent and Mossad agent?"

I was about to say no when Wakefield turned in her seat to face Leecy, saying, "I am very well-acquainted with the head of Mossad, and our agencies' relations have thawed a bit. They were almost frozen completely after the Pollard Case, but that was almost thirty years ago. Let me see what I can do. Maybe now is the perfect time for a joint operation."

I smiled, remembering the case she referred to, and thought if any one person could bring the two agencies back together, Leecy could.

Meanwhile, we had a puzzle to solve in Park City.

The drive to East Park didn't take long. I was seated in the second row seat of the suburban next to Leecy, who was next to Val. Wakefield was riding in the front passenger seat, and Ryan was driving. Following us in the second SUV were the rest of the team, including Julia and Zachary.

I listened to Tammy second guess herself and wonder aloud how she didn't see it. Valerie and Leecy sat in silence, staring out the window. I didn't pretend to have any answers for Wakefield, though I wanted to tell her not to be so hard on herself. The truth was, however, she'd be held accountable for having a rogue agent operating under her nose, even if we were able to clean up the mess. Fair or not, that was the way the agency would see it. I knew that's what she was worrying about. I also knew we could help her.

We stopped at the first red light in East Park.

"Where to now?"

"Straight for three lights," Valerie instructed. "Take the first right after the third red light. Follow that dirt road till it dead ends, and we'll get out there."

"Okay, will do."

"Why so far from Park City?" Wakefield asked.

"We left our Jeep a few miles from where the dirt road ends. Now that we know the APB was of limited scope, and I assume you'll counter it with a few phone calls, there's no reason not to drive the Jeep," I answered.

"Done and done," Wakefield said.

"Thanks for the lift," Valerie said.

"Our pleasure," Wakefield said.

"As far as Leecy's future is concerned," Valerie began, "let's talk when this is over. There are things to consider. I don't want her to rush into anything."

Touching her ear, Wakefield said, "Anytime."

Valerie didn't say goodbye or wait for the SUV to drive away before she started hiking for the Jeep. I saw her check her watch. "We have nineteen hours to find the mole, figure out what they're trying to steal, and stop it."

"Why do we have to do anything at all?" Leecy asked. "It seems to me the product is safe. I mean, if Porter and Moore could get to what they want, they would already have it. They failed, right?"

"No," Valerie said, "all they incurred is a setback. Guys like Porter and Moore aren't going to let that stop them. Yeah, they failed at taking you hostage, but what about Grandpa Reuben, my bothers, or Mom? They're all in danger. That's why after I called Lester, I called the family and told them what was happening. I don't care about CIA protocol, Ron," she said, and then, remembering her earpiece, "I don't care if Wakefield is pissed; my family needed to be warned. I told them everything. They're all hunkering down at INESCO. David and Isaac are busy working the files, trying to connect the dots."

"I thought the call with Lester went on a little too long," I said. "You made more than one call. That was risky. I thought we assumed Porter and Moore had our cellphone numbers and could listen in and track our locations."

"What does that matter now? We sat in the room with the bastard. It's my family, Ron; my parents," Valerie said. "I told David not to call the prepaid cellphone number unless it was an emergency, and even then, to just text me '911.'" She stopped and turned to face me. "I know it's exciting to be working with Tammy again. I also know she was never happy about having me around, but never mind that. What counts is we are up against Army Rangers, Ron. It's been almost twenty years since," she paused, checking her anger before continuing, "since that life I lived." She was fighting back tears, now. "I didn't have anything to lose back then, or at least, I didn't think I did. Now I have everything to lose, and for what? We don't even know."

I didn't say a word. I was angry with Valerie for taking that shot at me in front of our daughter. But I understood. She was scared, and lashing out at me was safe. She knew I could take it.

Leecy picked up on it right away.

"Wait, what did you just say? Did you and Wakefield have a thing back in the day, Dad?"

Valerie was staring up at the treetops, collecting her thoughts before leveling me with a stare.

"Let me make myself clear to you and anyone listening. If giving these guys what they want protects my family from harm, then I'll give it to Porter and Moore and whoever else it is that wants it, and don't even think about trying to stop me."

With that said, she turned and sped down the trail toward the Jeep. Leecy and I looked at each other, and then jogged to catch up to her.

The Jeep was just as we had left it. Valerie handed me the key from her Go bag as I climbed behind the wheel. It took an eight-point turn to get the Jeep turned around, but we were finally on our way. Leecy broke the long silence with a question.

"Mom, are you saying Dad cheated?"

Valerie turned sideways in her seat to face me. Placing a finger to her right ear, she turned off the earpiece. "Turn yours off, too." We did as she asked.

"I'm sorry," Valerie said to Leecy, "No, your dad didn't cheat on me. I lashed out at your father because I feel helpless right now and that makes me angry. I know all about your father and his time with the CIA. We've been together for twenty years. We have you. Please excuse me. I'm just a bit... scared."

"That goes for me, too, Leecy. I love your mother. I love you. I love our life together. I'll do anything to protect my family, and that includes your mother's parents and brothers."

"I knew the moment Wakefield smiled at you, Dad, that there was something between you two," Leecy said.

"Well, miss smarty pants, you're wrong. The only thing between us is a relationship forged in the fires of covert operations. Life and death situations have a tendency to bring people close. Our relationship has always remained professional. There were times when the bounds of that professionalism were tested, especially when she saved my life, but that was a very long time ago. End of story."

"Tell me how she saved your life."

"Sure. In 2035."

I smiled at my daughter in the rearview mirror, and we all

enjoyed a much needed laugh.

"So, what's the plan?" Leecy said, changing the subject.

"Valerie?"

"Well, hopefully my brothers will have a list of all the employees we've ever hired at INESCO as part of this state program. Assuming that's the connection. It's the most logical theory we have."

"That shouldn't take too long, right? A quick computer search and they're done?"

"Not really. For all the innovation we do at INESCO, there are some aspects of our business that are behind the times."

"Like what?"

"Like everything that doesn't involve production or research and development. We have very sophisticated equipment in those areas, but bookkeeping is still done the old fashioned way. Mainly because the building where the record keeping is done is the original office space from seventy years ago, and that building wasn't built with modern technology in mind. We looked into wiring it for computers and security systems and cameras, like the newer buildings have, but it just wasn't possible. We have plans to move into a new building one day, but that doesn't help us right now. All the searching your uncles and grandparents are doing is being done by hand."

Fifteen minutes later, the INESCO company sign came into view.

"We have work to do. Power up your earpieces and focus."

As we pulled into the parking lot, Valerie's family came out to meet us, pulling Leecy from the Jeep and showering her with kisses and hugs. They formed a human shield around her and walked her into the building. Once we were all safely inside with the door locked, Catherine Simon, Valerie's mom, took over.

"I knew it; I knew it," Catherine cried.

"You knew what?" her husband, Reuben, asked.

"I knew all this business with the government, all these secrets we keep and secret things we make, would put my baby in danger."

She was not referring to her daughter, Valerie, but Leecy, her granddaughter. I knew that because she was squeezing Leecy's cheeks so hard the poor girl was grimacing in pain.

"Don't be so melodramatic," Reuben scolded. "You're being ridiculous."

"We're okay, Catherine," I interrupted. "Leecy is okay; Valerie and I are okay. But to keep everyone safe we really need to focus on searching the files."

I knew my in-laws all too well. The situation could easily spiral out of control and into an argument about who knew what and when and don't forget about that time thirty years ago when it was entirely your fault and you know it. Like every other time I'd seen my in-laws argue.

"Have you guys had any luck with the files?" I asked.

David, the older of the two Simon boys, said, "Yes, let me show you what we found."

Everyone followed David through the small office and in and out of its series of doors to the file room, which was full of dusty, old four-drawer filing cabinets that lined the walls. In some instances, filing cabinets were stacked on top of filing cabinets. David led us to the table in the center of the room and the mound of paper there.

"It's here somewhere. I was just writing down the last name

when we heard you arriving. Where is it? Ahh, here it is," he said, handing a list to Val. "We found the file on Daniel Pickett and used it to reference the state agency called Georgia's Second Chance Program. Two names came up."

"So you were right, Leecy. But who hired Pickett and why?"

"I did," Val's father said. "But he wasn't the first one from the program. You weren't here, young lady. We were struggling to implement your plan for our future. We needed more help, but couldn't afford to hire any new employees. I heard about this program at one of my Chamber of Commerce meetings. I called them up, and they recommended Roderick Anderson."

"Rod Anderson came from the Second Chance Program?"

"Yes, and he's been a great employee."

"Yes, Dad, I know. He's also head of our R&D department," Valerie said.

"Of course," Reuben said. "And when we needed an entry level fork-lift driver, he recommended another guy from the program named Daniel Pickett."

"Roderick Anderson.... Wow...." Val said, and then glanced at me. "We go to Rod's house and find out what we need to know; then we'll be back here to get it, whatever it is."

"Good idea. Sounds like I may have trusted the wrong guy and now we're in danger," Reuben said as he stepped aside to let us out.

I walked past him, saying, "Don't worry. I'd rather die than allow any harm to come to our girls."

Reuben nodded. "Don't let it come to that, my son."

I smiled at the tough old man and left the room. Leecy was kissed and hugged by them all, and they locked the doors as we left. Valerie asked her brothers to call Lester and have him come and stay with them, but I knew they wouldn't do that.

"Let's go," Valerie said as the doors to INESCO closed behind us. "Anderson lives in Marion, Georgia. I know where his house is; he hosted the holiday party two years ago."

"I remember that. What? About twenty miles away?"

"That's right," Valerie answered. "Leecy, when we get to Rod's house, you stay in the car."

"No. If I'm going to be a spy, you can't protect me from the bad stuff. I need to see what you do and how you do it. I assume this guy isn't just going to tell you what he and the others are after. You and Dad are going to make him, aren't you?"

"We'll give him a chance to talk first."

"Okay. I can handle it."

I didn't offer any opposing view, because she was right. If being a spy was to be her career choice, she needed to see the unsavory side of the job. Wakefield's voice in my ear startled me.

"We're en route to Marion, but can't access the address for Rod Anderson. Please advise."

"Advising it's better to keep your distance. Those black SUVs will draw a lot of unwanted attention. Wait for us at INESCO instead," Valerie answered.

"Already have two men on scene at INESCO. Your family is well-guarded. We'll hold on the outskirts of Marion. Is that position advisable to offer support?"

"Yes, stay on State Road 27 at mile marker three. You'll be less than five minutes out if we need help. The address is 1719 Pine Knoll Lane."

"We have it here on the GPS. Good to go."

I was passing mile marker three at that very moment and

wondered where Wakefield might be. A few minutes later I saw Pine Knoll Lane ahead on my right, and slowed to make the turn.

"I'm going to pull right up in the driveway and play it casual," I said. "Like we're just in the neighborhood or something. I'm sure he and the family are eating dinner or cleaning up after dinner. What do you think?"

"Good idea," Valerie said, and then to Leecy, "Look in my Go bag and hand me my Glock, and look in your father's and hand him his straight knife and collapsible police baton."

I watched Leecy in the rearview mirror searching the bags for the items. She passed each item to her mother before asking, "This is about to get real, isn't it?"

"You tell me. This guy is working with a group that broke into our home and tried to kidnap you as a hostage to steal from our company and our country. Unless he has a very good reason why he did all those things, what do you think is about to happen?"

"Okay, sorry I asked."

"No, you haven't seen sorry yet," Valerie said.

Val opened the door to the Jeep before I'd brought it to a complete stop in the driveway at 1719 Pine Knoll Lane.

"Last chance to stay in the car," I offered.

Leecy's answer was to climb out of the Jeep. I stuck my knife in my right back pocket and the baton in the left, and followed the girls up the walkway to the front door.

Valerie rang the doorbell. I could hear the TV and other sounds of family life behind the door, and the faint sound of approaching footsteps. The door opened, and there stood Rod Anderson, INESCO's very own Mr. Wizard. He could pass for Bill Nye the science guy any day. He was still dressed in his work khakis and blue INESCO shirt.

"What a surprise!" he said. "Come on in. We were just cleaning up from dinner, so excuse the mess."

"Actually, Rod, we're here about work stuff, and it would be better if you came outside." Then pointing to the detached garage, Valerie suggested, "How about in there?"

He hesitated a moment and then called to his wife. "Honey, Valerie Granger is here about work. I'll be in the garage for a bit," he said.

He closed the front door behind him and walked between us back down the pathway toward the exterior garage door. He was startled and said, "Leecy? I didn't see you there. What are you doing here?"

"My parents have been taking me on a little family vacation during school break," she said.

He keyed the passcode into the garage door's keypad before he said to Valerie, "Is it okay for Leecy to hear about work?"

"Oh, absolutely she can. It concerns her," Valerie said, and followed Rod into the garage just as the overhead door stopped.

Leecy and I followed Valerie inside. I pressed the button on the interior wall so the garage door would close behind us.

The detached garage was as cold and uninviting as Valerie's mood was dark. She was standing in front of Rod now. Her right hand held the Glock steady at her side. She was listening, but I could sense her patience wouldn't last very long. The look on Rod's face said two things: 'I know why you're here, and please don't hurt me.' I thought for a moment he was going to cry, but he held it together. He just started talking instead.

"I had nothing to do with the kidnapping. You have to believe me. That was all Moore's idea. He said we needed leverage, and Leecy was the best we could get. I tried to tell him it was a bad idea, but these guys don't really listen to me," he said.

"Slow down, Rod," Valerie said. "It's okay. Everything is going to be fine. Just start from the beginning."

I took down a folding chair that was hanging on the wall with neatly-organized garden tools, and unfolded it for Rod.

"Sit," I said, "and tell the story."

Rod looked around at the three of us, and began. "I was hired by your dad back in '89. He gave me a job through the Georgia program for ex-cons. Did you know Reuben never even asked me what I'd done time for?"

"I don't care about that, Rod; that's not why I'm here," Valerie barked.

Rod was starting to get jumpy and scared. Valerie's exercise in control would be short-lived if he didn't get to the point soon.

"I'd done five years in prison for computer fraud. It was back in the early days of computers, and the old machines were easy to hack. I stole some money from a bank by hacking their system and triggering the ATM to release funds to my account. I was arrogant. I didn't cover my tracks like I should have, mainly because I didn't think the bank would be able to trace the transaction log so quickly. I got caught. Anyway, your dad hired me because INESCO was installing computers and needed a computer guy. I was thrilled to have the work, and you got to believe me when I say I worked clean till last year."

He looked from face to face for some sign of approval or agreement, but found none.

"So, last year I got a call from a guy that said he was running the Georgia Second Chance program now. The guy said the state wanted to highlight the program's thirty years of successfully placing ex-cons with local business owners, and they wanted to feature INESCO and me in the article. I checked with your father and his sons, and with their approval agreed to meet with the man in Atlanta."

I watched as Rod folded in on himself like a dying star. His head dropped and tears began to leak out of the corners of his eyes. He took a few deep breaths and slowly regained his composure.

"But when I arrived at the offices of Georgia's Second Chance Program, I met some of the most vile and terrible creatures on earth. These men, they threatened to do awful things to my wife and children if I didn't do exactly what they wanted me to do."

"Did they give you a reason?"

He started nodding before he said, "Yeah, they told me I was working for a company that was sitting on a gold mine. Porter, the black guy of the group, told me that I was going to help them steal an INESCO invention and they were going to make lots of money selling it. He told me they would cut me in on the take if I did exactly what I was told to do. And if I didn't do it, they would torture and kill my family."

Rod dissolved into tears again.

"So I had no choice. I told them what they wanted to know about INESCO. I told them what I knew about our security protocols. I told them everything. I was there for what felt like days, but when they let me go I realized it had only been hours. The one calling himself Porter drove me back to Marion. He warned me against going to the police or talking to anyone about what had happened. He showed me an FBI badge. He said he could get to me and my family anytime and anywhere, and to prove it, he showed me pictures he had on his phone of my wife shopping in Atlanta, at the grocery store in Marion, and of my kids at school."

Rod was crying again now. He was as rattled as any man I had ever seen. I realized his sobbing would have to run its course, but Valerie wasn't having any of it.

"Stop that, Rod," she said. "Those same men came after my daughter. Tell me what they want."

"I don't know. They never told me what they wanted. They only wanted to know how to get what they wanted. That's why I told them what I knew about all our security measures. I made it clear there was no way to walk into INESCO and walk out with their hands on any one project, because you, Valerie, coded all the projects. Only you know what the codes correspond with. No one else knows anything."

Valerie slapped him hard across his face and said, "That's why they came after Leecy, you idiot. You sent them to my house."

"No, no, no! I didn't mean for that to happen. You have to believe me. I was scared. I'm sorry, but I was scared. These guys were real tough military types. The one named Porter said that he and the others had been part of some special Army unit that killed people. I believed them. They scared me and threatened my family. We've been living in fear for a year. We started homeschooling the kids because of all of this. Please," he begged, "I'm sorry."

Valerie shoved her weapon inside the waistband of her jeans. She found some paper towels on a workbench and handed them to Rod. "Clean yourself up," she said, "and go back inside the house to your wife and kids."

He took the roll of paper towels from her and dried his eyes and blew his nose. He stood on a pair of shaky legs and walked toward the overhead door. He was about to push the button to activate the door when it began opening. Valerie started to draw her weapon, but stopped when two sets of small feet appeared beneath the slowly-rising door.

"Daddy?"

The word was said in a way that made every parent shiver with fear. When the door was halfway up, the two Smith boys rolled under the rising door, with AR-15 rifles aimed directly at Valerie and me before they were standing.

We didn't move a muscle.

Moore, who followed in close behind them, was the first to speak, shoving Rod's three children and wife roughly inside the garage.

"Very clever girl, your daughter," Moore said, pointing at Leecy. "I hadn't factored her into the equation. But I won't make that mistake again, will I?"

Porter answered like a seal at Sea World responding to its trainer when prompted with a fish. "No, not a chance, my friend."

"Leave Anderson and his family alone. You don't need them anymore. I'll give you what you want," Valerie said.

"Oh, you bet you will. Cause if you don't, I'm going to kill your daughter in the most unpleasant way imaginable," Moore said.

He walked between Valerie and me, taking Leecy by the arm, saying, "You're coming with me. Mommy and Daddy can have you back when they get me what I want."

Valerie was calm. No sign of anger or fear crossed her face.

Her hands were as loose and easy at her side, as was her voice when she said, "Just tell me what you want, and I will bring it to you myself."

The one calling himself Briggs Smith lowered his weapon.

"Not yet, Boss. I owe this one big time."

He slammed the butt of the AR-15 into my stomach, and as I doubled over he brought the butt of the rifle down on the back of my head. I fell to one knee. I was fighting for consciousness. My vision was blurry and there was a ringing in my ear. Maybe it was Smith yelling at me, but I wasn't sure.

"'Considered dangerous,' my ass."

He kicked me in the face, and then I only saw black.

CHAPTER
SEVEN

I woke up on the cold concrete floor of Anderson's garage. I didn't know how long I'd been out, but at least I was alive. I knew where I was because the first face I saw was Rod's, staring down at me.

"What happened?"

"Well, after that guy kicked you in the head and knocked you out, he left with the others and your daughter. Your wife is inside the house with this lady named Wakefield, four guys and another lady named Julia. How's your head?"

"It's been better. Got any aspirin?"

"Sure, sit tight. You probably have a concussion. Don't move," I heard him say as he ran from the garage.

I stood slowly and was immediately dizzy. I fought the urge to vomit. Rod was right; I probably did have a concussion. I walked on very unsteady legs toward the open overhead door and the fresh night air. I used the track for the overhead door to steady myself before pushing off and walking toward the front door of the house. The pathway looked like it was a mile long and curved like the letter S, but I managed to make it to the front door. I fell up the two steps, pushing the front door of the house open. I saw with blurred vision heads turn and look in my direction. I couldn't make out any of the faces. I heard talking and the sounds of soothing voices, but I didn't understand what was being said. Valerie's face came into focus. She was crossing the floor toward me. She was unharmed.

"You've got a really nasty black eye and busted lip. Here, look in the mirror," she said as she steered me to the left.

I saw myself. The left side of my face was red with black and blue streaks. My face reminded me of pictures my Great Uncle John had of Indians ready for battle with faces painted with war paint.

I was still admiring myself in the mirror when I remarked, "I've seen worse. Will someone get me some ice or frozen peas for the swelling, please? What happened after I lost consciousness?"

Val steered me to the kitchen table and helped me sit down. She found some frozen vegetables in the freezer and placed one bag on my face and one on the back of my head.

"You have a hematoma on the back of your head the size of a baseball. Sit here. Rod is getting the aspirin." She turned to walk away but I grabbed her hand and said in my firmest voice.

"Look, I've been shot twice, stabbed in the back and chest. I've broken both arms and one hand. This is nothing. Tell me what happened."

"Moore and Porter have Leecy. Wakefield's team found cameras and microphones all over the Andersons' home. Moore has had the Andersons under surveillance for who knows how long. Julia and Zachary are trying to use the cameras and their signal to trace back and find a location for Moore and Porter. Julia says the surveillance cameras were using the Andersons' home WIFI connection to transmit their signals. The cameras and listening devices were sending their data to another IP address. Julia thinks the location of the receiving IP address might lead us to Leecy. Julia also said that Moore is bouncing that IP address signal off of every unsecured WIFI in the area, and in some cases, even a satellite or two. So tracing the IP address signal back to its origin might take a while. Julia is also concerned that if the Andersons' home was being watched, then INESCO might be under surveillance also. She and Zachary are preparing to sweep INESCO for transmission signals similar to the ones found here when we get back to the office."

Valerie freed her hand from my mine and walked a few steps away to lean against the kitchen counter. "Zachary and Ryan are also trying to locate Leecy using the earpiece she's wearing, or hope she's still wearing."

There was something else she wasn't telling me. I could see it all over her face. I felt whatever it was had to be pretty bad in her mind, because she was reluctant to share it.

"Tell me what you don't want to tell me."

She was silent, but finally spoke.

"Moore gave me the DOD code that corresponds with the internal alphanumeric code I assign a new product. I don't know how he got it. Wakefield thinks he hacked the DOD, but we don't know for sure. It doesn't matter. I know what they want."

I waited, but Valerie didn't say anything else. She pushed off the counter, walking across the room to the dining room table, where Wakefield's team was working on a laptop.

I stood to follow her, but I saw Rod enter the kitchen from what must have been a hall and say, "I got you aspirin."

"Great, thank you," I said. "So what are Moore and Porter

after? Do you know?"

"Yes," he answered, "and it turns out it's a project of Valerie's. It's a new monomer technology. Funny thing," he paused as he remembered, "she discovered it quite by accident, and wouldn't have submitted it to the DOD if some of our other products had tested better. Regardless, Valerie's little beauty is amazing. The compound can be made into a pourable liquid and molded to any shape. The resulting mold is undetectable, as is any object that is dipped in or sprayed with the compound. The compound bonds to the object on a molecular level, and the resulting polymer doesn't alter the object in any way. The gun still fires, the C4 still explodes, but they are now undetectable to any current detection devices. Do you follow me Ron? You look like you don't."

My head was pounding and my face was hurting badly, but I managed a nod to indicate I was with him. In fact, I was thinking of the havoc that would be caused by a product like the one he described. I was running down the list of objects that could be molded to conceal a bomb and stopped after ten. I realized the possibilities were endless. I could see Rod was still talking to me, and forced myself to listen.

"She ran the entire barrage of necessary tests. I think she was as shocked as anyone. Not one of the objects tested was detected by metal scan, x-ray, or millimeter-wave machine scans. You can see the object with the naked eye, but the object remains invisible to any form of man-made detection, unless, of course, the person carrying the object is being physically patted down. There's a group at Duke University and another group over in Texas working on cloaking technology as in the Harry Potter movies. They've had some success bending light waves around one side of an object. But those groups haven't achieved the level of invisibility this compound can produce. Valerie's invention may not make the object invisible to the human eye, but if the object can't be detected, it might as well be invisible, you know?

"Anyway, Valerie's compound, or VS621-971, is the first real breakthrough in cloaking technology." He was leaning in toward me real close now, and I was about to ask him what he was doing when he said, "I can see the print of the boot that kicked you."

I turned my face away from him to see Valerie walking toward me. I could see she was wearing the responsibility of the situation like it was hers and hers alone. I reached out my hand and she took it, and I pulled her to me. I held her there for a long moment. I felt her melt into me. She sighed deeply, not wanting to be the strongest person in the room at that moment, but just wanting to be a mother and a wife.

"They have her, Ron," she whispered. "They have our baby. Those men who threatened Rod by saying they'd do such horrible things to his family. They have our Leecy."

"Moore and company won't do anything to her. They want something and they need Leecy to get it, that's all," I said, trying to calm her, and I hoped I was right.

Wakefield's voice was the next sound I heard in my ear. "Let's not forget it was your baby that figured all this out. I think she'll be just fine. How's Moore going to contact you?"

"He said he'd call the offices of INESCO at midnight with a time and place to make the exchange," Valerie answered.

Looking at her watch, Wakefield said, "It's now 8:30 p.m. We have more than three hours to prepare. I suggest we turn the tables on these little shits and use what they want against them."

Valerie looked around the room and then said, "Let's get back to INESCO."

We made the drive to INESCO in a little less than ten minutes. The earpiece chatter was constant. Wakefield and her team were trying to track the IP address they'd discovered with no luck, and also preparing a signal sweep for listening devices at INESCO. I was about to ask a question when Julia's voice came through the earpiece.

"If our security sweep of INESCO indicates surveillance is in progress, I don't think we should disable whatever it is, but instead use it to gain an advantage."

"How do you know they aren't listening to us right now, and have been all this time?" I asked.

"Mr. Granger, we made that assumption the moment Agent Moore revealed himself to be working for his own self interests. I sent each earpiece a recalibration signal that blocked him as soon as we left Atlanta."

"Wonderful," I said.

"Everyone stay in their vehicles," Wakefield ordered as we pulled into the INESCO parking lot. "Hodges, you and Franks bring the Simon family outside and secure them in your SUV. We'll hold our positions and maintain radio silence, just to be on the safe side. Julia and Zach, you two run the diagnostics and report back to my position with the results."

I heard 'ten-four' in my ear five times, and added one of my own. Valerie and I watched from the Jeep as a black SUV rounded the corner a block away and headed for the parking lot. The Simons exited the building under Franks' watchful eye as the SUV, driven by Hodges, came to a complete stop.

With David, Isaac, Reuben and Catherine safely tucked away inside the SUV, Julia and Zachary excited the vehicle they were sharing with Wakefield and Ryan.

Julia's voice was in my ear again saying, "Zachary will check the phone lines for listening devices, and I'll sweep the rooms for the same."

There was nothing to do but wait and watch. I looked at the dashboard clock; it was 8:45 p.m. Leecy had been gone for almost an hour. I reached out and took Valerie's hand. I wanted my daughter back safe and sound. I wanted my family back together, and I wanted to get my hands on Moore, Porter, and the Smiths. I realized I was squeezing Valerie's hand too hard when she punched me in the arm mouthing *ouch* at me.

The doors of INESCO opened. Julia and Zachary exited the building. The two computer techs made a beeline for Wakefield's SUV and gathered at the open window on the passenger's side. I was just about to break the radio silence when Julia walked toward our vehicle. She came along the driver's side to my open window.

"We have multiple listening devices inside the main office, but no tap on the phone line. Zachary wants to extend the sweep to the production areas and the R&D labs, but we need access. He's asking your brothers and father now, but I wanted to check with you, Valerie."

"Do it," Valerie said, "but I think it's highly unlikely they gained access to plant listening devices to those newer areas of the facility, and I don't think Rod planted devices for them. He would've told us, but better safe than sorry. Do your sweep."

Planting a listening device in the unsecure office wouldn't

have been too difficult. The Simons didn't remember to lock the front door at night half the time. Gaining access to the new building located behind the office wasn't so easy, but it could be hacked by someone. That someone would need a key, key card and passcode, or the ability to hack all of those security measures plus disable an alarm system and cameras. Tough, but not impossible.

I watched the minutes pass on the clock on the dashboard of the Jeep. Nine o'clock came and went, and then 9:15 rolled over to 9:20 before Julia, Zach and David exited the building. David took his seat in the SUV with Hodges and Franks, while Julia and Zach met with Wakefield. It was 9:30 p.m. before we heard Wakefield's voice in our ears.

"No devices were found in the production area or in R&D, but we do have devices throughout the office area to deal with, and Julia has a very interesting plan. We're going to use the fact that Moore is listening to gain an advantage, but first we need to make a few recordings. Everyone listen to Julia, and do exactly what she says."

"Okay, gang, if this works, we'll be able to be in two places at one time."

The next ten minutes were spent repeating phrases and key words that Julia and Zachary compiled into a database for a program Julia had written to utilize. We were all playing a part, including the Simons.

With the recordings completed, Julia explained to us what she and Zachary were doing. "We'll use these new recordings and the recording of the meeting with Wakefield and the Granger family in the hotel to create a virtual conversation. David, Isaac, Reuben and Catherine will role-play with our computer-simulated conversation, so the Simons will be having a conversation with my modified laptop computer, which is running a program I wrote called Talktome. Once I activate the program, it will not only be able to listen to what's being said, the audio playback will be crystal clear through the wireless Kronos speakers, and Franks will be wearing a wireless Bluetooth headset to monitor the situation."

"I thought all the computers were destroyed by Moore," I said. "How did you get a copy of the meeting in the hotel room?"

"The back of the SUV Wakefield's in is also our mobile command post and tech center. Our earpieces and the equipment in the rear of that SUV are synched, and pick up everything any of us have said or heard."

"A couple of points before we begin," Wakefield said. "We'll all go and start the charade in person while the program is booting up and all the equipment is put in place. Then we'll temporarily jam the listening devices Moore has installed before we start the operation. Julia tells me it's very common to have listening devices like the ones Moore installed experience periodic static burst, so this shouldn't arouse suspicion. While the jamming is in progress, Franks will set up outside INESCO to listen to the conversation and provide protection for the Simon family if it's needed. The rest of my team, along with Ron and Valerie, will take up a position behind Hodges' SUV. We'll transfer our gear to David and Isaac's vehicles in the event we need to roll. We can't drive around Park City in the big black government cars, but we can go unnoticed in a Honda Civic and Toyota 4-Runner. The plan is to leave the INESCO parking lot when we get the call from Moore. If we pinpoint Moore's location before midnight, I want Hodges and Ryan ready to move. I want eyes on Moore and his partners to make certain they are where we think they are and not running some game on us. Understood?"

We all nodded yes.

"Everyone go inside the main office building. Let's leave earpieces on for now. If there is a meeting room, let's use it."

Valerie spoke for the first time since leaving Marion and the Andersons.

"Wait, there's one more thing we need to discuss before we go inside. We need to discuss what Moore and Porter are after."

"What's there to discuss?" Wakefield said. "You can't give them what they want. Our plan will work. We'll find Leecy and extract her, taking Moore and his boys down in the process."

"With all due respect, Agent Wakefield, that's not a call you get to make on your own," I said.

"Your plan hinges on pieces of this puzzle that aren't in our possession suddenly falling in our lap," Valerie said. "I don't like the risk that poses for my daughter. There are still too many variables."

"Okay, what do you propose?"

I looked at the clock; it was 9:40 p.m. Where was the time going? We had two hours and twenty minutes to figure this thing out before Moore called to make the exchange. At that time, Valerie would be forced to give away a technology that could result in unprecedented terrorist action around the world. If the technology Moore was after lived up to its billing, bombs – undetectable bombs - could be molded to take the shape of everyday objects and placed anywhere and everywhere. Part of me, the CIA agent part, wanted to argue against giving away the technology, but the other part of me, the father in me, didn't want to take any chances with my daughter's safety.

"I need five minutes in R&D to prepare to make the exchange."

There was silence as each person listening through earpieces realized what Valerie was saying. Wakefield broke through the silence when she said, "Ron, you and Valerie go ahead. Let's sync our watches. I have 9:42 p.m. in three, two, one, go."

Valerie and I did as Wakefield instructed and entered the building. We made our way through the series of security doors and entered the R&D lab. We could hear the doors to vehicles closing outside. They were waiting for us to do what we needed to do. Valerie touched her earpiece to power it off, and I did the same.

I watched as Valerie powered up three different computers and began her download. She filled a one GB memory stick and said, "Okay, that's it."

I'd been watching her the entire time and asked, "Are you sure this is the way you want to handle this?"

Sticking the memory stick in her jeans pocket she said, "I have a plan. This is part of it. It's the only way."

We powered up our earpieces as we walked back through the maze of doors and rooms to find the team assembled in the kitchen. I leaned against the far wall and watched Zachary set up the computer and the speakers. Julia was busy typing away on the modified laptop's wireless keyboard. The Simons and Valerie were seated in the chairs around the small kitchen table. The room was small, and filled to overflowing with bodies. Wakefield was standing in the doorway looking at her watch. Hodges, Franks and Ryan were just inside the door.

The mood was somber. The air was heavy. I felt like I was suffocating. I wasn't one for dwelling in the past or prone to worry about the future. I tried to stay in the present moment, but the weight of the moment was becoming a burden. I was worried about my child, and the choice Valerie had made in R&D. Valerie was formulating a plan. I only had my trust and belief in her.

As if on cue, Ryan, Hodges, and Franks announced they were heading outside to check their weapons and gear. Wakefield, for the benefit of those listening, made a formal request of them for a status update in five minutes. Then she pointed at her watch and to the group, making sure we were all on the same page. The time was 9:50 p.m. Julia began signaling she was jamming the listening devices by holding up her hand and counting down with her fingers from five. Valerie kissed her mother goodbye and hugged her father silently. I thought I saw her whispering in Reuben's ear. Probably one last I love you. We left together with Wakefield, Julia, and Zach. Wakefield's plan was off and running, for better or worse.

We were all standing just outside the doors of INESCO. I saw Franks pulling on his headphones to monitor the conversation taking place inside. I heard a buzzing and crackling in my ear, and I looked at the others. Each person had a hand on an ear. I was about to ask if the resulting sounds were part of the jamming Julia had done, but before I could say anything the crackling subsided. It was replaced with the sweetest voice I'd ever heard.

"Damn it. What's wrong with this thing? Why won't it

work?" Leecy's voice could be heard saying in my ear.

Wakefield answered saying, "Well, kid, if you want to be an agent you have to be able to work the equipment."

"I can hear you! I can hear you! It's me, Leecy!"

I wanted to scream, but I took my cue from the smiling Ryan and just smiled the biggest, happiest grin I could.

"Are you okay?" Valerie asked.

"Mom! Mom!" and Leecy's voice trailed off. We heard her fighting back tears before she said, "I'm fine. I'm not hurt."

"Where are you?" Ryan asked.

"Who is this?" Leecy asked.

"It's Ryan. We met briefly in the hotel. Can you tell me where you are?"

I looked at Wakefield and she gave me a wink. Ryan was getting down to business. He was taking point, doing what he was trained to do. Valerie hugged me tight as tears of relief streamed down both our faces.

"No, I don't know where I am. The room is dark."

"Tell me everything you remember happening to you after Moore and Porter took you from the Andersons' house," Ryan instructed Leecy.

Wakefield waved us away from the building, because we'd all stopped walking at the sound of Leecy's voice. Hodges popped the lift gate on his SUV and we all gathered under it. Julia and Zach opened black metal briefcases, connecting wires and cables between the cases and a stack of electronic equipment mounted in the SUV's cargo area. I could see one three-component stack was marked SAT ONE RELAY, and the other was marked SAT TWO RELAY. I watched as Julia and Zachary began blazing away on the computer keyboards.

"Okay, well they put a sack over my head, and put me in

the trunk of a car. I tried to time the trip with my watch, but I don't think it worked. The glowing hands of my stopwatch function indicated I was only in the trunk for twelve minutes. I felt the car drive over a speed bump, or something like that, just before the car stopped and the engine was turned off. That's when I stopped the watch. I was pulled from the trunk by two men and told to walk. I was scared, but not as scared as I pretended to be. I fell down on purpose because I knew I wasn't standing on pavement, and I wanted to know what it was. I felt grass. I was walking across a lawn, maybe, steered by a hand on my left arm. I counted thirty-seven paces before I was told to stop. That's when they loosened my hood or sack thing enough for me to see my feet, but nothing else. I could see that I was standing at the top of a set of concrete stairs. I counted ten steps down. I was stopped at the bottom and the hood was refastened. I heard what I thought was the sound of a door opening, and was led by the hand where the person wanted me to go. I counted forty-five paces before I stopped walking. I want to say there was a light on somewhere, because the front of the sack on my head was brighter, but it could have been a flashlight. I couldn't see anything, but the bag looked brighter, you know what I mean? Anyway, I heard the sound of metal sliding on metal before I heard a door open. I was sure it was a door, because the sound was similar to the sound the door on Grandpa Reuben's barn makes. I was pushed to my right and fell. The floor is either made of stone or brick. I heard the door close, the metal on metal sound, and then a voice tell me I could remove the hood. That's it. That's all I know about where I am."

I was losing the battle I was fighting to control my emotions. My initial relief was replaced by anger. I wanted to scream. Valerie appeared to be calm and unaffected by Leecy's words, but I knew that was a façade. I knew she was killing Moore and Porter in her mind.

The small group was huddled behind the SUV, listening to the conversation between Ryan and Leecy like we were in front of an old radio, listening to an episode of the Lone Ranger.

"Okay, that's great," Ryan, said. "Everything you did was perfect. I know seasoned agents that don't think as well as you did under pressure. Now, I need you to do something for me."

"What?" Leecy asked.

"I need you to run your hands over the walls for me. Tell me what the walls feel like and give me an idea of the size of the room you are in. If you can, find the door and start there." Ryan said.

"Okay, I think I can find the door."

We listened as Leecy shuffle-walked for a few seconds before she spoke again.

"Found the door. The door feels like it's metal. Definitely not hollow. I found the wall and it feels like..." There was another pause.

We listened as the sound of her hands sliding over a very rough surface came through our earpieces.

"The walls feel like brick. I've reached a corner. I'm going back to the door now. Based on the rough measurement I just made, the room is six feet wide. I'm going to place my back to the door and walk until I find a wall now."

We listened to the sounds of shuffling feet and then heard her say excitedly, "Six feet deep. I'm in a six by six room."

"Great work, Leecy. I'm going to turn you over to your parents and get to work on your location. One last thing before

I sign off, we aren't receiving the tracking signal for the earpiece. Did it get damaged somehow?"

"It did fall out of my ear in the trunk, and I rolled on top of it. I got it back in my ear with no problem, but it may have been damaged. I've been trying to make it come on for the longest time."

"Not a problem," Ryan said. "Because of your great work we know we are looking for a basement. We know how long you were in the car, and we know the room you're in is made of brick and stone."

"Mom? Dad? Are you there?"

"Yes, dear; we're listening, as is the rest of Wakefield's team," Valerie said.

"I'm here, angel," I said, just so she knew it was true.

"There's something else you guys and Wakefield and Ryan need to know."

"What's that?" Valerie said.

"I heard them talking when I was in the trunk."

"Okay, what did you hear?" Valerie asked.

"They are selling the thing they want from INESCO to a buyer coming in from the Middle East. They're getting some type of certificates or something in exchange for the INESCO product. I don't know who the buyer is, but I do know they are meeting the guy at the Atlanta airport. I heard them say his flight was delayed and would now land at 9:00 a.m. Sunday morning- tomorrow. They're making the exchange in baggage claim."

"Great intelligence report, Leecy," Ryan said. "Anything else about this guy?"

"Nothing about the man, but I did hear them say they were going to remove the bag of the guy coming into Atlanta from the baggage carousel, and replace it with one identical to it. The bag is green, and it is monogrammed. That's all I heard."

"Great work," Ryan said again, "What else do you have for us?"

I could hear Leecy starting to cry now. She was coming apart on us and there was nothing we could do to comfort her. If not for the sound of her gentle crying, there would have been only silence in my ear. Valerie was the first to speak, and when she spoke it was clear who was in charge now.

"Leecy, I need you to listen to me. Are you listening?"

"Yes, Mom."

"Here's what's going to happen. We are going to locate you, and come and get you. Your father and I will take care of Moore and his band of ex-Rangers. You sit tight. We're on our way. No more talking. Just listen. You be ready to move when your father opens that door. You got me?"

"Got it," Leecy said.

At that, the conversation was over. No more talking. It was time to get to work. Valerie jogged toward the Jeep and opened the door to the passenger side. I could see her fishing around in the glove box. She found what she was looking for and held up the paper map folder. The maps were courtesy of our AAA membership, but I don't think we had ever used them. Valerie was searching the contents of the folder as she slowly walked back in our direction. When she found what she was looking for, she ran back to the rear of the SUV and unfolded the map. With all the members of the team looking over her shoulder, Valerie began by placing a finger in the center of the map.

"The only buildings in town that are a twelve-minute drive from Marion and which have a grassy area, and a basement made of brick and stone, are city hall, the Theatre Cinema Playhouse, the first National Bank of Park City and the pharmacy. All of these buildings are located around the town square." She paused and asked, "Anyone have a pen?"

Ryan handed her a black marker. Valerie pulled the top off the marker with her teeth as she held the map in place on the floor of the SUV's cargo area with the other hand. She marked the locations of the buildings in question by circling them with the marker.

"City Hall faces south, and is located in the center of the town square," she said as she circled its location. "The streets run north and south through the town with odd numbered streets on the west side of City Hall and even numbered streets to the east of City Hall. The avenues run east and west. The odd numbers are to the north and the even numbers are to the south of City Hall. You guys with me so far?"

"Got it," Wakefield said, answering for the group.

"The Playhouse is located on the eastern side of the square on Second Street. The pharmacy is one block north of Howells' restaurant on the western side of the square on First Street. The bank is here," she said as she drew the last of the four circles, "on the south side of the square directly across from the front of City Hall on Second Avenue. All of these buildings fit the description Leecy gave us."

"There's no way to cover all those locations; we don't have enough manpower. Is it possible to eliminate one or more of these?" Wakefield asked.

Valerie studied the map.

"The bank, the pharmacy and City Hall are active properties. The Playhouse has been vacant for decades. I don't think they would use the Playhouse, though."

"Why not?" Ryan asked.

"I agree it sounds perfect. But the Playhouse is located on the side of the downtown square that backs up to a residential area, and all of the buildings on that side of the square are vacant."

"Still not seeing why that's a bad location," Ryan said.

"It's bad because no one ever goes over there. Any activity would be noticed."

"I agree the movie house is out," I said, "and I think the bank is a non-starter. Their basement was converted to storage years ago. Leecy would have felt smooth floors underfoot, plus the security system alone is enough of a deterrent."

"Agreed," Valerie said.

"The pharmacy or City Hall?" Wakefield asked.

"Both are excellent choices. The pharmacy's basement access is in the alley behind the building. There's a sidewalk that runs down the center of a small grass courtyard, connecting the rear door of the pharmacy to the asphalt of the alley. The basement access is located off the rear courtyard. There is a privacy fence back there to offer cover. It's a smart choice, and I know Mr. Loather, the pharmacist, doesn't use his basement," Valerie said.

"What about City Hall?" Ryan asked.

"It's a better choice than the pharmacy," Val said. "The town council turned the old basement jail into a tourist attraction when the state of Georgia declared the site a Historical Landmark. The tours are once a week, usually on a Wednesday. The old jailhouse door is the original cast iron with barred window and all, and can't be locked, so the jail is accessible to anyone at any time. Access is clearly visible from the dispatcher's desk at the PCPD across the street, so there's never been a problem with vandals or anything."

"Moore or some other member of his group could have scouted the basement jail by taking the tour," Ryan said.

"City Hall is the most likely candidate," Wakefield said. "They could've scouted the location well in advance, and the entry door issue gives them unfettered access."

"But what about the PCPD? You just said the access stairs leading to the door of the old jail could be seen from the police station," Ryan argued.

"True," Valerie said, "but if a person is flashing FBI credentials like the ones you, Hodges, and Franks have hanging around your necks, I don't think the local cops would question anything."

"I see," Ryan said. "They come to town and scout the place by taking a tour. They learn the tour's schedule and know they're safe using the location to hold someone. Furthermore, they learn that even though the door can't be locked, no one goes down there during off-hours because the local cops can watch the location. Moore and gang flash FBI badges, issue a phony APB, and they have all the reason they need to be there in the PCPD. They kill two birds with one stone. They can watch the old jail, and have a legitimate reason to be in town and in the police station."

"So, how do we make certain Leecy is in the old jail?" Wakefield asked.

"I think we can verify that theory," Zach said.

Zach and Julia had been busy over their keyboards this entire time. The sound of his voice reminded me he was still there. He stepped back from the SUV, stretching and shaking his hands back and forth.

"How can you help?" Wakefield asked.

"Julia and I have been trying to trace the IP address linked to the surveillance equipment we discovered at the Anderson home. That search has turned out to be as successful as a dog chasing its tail. But if the new theory is correct, we can focus on the Park City Police Station. If Moore is in the station, he'll want to listen to all that audio surveillance coming from inside INESCO. If that's where he is, the bandwidth usage will be off the charts."

"Will Moore know you are snooping around on the lines or whatever it is he is using? How will that verify where Leecy is?" I asked.

"There's a chance he is running detection software, but I doubt it," Zach answered. "Having spent six months working with him," he began typing on his keyboard again, "I know Moore will think no one will think to look for him at the police station. As far as helping verify Leecy's location, I figure if he's listening here at INESCO, he's watching her wherever he is. It's worth a shot, I think."

"Do it."

While Zach typed, I wandered away from the group to snoop through the bags of tactical gear in the rear of the 4-Runner. I passed Franks seated in the rear of the unused SUV with his headphones on, listening intently, and he gave me a thumbs up sign. I nodded as I continued toward the Toyota, and found Hodges seated in the rear cargo area under the raised cargo door. I looked at the two black bags, and then at Hodges. Hodges didn't need another hint. He stood and unzipped one of the bags.

"What are you looking for? Cause we have it all."

"I need a six-inch straight knife and sixteen-inch collapsible police baton. I seemed to have misplaced mine back at the Anderson house."

"No, you didn't misplace them. Your wife told us the guy that kicked you in the face took them when you went down. Here, we have exactly what you need," he said.

I spread the mouth of the bag open to reveal guns, ammo, knives, batons, wire tie handcuffs, and concussion grenades. I found the knife I was looking for, and it even came with a scabbard and belt. A baton was also there in a handy little carrying case. I slid it on the knife belt.

"Thanks," I said, and then asked, "What's in the other bag?"

Hodges answered. "Night vision gear, directional microphones powered by the same technology as the earpieces and synched with them, a couple of small drones we can fly with our cell phones. You know, the real cool stuff. You want a pair of night vision goggles?"

"No, thanks; my night vision is just fine."

Just then, I heard Zach's voice in my ear.

"I've got something. You all need to see this."

Everyone crowded around the rear of the SUV to see a picture of a steel door on the screen.

"What is that?" Ryan asked.

"I was looking for the audio stream that should be here if Moore is listening via the devices planted at INESCO, but it isn't here; it isn't anywhere. Julia, you're sure you found listening devices on our sweep?" Zach asked, "because the only thing being pulled down from the PCPD Internet connection is this video feed I found. Maybe that's the metal door Leecy talked about?"

I looked at the computer screen Zach was using and saw the image of a steel door, and then I looked at Julia. She was backing away from the group, nervously clutching at her necklace. I turned to walk toward her, but Valerie ran past me and got to Julia first, grabbing her necklace.

"You've been fiddling with this thing since the hotel. At first I thought it was just some nervous tic you had, but now I think you're hiding something. Or lying about something. Or is it both? I'll give you one chance to tell me what's going on before I make you tell me. Do you understand me, Julia?"

Valerie was nose-to-nose with the technology advisor. Val wound the necklace tighter and tighter around her fingers, and Julia's neck. Tears were flowing down Julia's cheeks. Her mouth was quivering, but no sound was forthcoming. Valerie turned and walked away from her, but didn't let go of the necklace. Valerie led her by the throat to the rear of the SUV and whipped her around like a rag doll, slamming her into the tailgate and forcing Julia into a sitting position.

"You want to cry?" Valerie said, letting go of the necklace in favor of grabbing Julia's head with a hand on each side. She turned it to face the computer screen. "My daughter is alone in that room behind that door, why? Is it so your boyfriend can make some money selling something he wants to steal from me? That's what Moore is to you, isn't he? Your boyfriend? You better start talking to me, Julia, or I'm going take that little gift from Moore you wear around your neck and make you eat it," Valerie hissed, inches from Julia's face.

Valerie had scared her to death, and now I needed to play good cop to Valerie's crazy cop. I grabbed Valerie by the arm and pulled her away gently, though Valerie made it look rougher than it was. I said in as soothing a voice as I could muster, "No one wants to hurt you, Julia. Just talk to us. Maybe there's an explanation for why you said there were listening devices and there aren't any. Help me understand, okay?"

Julia straightened her blouse and rubbed her neck. Then she made mistake number one, glaring at Valerie. Then she lied. Mistake number two.

"Zach is mistaken. I found listening devices. I don't know what you're talking about."

I knew she was lying because her hand reflexively reached for the pendant. It was her tell.

"Ditch the earpieces," I said. "Moore's been listening to us all along. She never recalibrated anything. It's all one big game."

I turned away from Julia in mock disgust. I caught Val's eye, and she drew her weapon as I said, "Valerie, she's all yours."

"No!" Julia screamed. "The earpieces were recalibrated, but yes, the listening device thing was a lie. Yes, Moore is my boyfriend, and yes, I was supposed to waste your time and keep an eye on you, and make sure you were all busy till midnight, but that's it, that's all I was asked to do."

Wakefield grabbed Julia's hands and restrained her. As Valerie patted her down, I noticed Zach had already started working the computer Julia was using.

"Nothing on the computer communicating with Moore," Zach announced.

"Two cellphones on her person. Could one of these be used to contact Moore?" Valerie asked as she handed them to Zach for inspection.

"Give me a few minutes and I'll let you know," he said.

"Where is she?" Valerie asked. "Where's my daughter?"

Julia's hand shot up from her side to grasp her pendant, but Valerie caught her by the wrist and said, "No, not this time," and jerked the chain from around Julia's neck. She handed it to Zach, saying, "She plays with this too much. Check it for me, will you?"

Zach stopped what he was doing with the phone and took the necklace from Valerie. I watched as Valerie kept a close eye on Julia. Julia attempted to level her stare back at Valerie. She was about to make mistake number three; she was about to challenge my wife. Julia's blonde locks hooded her eyes, but I was sure she was staring at Val. Wakefield wire-tied Julia's wrists together behind her back. There would be no more freedom for Julia now, and Zach didn't have the necklace long before he made a discovery.

"Bingo," he said. "Micro recorder and transmitter inside the pendant. Touching it activates the device. The transmitter is just a basic cell phone connection. Looks like it sent bursts of recorded data to a cellphone number every time she touched it. It's safe to assume he knows everything we know."

"So we're blown?" Ryan asked.

A new voice entered my ear now, "Franks, here. If the listening devices aren't present, can I shut this down? Catherine and Reuben have been arguing for the past fifteen minutes, and it's getting worse. Franks out."

Wakefield said, "Yeah; shut it down, Franks, but tell them to remain inside for their safety."

"Well, are we blown?" Ryan repeated.

"Maybe, I don't know yet," Wakefield said. "Zach, is there any way for us to know what information Moore's been sent?"

"No, but I may be able to find out what's stored on the device awaiting transmission. That might help us. Give me a minute, here. I need to disable the device's transmission capability. There...got it. Now I can read the file. Let me plug this in here, and that should dump the file onto the memory stick."

Wakefield interrupted by saying, "Zach, we don't need a play-by-play."

I could see the kid laughing to himself as he worked the keyboard. Valerie was locked in a stare-down with Julia. That situation was going to end badly for Julia; she just didn't know it yet. Zach turned away from his computer and smiled.

"Okay, we are in the clear. The pendant has Ryan's conversation with Leecy queued up and ready to send. Looks like we caught it just in time, or Moore would've known we were on to him. This thing is really cool. The transmissions from the pendant are very small. Each transmission is about a hundred and twenty characters of dialogue. The transmissions are about the size of a text message, but plays back on Moore's end as audio. The mechanism takes the recorded audio and breaks it into bite-sized, manageable pieces before sending. Every time she touched the pendant she activated the transmission. No wonder Julia was constantly messing with this thing. But lucky for us, Moore hasn't heard anything that can compromise us. No, we are good to go," Zach said with complete confidence before asking, "What do you want me to do with the thing?"

"That's a good question. I think we should use it to our advantage, but that all depends on Julia," Wakefield said.

As if hearing her name for the first time, Julia snapped her head toward Wakefield and said, "What are you talking about? I'm not helping you, and I've got nothing to say."

"Zach, I want that device from Julia's necklace up and running and ready to be used ASAP. I want to know the origin of that camera view and where it's sending its video. I want to know how we can use that video to our advantage. I want to know where Moore and his crew are, and I want you to be as certain as if your life depends on it, and I want to know all of that..." she paused and looked at her watch. "It's ten o'clock now. I want to know all of that in ten minutes."

Wakefield waved the rest of the group toward the doors of INESCO, and we followed. Valerie walked with one hand firmly grasping Julia's arm and the other on the butt of her gun. I brought up the rear behind Franks, Ryan, and Hodges. Zach was left standing at the rear of the SUV, working on Wakefield's to do list. I didn't know what Wakefield had planned, and I was reaching the end of my patience with all the high tech stuff, but I didn't really have a choice; I had to be patient. We moved through the offices of INESCO until we found the kitchen and Franks. He was telling the family the hoax was over.

Wakefield said, "Not so fast. I think we might be able to use them and this equipment to help us after all. Simons, take a break, but don't leave the building. I'm going to need you, so don't go too far."

Reuben stood stiffly and said, "Okay, we'll be right back," and he, his wife, and sons left the room.

Wakefield pulled out a chair, and as she cut Julia's wire ties with a pocketknife, she said, "Have a seat, sweetheart, and spill. Or I'm going to leave you alone in this room with Valerie."

Julia huffed, "Whatever," to Wakefield, but kept her eyes trained on Valerie.

"Oh, I see you don't think that's a problem for a gal like

yourself? You may not be a full-time field agent, but you did go through the standard CIA training. You know the basic self defense techniques, and I understand that affords you a certain level of confidence over your average citizen, but," and Wakefield paused here for dramatic effect, "Valerie is no average citizen."

I thought that got Julia's attention, but I couldn't tell for sure, because Julia remained focused on Valerie.

"There isn't anything average about Valerie at all. Quite the opposite, really. And of the long list of things that make her extraordinary, there is only one item on that list you should be aware of."

"What's that?"

"Valerie," Wakefield glanced at Val, and receiving the go ahead nod, said, "is a former agent of the Mossad."

Julia whipped her head toward Wakefield.

"Bullshit. There is nothing in her background that indicates membership in any organization, let alone the Mossad."

"That's right; there isn't. Why would there be? Unlike the US intelligence agencies, the Mossad keeps their agents' secret forever. They never reveal their identities, and the agents aren't allowed to reveal they were part of the Mossad, but I think we can make an exception to that rule tonight, given the circumstances."

Wakefield paused and took a seat at the table.

"Do you know what Mossad agents do, Julia?"

"No," she said, "not really."

"Their primary function is that of assassins. See, that's another thing the Israelis do that the US agencies fail at. The Israelis make it clear what agents of Mossad are all about. The US agencies like to hide their true purpose behind the veil of intelligence gathering, but that's all bullshit. If you don't be-lieve me, just ask Ron. Oh dear, I almost forgot about Ron. See not only did you and your boyfriend target the child of an agent for the Mossad," Wakefield informed her, "but that child is also the daughter of a former CIA kill squad agent. In fact, he was so good at his job that he was a squad of one. Those rumors Moore talked about in the hotel? Well, those are all true, and the man those rumors are about is standing right over there." Wakefield pointed at me and then said, "So pick your poison, Julia. You can talk to me and tell me what I need to know and live, or you can die. Which is it?"

All the color and anger drained from Julia's face. She was as pale as her shirt now. She reached for the pendant that was no longer around her neck. Her security blanket, as it were. She looked away from Valerie's face, to me, and then back to Valerie.

"Okay. I'll talk."

CHAPTER

EIGHT

"We're listening," Wakefield demanded.

Julia was crying now.

"It started eighteen months ago. Tom and I had just begun our relationship. We'd been working together for about six months, and finally decided to date each other. Anyway, we were reading the news one rainy Sunday morning when I stumbled across an article online. The article was about government waste, like that was something new, but this article detailed hundreds of millions of dollars being fraudulently sent to people by the IRS. The problem was, the people receiving the money didn't exist. The IRS eventually tracked down the group perpetrating the fraud, but never got back all of the money. I made a silly observation that Tom took seriously. I commented how the perps in that case could've avoided being caught and totally gotten away with it. He begged me to tell him how. So I did," she paused, and the tears turned to sobs as she said, "but I never thought he would try to do it for real. I swear."

Wakefield slammed the flat of her hand down hard on the tabletop. The resulting noise snapped Julia out of the personal pity party she was having.

"Listen to me, Julia. I don't care about that crap. I want to know where the girl is being held, and where Moore and his crew are. I want to know to whom they are selling the technology. We've made an educated guess as to the location Leecy is being held, but I want confirmation. We know the buyer is coming in from the Middle East, but I want a name. I want details. Start telling me what I want to know or all bets are off, and you have option two chosen for you. Stop wasting my time."

"I don't know any of that stuff! Tom kept me out of the loop about details like that."

Julia tucked her long blonde hair behind her ears and wiped her face with shaky hands. "I can't tell you what I don't know. You think you're the first person to ever threaten me? Think again!" She was laughing and crying, but this time uncontrollably. "And threatening me with Susie homemaker here," she said, jabbing a thumb in Valerie's direction, "won't change a thing. I suggest you give Tom, Porter, and those two Smith guys what they want, or," she reached for the missing necklace again, this time clasping her shaking hands together, "or Tom and his friends will make sure that girl suffers. This is something I do know; it's not an empty threat. Other than that, you can go fuck yourself, Special Agent Wakefield," she said, turning to face Valerie, "And you, you can..."

Valerie shut Julia up by landing a right cross on her chin. The punch landed with enough force that Julia was thrown out of her chair and slammed into the adjacent wall. Julia was KO'd. Valerie was still sitting in her chair as if nothing had happened. It was like watching a black mamba strike and recoil. Valerie was that quick, and that powerful.

"What the hell?" Wakefield exclaimed when she saw Julia's head bounce off the wall and her limp body slide to the floor.

"She was useless. She's obviously suffered some trauma at

the hands of Moore or someone else. No point in dragging it out," Valerie said, as she stood to leave the room.

"Was that necessary?" Wakefield said.

Valerie whipped around to face Wakefield from the open doorway of the kitchen.

"You gave her two options. I assumed you weren't bluffing. If I misread the situation, that's my bad, but you said it your-self: I'm an assassin. I don't make idle threats, and I don't ex-pect the people I work with to waste time, either. Julia is going to remain loyal to Moore till the bitter end. She was going to waste our time with some long, sad story and say nothing help-ful. The best thing we can do for her is get her some help, but until then, our choices are to waste manpower watching her, kill her, or incapacitate her until she can be useful. So I gave her a version of the option two you mentioned because I didn't want to kill her. She can still be of some help."

Wakefield thought a moment and then said, "Sounds like you have a plan. Do you want to share it?"

"Not yet."

"Okay. Fair enough. But what do we do with her now?"

"I'll take care of it," Valerie said, and turned away from Wakefield, signaling that she was finished with that conversa-tion and moving onto something else. "Ron? I'll grab some of those extra large black bags from the warehouse and a roll of duct tape. Bring Julia and meet me in the rubber lab. Franks, if you will grab her feet, you and Ron can move her."

"Okay," Franks said, "which way to the rubber lab?"

"Just follow me," I said, grabbing Julia's body under her arms and walking out of the kitchen.

I heard Wakefield's voice in my earpiece. "I'll be outside with Ryan and Hodges talking with Zach. Find me there when you three are finished in here. I'll tell the Simons to wait for us in the kitchen."

I led Franks through to the rubber lab, which was nothing like R&D. The place was covered in a thin layer of carbon black from all the rubber compounds being produced and tested in the lab. Valerie was waiting for us.

"Now what?" he asked.

"Now, we wrap her up in the bags and tie her up with duct tape. Make certain she can breathe, though. We don't want her dying on us, but we don't want her making any noise, either. So make the package snug so it's easy to transport. We'll need her later," Val said.

We loaded Julia into the trunk of the Honda.

Frank said, "Will she be okay in there in this heat?"

"Sure, but to be safe we'll leave the lid of the trunk open till we have to close it," I said, as we turned and walked toward the others.

"Good news." Zachary said. "Leecy is in the old jail beneath the City Hall, exactly where you thought she might be. She..."

"How do you know?" I asked, cutting him off.

"The camera filming the image of the door is sending what appears to be video through the WIFI signal from City Hall."

"Why do you say appears to be video? Again, how do you know?" Valerie asked.

"Long story short, I hacked the phone company and determined City Hall uses the phone line for Internet access, but spreads the signal throughout the building via a WIFI router the phone company installed. That WIFI signal is being hacked by a computer using the PCPD Internet cable. I've identified the computer at PCPD by the IP address we've been searching for. So, I've found the computer, and I've found Moore," Zach said, almost admiringly.

"And the video?" Wakefield ordered.

"Oh, sorry," Zach said. "The bandwidth usage at the PCPD is off the charts. That's not surprising, given the images coming from the old jail. And Moore is also routing the transmissions from the pendant to his computer. I assume he's doing this to prevent his phone from being tracked in case we got on to Julia."

"What about the video? The video!" Valerie demanded.

"Just a second; let me verify one thing," Zachary said, before pointing at his screen. "If you look closely at the image of the door, you will see that it's not a streaming video at all. I found a code embedded in each image. That code is unique to the image it appears with. It's actually very ingenious, because the images cannot be looped to fool the person watching the camera view of the door."

Wakefield asked, "Can we get eyes on Moore and verify he is actually in the police station? I don't want to fall for some elaborate hoax."

"The schematics we found for the police station don't indicate security cameras being installed," Zachary replied. "So I can't hack what isn't there, but because the computer viewing the camera images from the old jail is plugged directly into the phone line, I might be able to activate the computer's camera. I would need to trick the person watching the screen into opening a virus to do it, though."

"How?" Wakefield asked.

"I could load the virus on the pendant as part of an audio file transmission. We click the pendant; it sends the file. The file arrives on Moore's computer in the form of an email. As long as someone opens the file, the virus will be uploaded."

"Do it," Wakefield said, "and while you're at it, we need to lay out the plan."

"Valerie?" I said.

Valerie pointed to the map.

"One thing first. Zach, can you kill the feed to Moore's computer?"

"Sure, no problem."

"Great, that's exactly what I wanted to hear," Val said. "Ryan and Hodges will take up positions here and here. I want you both on the roof of Howells' restaurant. The left side of the building is directly across the street from the front door of the Police Station. The front right corner of the roof has a direct line of sight to the entrance of the old jail. You guys can park here.

"All of the buildings on that side of town are vacant except for the pharmacy, Howells' and the hardware store. All the storefronts in the town square face City Hall. The alleyways run behind the buildings. The alleys will allow you to move around unseen. Once you've parked, walk one block south along the alley; you can access the roof of the restaurant from the adjoining hardware store roof. There's an old fire escape on the alley side of the hardware store. Once in position, signal Ron and me with the word 'ready.'"

"And where will you and Ron be?" Ryan asked.

"Here," Valerie said, and pointed to the opposite side of the town square, "on the East side of City Hall, directly across from your position on the roof of Howells', at the old movie house. We'll park in the alley behind the vacant theatre. This position gives us a clear field of vision of the back of City Hall and the old jail access point. We'll be able to see anyone approaching the entrance to the old jail, and the City Hall building itself will act as a shield blocking our movements from anyone watching from the PCPD."

"Sounds like we have a plan." Wakefield said, "I'll remain here with Franks and Zach and advise everyone of any changes. We'll roll to your location once contacts with Moore and company have been made."

I looked up to see Zach jogging in our direction from IN-ESCO.

"I've sent the transmission." He retook his position at the computer. "Now we just wait and see if someone takes the bait."

"What did you send them to listen to?" Ryan asked.

"Oh, I sent them the sweet sound of the Simons arguing again. It really doesn't take much to get them started, does it?"

"It's just how they talk to one another," said Valerie, smiling. "If they didn't argue I'd think something was wrong."

"We're in; the file has been opened. Give me a few seconds," Zach said. "Here! Look at this."

The image of Agent Thomas Moore filled Zach's computer screen. We watched in silence as Moore stood. We could now see the image of the man calling himself Porter seated behind him, and heard them talking.

Moore was saying, "Damn, those two old birds argue enough."

"Old Jewish people love to argue," Porter said. "Christ, this is painful to listen to. Turn it off."

"It's a thirty-second burst," Moore said. "See, it's over. At least we know what's going on with Wakefield."

"Yeah, absolutely nothing."

"Speaking of what's going on, when is the Captain - what's his name? Lester? - due back?"

"I don't know. He went to check on his pregnant wife. Don't worry about him or his officers. They're staying out of our way."

"Travis!" We heard Moore call. "You and Briggs go check on the girl. I don't trust the WIFI connection. The Internet is crap in this town, and we've only got an hour till I call for the meet."

We all stared at the screen. We watched as Porter stood and walked out of the view of the camera, and Moore retook his seat.

At that moment, Zach killed the feed.

"Why did you do that?" Ryan asked.

"We couldn't risk staying on the camera any longer. The red light that illuminates when the camera is in use might have been spotted. Better we play it safe. We got what we needed, right?"

"Yes, we got what we needed," I said. "Switch over to the feed from the old jail door, will you?"

We all looked from Zach's computer to the one Julia had been using in time to see the Smith boys enter the camera view. Their movements weren't fluid, but more like stop action animation. I watched as the two men stood in front of the metal door. Briggs started to speak, and I heard his voice in my earpiece.

"Not much longer now," he said. "Your parents will bring us what we want, and it'll be over."

Leecy didn't respond. We watched as the two men then grabbed their crotches and thrust their pelvises at the door.

The one named Travis couldn't contain himself. He threw his head back and laughed. "Yeah, and then we're going to have a party with you."

I closed my eyes. I could hear my daughter crying quietly in my ear.

Valerie had all the information she needed. She handed her cellphone to Zach. "Make sure all INESCO incoming calls are routed to this cellphone so I don't miss the call from Moore. More importantly, be listening for my signal to cut the feed from the old jail. That's when our game begins. The timing has to be perfect. Got it?"

"It'll take me a minute to forward the calls, but not a problem. I'll be ready to cut the feed."

"Wait," Ryan said, "wait just a second. Are you going to dash into the basement jail and back out with your daughter? Let's say by some miracle you beat the two Smiths to the metal door and retrieve your daughter. Moore and Porter won't be too far behind. What do you plan to do about them? You and your husband are going to face down four armed Rangers with your daughter by your side? With what? One gun, a knife, and a police baton?"

"Something like that. Don't forget; I have what they want," Valerie answered. She pulled the memory stick from her pocket.

"But I never said anything about running in and out with my daughter. You said that. I just want Zach to cut the feed from the old jail when I tell him to do it. I want to force the Smith boys to show themselves. Sure, I could assume they're back inside the PCPD, but why assume when I can be certain? I figured if Moore were worried about the Internet connection, then cutting the feed wouldn't alarm him. Moore sent the Smith boys over once to check on Leecy. I figure he'll send them over again. That's all. I just want all the players on the field so there will be no surprises."

"Boss?" Ryan pleaded with Wakefield. "We've got three experienced operators she's not using properly. Two of us are on lookout duty, and Franks is babysitting."

"Look," Valerie said, and this time her voice was devoid of any semblance of patience, "I appreciate your concerns, but I was doing this stuff before you were out of diapers. I've planned and executed missions on five continents. I've killed people in more ways than you can imagine. If I thought I needed your help I would ask for it, but I don't. I want those four bastards. I want them in that old basement jail for two reasons. First, I want to minimize the risk to the local police force. I don't want Lester or any of his officers involved in this."

"And the other?"

"Once down in that basement, there is nowhere to hide."

I was already walking toward the driver's side door of the Honda Civic, closing the trunk as I walked past, not waiting for a reply from Ryan. I didn't want to talk anymore; I wanted to act. I sat down behind the wheel of the Honda, only to hear Valerie ask, "Do you mind if I drive?"

I was about to answer her when I saw her finger pressed to her lips. I walked around the car in silence, meeting her gaze over the roof. I opened the passenger side door. She touched her ear with her right index finger and I followed suit, turning off my earpiece.

"You want to keep secrets?" I said, sitting down inside the car.

"I like playing my cards close to my chest, if you know what I mean."

"I do. That's one reason I never beat you at cards."

"I understand Ryan's concern about being cautious, but I think it's time to take some calculated risks," she said, smiling.

"Risks?" I asked, and then added, "I'm starting to think you're having fun."

"No, nothing like that. But if I told you I'd figured out a way to rescue our kid, bring the bad guy out in the open, and trick him into telling us everything, what would you say?"

"I would say great, but what about the Smiths? You assume they walked back to the PCPD?"

"I may not know exactly where they are, but I know they aren't waiting for us down in that old jail. No, Moore and company think we'll play it safe because of Leecy. That's why we're going to do the exact opposite."

"I like it," I said, gesturing toward the trunk. "And Julia?"

"We need her to play a part. If it weren't for that, I wouldn't involve her. She's manic."

"Abused?"

"If not physically, definitely mentally. We'll use her, but treat her with kid gloves."

"I can do that," I said.

"Anything else?" she asked.

"Just waiting to hear the plan."

"I'll fill you in on the details in a minute. First, let's make sure Ryan and Hodges do what I need them to do. Earpieces back on."

"Earpieces back on," I replied, kissing her cheek in the process.

The Honda rolled forward, and Valerie turned left onto State Highway 64, heading south toward town. "Listen up people," she announced. "This is the road that will take us to the center of town. In about five minutes, we'll arrive at our first stop sign. Ryan, you and Hodges make a right at the stop sign, drive west one block, and make another right. That's the alley. Park there, and walk the one block south to the rear of the hardware store. Ron and I will continue driving south on what will become First Street. We will make a left on Second Avenue and another left at Second Street. Do you copy?"

"Copy," Ryan responded immediately.

"Copy," was then heard from the rest of the team.

"I think we should consider keeping Hodges on the ground to offer additional support," Ryan suggested.

"Considered and denied," Valerie answered. "I need you both covering the roof. The Smiths could be hiding somewhere on the grounds of City Hall. I need a bird's eye view of that location. I also need eyes on the doors of PCPD. I need you both on the roof. Confirmed?"

"Ten-four," came as reply.

The drive didn't take long. Val turned left after stopping at the stop sign at the intersection of First Street and Second Avenue. I resisted the urge to look to my right at the PCPD located on the Southwest corner of Second Avenue. I followed the headlights of the Honda instead, and saw the third stop sign come into view. Val stopped, then turned left and slowly drove north on Second Avenue. I eased open my door and stepped out of the moving car. Valerie popped the trunk, and I removed the tightly-wrapped package. I hoisted it over my shoulder and closed the trunk. Valerie continued north for another block, then turned right between the vacant movie house and the row of vacant storefronts and parked the car.

I was running now. I reached the northeast corner of City Hall, and stopped. I turned around in time to see the tail lights of the Honda disappear down the alley. I waited. I watched the grounds of the mostly dark town square, and tried not to think about the girl thrown over my shoulder. I felt for Julia. Any women suffering any kind of abuse needed help and protection, but in this situation, we needed her; I only hoped she would rise to the occasion.

The good news was, it was very dark around the town square because there weren't any working streetlights in downtown Park City. The town council had ordered the power to lights be disconnected a decade ago. They reasoned there weren't any stores open after dark or people walking around, so there was no need for lights. There were a few up-lights to illuminate the building, like the one shining on the historical marker. The series of low-wattage up-lights were located in the planted foundation flowerbeds at various intervals around City Hall. I was pressed up against the red brick building in the shadows between two up-lights waiting for my wife to come and join me. I heard Ryan speaking in my ear.

"In position. I have eyes on PCPD. No activity. Thirty minutes till kickoff."

Hodges followed with one word. "Ready."

I was wondering if Ryan was going to be a problem, or if that was just his way of defying Valerie's authority, when I heard movement to my left.

I dropped to a crouch, shifting the bag to the right shoulder from the left, and readied myself, but it was Valerie. She eased up next to me. She turned off her earpiece, and I followed suit.

"Time for radio silence," she said, and then turning her earpiece on again, announced, "We are in position and holding. Hold your positions. Wait for the call to converge. Radio silence unless status changes." She turned her earpiece off again, not waiting for a reply.

Val passed in front of me, kissing my cheek as she did so. She was taking point. I followed her lead, staying close to the building. The pine straw beds made little noise under foot, and the small shrubs didn't slow us down. She stopped as we reached the middle of the building where the rear entrance staircase was located. The up-lights gave way to two small wall sconces mounted on either side of the entrance. The lights made a cave-like shadow of the recessed doorway.

We could see the northwest corner of City Hall now. It was directly in front of us about fifty feet away. The iron railing marking the entrance to the old jail shimmered in the moonlight a few feet before the end of the building.

"Do you think this is too big a risk?" Val asked.

"For both of us? Yes. You stay put and keep watch," I said kissing her cheek before I left her side.

Dodging in and out of the shadows of the building, I reached the metal railing and paused. I peeked over the railing into the abyss. I clutched the bag and the body inside tightly, and then vaulted quickly over the rail. I held on to the metal pipe to effect a soft landing on the steps below. I was immersed in complete darkness. I blinked my eyes rapidly, and my night vision slowly improved. I could see the steps and the door at their end. I took the remaining steps two at a time, eased the door open, and stepped inside the old jail, closing the door behind me. The glow of the infrared camera's light caught my attention, and I ran toward it. Finding the metal door, I pushed back the slide and whispered, "It's me, kiddo."

Leecy rushed into my one empty arm and said, "I knew it. I knew you two were up to something."

I deposited my bag in exchange for my daughter. I ripped the plastic away from Julia's still unconscious body and threw the debris into the corner of the room. It was then that I saw the clothes Julia was wearing, and realized I needed to improvise.

"Leecy, strip off your clothes, and let's put them on Julia. You wear her stuff. You guys are almost the same size, right?"

Leecy answered while she undressed, "she's a little taller, but everything else is close enough. My pants might be a little short, but no one will notice in the dark."

"Get dressed and get out of here. Keep to the right on the stairs and stay in the shadows. Crawl between the railings on your right. Hug the wall of the building. Mom is waiting by the rear entrance of City Hall. Now hurry."

I undressed Julia and swapped her clothes and shoes for Leecy's. Leecy was dressing in Julia's suit.

"What? You're not coming with me? Why?" Leecy asked.

"Like you said, we're up to something. Mom will fill you in on what you need to do once you two are safely away from here. Now go. We don't have a lot of time."

She kissed me and was gone.

I finished dressing Julia in the dark, and retrieved the black plastic bags. I peeled a strip of duct tape away from the plastic and used it to cover Julia's mouth. I spent another moment searching the floor of the room before finding the hood Leecy had been wearing, and I placed it on Julia's head. I tied a knot in the drawstring that would be difficult to undo, and most likely need to be cut. I left the room, closing the steel door behind me, and walked down the short corridor to the main body of the old jail.

I turned on my earpiece and said, "Granger, here. Status update: all clear."

I heard 'all clear's from the team and smiled. I felt my way around the main room of the old jail. It was smaller than I remembered, about the size of a large master bedroom. I looked at the glowing face of my watch and saw that it was 11:37. We were eight minutes ahead of schedule. I took a seat on the floor against the wall, about four feet to the left of the entrance. Valerie was up next. I thought she would begin her part in the next thirty seconds. I figured it would take her that long to get to safety with the kid.

I was wrong; Valerie was early when she said, "Ryan, any movement?"

"No, nothing."

"Hodges?" Valerie asked.

"All clear."

"Zach, cut the feed to the metal door."

"Cutting feed now."

"I have four armed men exiting the PCPD," Ryan announced. "Four men are now on the move from PCPD. Two men are on foot. Two men are in a black Suburban. I'm bugging out to support position on the ground."

"Do not, I repeat, do not move. Hold your position. I repeat, all hold. This is a test. I want to see how Moore and his crew respond. Hold your positions," Valerie ordered.

Hodges came over the earpieces next. "Two armed men heading across First Street on foot, and moving fast. The two males are descending the stairs and entering the old jail. I've got the Suburban backing up over the curb onto the lawn of City Hall. Looks like two men in the front seat. The SUV is backing up to the entrance of the old jail. The vehicle has stopped. The two coming up from the old jail are meeting the two men exiting the vehicle. They are gathered at the rear of the vehicle. I think I can get a directional microphone on these guys. Hold on. If it works, you'll hear them in your ear ... now."

There was a burst of static and then another voice came in loud and clear.

"Girl is in the room asleep on the floor," Briggs Smith could be heard saying. "She never even bothered taking the bag off her head."

"Okay, then it was just a loss of video, probably because of the crap Internet," Moore offered. "Besides, we were here too fast for anyone to get in and out of the jail. But to be on the safe side, Smiths, you stay put here at the top of the stairs and keep an eye on everything. At five minutes to midnight, head on down and get ready. Porter and I will head back over to the police station in the SUV. I need to get back to my computer. You two keep your heads on a swivel. We've come too far to blow it now."

"Hodges here, Moore and Porter are walking toward the SUV now. No, check that."

Moore's voice replaced Hodges' voice in my ear. I heard, "Remember boys, I want the kid stripped down, but unharmed."

"Hodges here, Moore is removing something from the rear of the SUV. It appears to be a bag."

"Travis," Moore said, "there's an air-powered nail gun loaded with masonry nails and some rope in the bag. Shoot some nails in the floor and tie the girl down spread-eagle, but no funny business unless Valerie refuses to cooperate. You read me?"

I heard, "Ten-four, boss."

"You boys lay it all out for Mrs. Granger like I told you. You make sure she understands I want a copy of everything her company sells to or makes for the government. The sight of her kid bound naked on the floor should be all the persuasion she needs. If mommy refuses the offer and won't work for us like I want her to, one of you boys come and find me at the PCPD. Porter and I will want to take part in the persuasion party. Everything I've read and seen on using this method to break someone indicates the more vicious the process, the sooner the results. I want to scare the woman to death. Even if that means we have to beat and rape her and her daughter. Do you understand?"

"Normally, I wouldn't go in for that kind of approach, boss," Briggs said, "but I can make an exception with two women that look like they do."

"Yeah, me too, boss. I don't think we'll have any perform-ance anxiety," Travis added.

"Good to know, boys," Moore said.

"What about the husband?" Porter asked.

"If the husband shows, which I highly doubt after the boot to the face Briggs gave him, shoot him on sight," Moore said.

"That will be my pleasure," Briggs said, "I only wish I had done that earlier."

There was a moment of silence. I think that silence would have stretched into tomorrow had Hodges not reported in.

"Hodges here. SUV is driving away."

"Ryan here. SUV is pulling into the PCPD parking lot."

The normally quiet town square of Park City was buzzing with activity. Hodges and Ryan were calling the action as they saw it happen, and the earpiece in my ear meant I didn't miss anything going on in the streets above.

"Hodges here. I got a car moving north on Second Street. It looks like a Honda Civic. Is that you Valerie?"

"Nope, not me."

"Hodges again. The car has the same plates as the car you and Ron were driving."

"I didn't say it wasn't the car I was using," Valerie retorted.

"Hodges here. Who is in the car? Ron?"

"No, it's not me," I replied.

"Who is in the damn car?" Wakefield asked.

"It's me, Leecy. I'm rolling to your location, Wakefield."

I heard Ryan bark, "What the fuck is going on?"

"Settle down people," Val said, "it's all part of the plan."

"Let's not forget there are two armed Rangers positioned at the top of the stairs, and two more armed men soon to be at that location at midnight," Hodges said.

"Good, that's where I want them to be. Valerie out."

"Granger out," I said.

"Wait! Don't turn off your earpieces. Zach, are they gone?" Wakefield asked.

"No, I'm receiving their transmission signal. I think they're just being quiet."

"That's advisable. Radio silence till we receive the call from Moore about the meet," Wakefield said. "I see headlights coming our way. It's Leecy," Wakefield said.

I was feeling good. All was going according to Valerie's plan. Now, Leecy needed to get Wakefield to do what Valerie wanted. I could hear Leecy's voice coming through my earpiece as she made her pitch to Wakefield.

"We need to get everyone out of here and into town. We need to meet my mom in the alleyway behind the pharmacy," Leecy could be heard saying excitedly. "Zach, Mom said to bring that voice analyzer thing. And I have a list of things I need from the lab. Grandpa, give me hand? Hurry up; we need to get moving. We need to be in position before Moore makes the call at midnight."

Wakefield didn't hesitate one second. "Franks, hustle the Simons out here after Reuben helps the kid, and split them between the SUV and the 4-Runner. Zach and I will ride with Leecy in the Honda. Rendezvous in the alley behind the pharmacy. One of the Simons can direct you where to go. Let's move."

The sound of closing doors and revving engines flowed from the earpieces. The Leecy-led brigade would be cutting it close, I thought. Checking my watch, I saw it was 11:45 p.m., fifteen minutes till Moore made the call. Depending on driving speed, it was a three to ten minute drive from INESCO to the town square. Valerie had driven the distance in less than five minutes earlier tonight. I figured Leecy would cover the distance a little quicker, given her level of excitement.

"What's the plan, kid? And how did you get out of that room?" I heard Franks ask.

"Let's get into position and Mom will brief you," was Leecy's answer to the first question. To the second, I heard her say, "My dad opened the door. I walked out. Kill your lights, okay? We're almost there."

"But it's pitch black. There are no street lights anywhere," Franks objected.

"It's only a few more blocks. You'll be fine," Leecy said. "Just get on my tail, and I'll lead you there. I'm turning right in three, two, one," Leecy instructed.

"I'm with you," Franks said, and David's voice could be heard over the earpiece as he offered his help, "Get ready to turn left now. See the alley? Good, Val is just ahead. I can see her holding a flashlight."

"Got it, thanks," Franks said.

I was a spectator now. All I could do was listen to the action on my earpiece. It reminded me of the stories my grandfather and Uncle John told about their childhoods. They reminisced about listening to the radio at night before they went to bed. I imagined them sitting on the floor listening to the radio, just as I now sat on the stone floor of the old jail listening to the show unfolding on the streets and alleys of Park City.

It was 11:50 p.m. now. We had ten minutes before Moore would make the call. Ten minutes was more than enough time.

"Ryan, you and Hodges still in position?" I heard Val ask.

"Ryan here. All quiet at the PCPD."

"Hodges here. Two Smiths at the top of the stairs leading to the old jail. No change."

"Hodges here. How did you, Valerie, cross town square unseen?"

"I hitched a ride with Leecy when she drove out of the town square. I bailed out of the car at the intersection of Second Street and Third Avenue on the northeast side of the square. I used the alley behind the vacant buildings that face First Avenue and walked here, and I made a few phone calls along the way."

"Who did you need to call?" Wakefield asked.

"I needed to get in touch with the local cops. Like I said before, I don't want them involved. I didn't want to risk Moore or Porter flashing a badge, fake or not, to coerce the locals into doing something, or have one of those guys get caught in the crossfire. So I called Lester and brought him up to speed."

"Lester is the one with the pregnant wife Moore and Porter were talking about, right?" Zach asked.

"That's right," Val said.

"Hodges here. What good does that do us? Lester's not the Chief."

"Lester is not the Chief in title only," Val replied.

"Ryan here. So what about the local police? What are they doing?"

"They are holding positions around the square, Ryan," Val answered and then instructed, "Hodges, check your six, twelve, and four o'clock; you'll see," Valerie explained.

"Hodges here. I got a patrol car in my sights two blocks southeast at the corner of Second Avenue and Fourth Street. There is another car one block northeast at Second Street and Third Avenue. And the last car is directly behind my position at the corner of First Avenue and Third Street. You guys should've seen that car on your drive down the alley."

"I could barely see the Honda in front of me," Franks said.

"That's real nice work, Valerie; seems you thought of everything," Hodges said.

"Slow down, Hodges," Wakefield said. "All that is well and good, but it doesn't explain why we all have to be here in this alley. I don't like all these civilians on scene."

"Lester will be rolling up at the police station any second now," Valerie began.

Ryan cut her off, saying, "I've got a car pulling into the PCPD now."

"This is why I brought you four down here," I heard Valerie say. "David, you and Isaac bring Mom and Dad to the police station. I need you guys to create a little distraction for me. I want the four of you to drive over there and raise as much hell as possible. Demand action on whatever you can think of. Like, use the APB as your reason for being there. Just be loud, obnoxious and angry. Lester is expecting a good show," she explained.

"From what I've heard, that shouldn't be a problem," Franks added.

I heard Reuben's voice in my ear. He asked, "Valerie, you want me and Catherine and the boys to go into the Park City Police Department and raise a ruckus? Why? Why should we do that? We have Leecy. Leecy is all that matters. Let's just leave. Let's go."

Leecy said, "You're just scared, Grandpa. I'm scared, too, but I need you to do this." Following her mother's lead, she said, "We need to help Wakefield and her team. Please, Grandpa, do this for me."

Reuben responded, "Valerie, I know there is more to your involvement than just INESCO. I feel that in my bones. I will help you now and you explain everything later. Come on; let's go."

"Thank you, Dad," Valerie said. "We'll talk when this is over."

"You don't forget that," I heard Reuben say before the sound of a car engine filled the earpiece.

"Ryan here. I got a Honda pulling into the PCPD parking

lot. The Simons are on-site."

It was five minutes to midnight. I expected to see the Smith boys at any moment. Moore had instructed them to get the girl ready before the meeting took place. I listened to the ear-piece chatter and readied myself.

"That didn't take long," I heard Ryan say. "I've got a visual on Moore and Porter. They're outside the PCPD and moving toward City Hall."

"Hodges here. I should have Moore and Porter up on the microphone in a few seconds. Be advised, Smiths are moving down the stairs of the old jail. Granger, if you're down there, I hope you can hear me."

I whispered, "I am, and I do."

Moore's voice came over the earpiece. "That's exactly why I could never be a small town cop. I'd just slap the lot of them and throw their butts in a cell for causing a public distur-bance."

Porter's laugh followed, and then his voice. "Yeah, I hear you, man. Looks like the Smith boys are doing their job. I don't see them outside. Are we heading over now, or what?"

"Let's walk over and wait outside. It's too soon to make the call just yet."

I clicked off my earpiece; I didn't want the distraction. I was about five feet away from the door to the old jail when I saw them. The two Smith boys walked through the open door and into the shaft of summer moonlight reaching across the floor of the old jail. I watched them walk to the metal door, and heard the slide of the bolt. I crossed the stone floor. I lis-tened for the sound of the door opening, and timed my move-ments with those of the door. I was behind the two men now. Two feet of floor was all that remained between us.

"Looks like we got a live one, Travis. She's kicking her legs and rolling all over the floor," Briggs Smith said.

"Give her a smack on the head; that'll calm her down," I heard Travis instruct his partner.

I wasn't about to let these two do to Julia what Moore had told them to do to Leecy. But I didn't want to act too soon, either. I needed the two men to be fully engaged in the task at hand. I needed them distracted.

"No, man; I'm not hitting her. Moore said no rough stuff unless he said so. Just come hold her legs for me and stop her kicking. I'll get the bag off her head. Maybe that'll calm her down."

"Okay, I'll hold her legs, but leave the bag on over her head. I don't want to be looking at her face if Moore wants us to rape her. Move over a little and let me slip past you so I can reach her feet. You grab her by the arms and we'll carry her out of here into the main room."

I could tell the mention of the word rape had sent Julia into a panic. I could hear her trying to scream through the duct tape gag. That was enough for me. I engaged my earpiece and covered the last two feet of stone floor, making my presence known.

"Hello, boys. I think that'll be all for the day," I said.

I got an immediate response in my ear, and regretted powering up the device. "Hodges here. Did everyone copy that?"

"Shut up, Hodges. We copy," Wakefield ordered.

The shaft of moonlight stretching from the open cast iron jailhouse door illuminated the area directly in front of it. I could see Travis Smith was the closest one to me. He was bent at the waist, holding Julia's legs by the ankles. He reacted quicker than I thought he might, launching a back kick in my direction but missing his target, my knee. I caught his ankle and drove my right elbow down into his knee joint. The resulting snapping and popping was joined by screams from the now disabled former Ranger. Travis collapsed on top of Julia momentarily before rolling to the right and off of her.

"One down," I said, as Briggs Smith met my eyes. We both stood slowly, with only the length of Julia's body between us. I was awash in the moonlight. He was in almost total darkness.

"Jesus, old man," Briggs laughed. "My boot print would look good on your face if it weren't so damn spooky in the moonlight." He looked at me sideways and then continued. "No gun? Doesn't seem like a fair fight."

"I agree. The fight was fair till your boy went down in a whiney heap, but that's what Rangers are known to do, right? That's why the Marines have to come save your asses all the time, isn't it?"

I didn't have to say anything else; that got the reaction I was looking for. He drew his sidearm and I threw my knife, burying it up to the hilt in his right shoulder joint. I'd missed. I guess I was rusty after all. I was aiming for his throat. The gun fell to the stone floor shortly before its owner hit the ground, screaming in pain. I stepped over and around Julia's body and retrieved my knife from Briggs Smith's shoulder, wiping it clean on the Ranger's shirt.

"Shut up," I said. "Time for you to take a nap."

I finished him off with a boot to his face.

"Two down; two to go," I said.

The howling screams of pain from Ranger Travis got my attention next. "Do you want to live tonight?" I asked.

"Yes," he grunted through gritted teeth, "I do."

"Then shut up. Do that, and live to see the sunrise."

CHAPTER
NINE NINE

With Travis Smith disabled and quiet for now, and Briggs Smith unconscious, I was free from any immediate threat. I was busy cutting Julia out of the hood. I was worried. She wasn't moving. I thought she'd been injured when Travis fell on top of her. I pulled her head free, and heard Hodges in my ear.

"Moore and Porter are on the way. Ron, if you are planning on leaving, now is the time to get out of there."

I wasn't going anywhere, but I wanted Julia free and clear before Moore and Porter arrived. I was about to ask her how fast she could run, but even there in the limited light, the lifeless quality of her body told me she was in a state of shock. I moved her into the shaft of moonlight. Her blank stare looked up at me. I checked her pulse. It was slow, but strong. I checked her breathing. It was shallow. I needed to get her moving. I slapped her lightly on the cheek. I called her name. I didn't know what else to do with her. Her eyes blinked suddenly. She slowly raised a hand to her face.

"Damn it. Is everyone going to hit me in the face tonight? First your wife knocks me out, and now you slap me. Who's next?"

"Sorry, but you looked like you were in shock," I said. "I didn't know what else to do."

"I guess I kinda was. I don't know," she said as I helped her to her feet. "Whose clothes am I wearing? Where in the hell am I?"

"You switched places with my daughter, but now it's time for you to get out of here, too."

"I heard one of those Smith guys say the word rape," she said looking at herself in the moonlight. "I freaked out a little bit. Thanks, by the way. Thanks for not letting that happen to me."

"Never going to get that far," I said, and against my better judgment asked, "Are you able to run?"

This was the one part of the plan I didn't agree with. I was worried about Julia in more ways than one - she'd already shown her loyalty to Moore - but Val had asked me to trust her where Julia was concerned, so I did.

"I think I am. Why?" Julia asked.

"Because Moore and Porter are on their way and should be calling my wife in," I checked the time, "the next ninety seconds. And for whatever reason, Valerie doesn't want you down here when we take on Moore and Porter." Then something occurred to me. "And after hearing Moore talk about his time with the sex trafficking task force, I think I understand my wife's reasoning."

"You know about that, then?" Julia asked.

"Yeah, I know about it."

She gestured to the two Smiths and said, "Tom brought them around a few times. They stayed at my place before. With Tom there, of course. You know those two would've hurt your daughter badly."

Travis protested from the floor. "That little lying bitch doesn't know what she's saying."

I left Julia's side, and it took me two long strides to cover the distance from the metal door to the back wall of the room, where Travis sat holding his knee. I led with my right leg and when my left foot touched the floor, I said, "I thought I told you to be quiet," and drove a right front kick into the face of Travis Smith. He joined his partner Briggs in a nap.

I said to Julia as I took her by the arm, "But they didn't hurt my daughter, and they can't hurt you now. Did they hurt you before?"

She started to cry, but stopped herself immediately. She shook her head instead. "No, I'm not going to do that. I played that game before, and I don't want you to think I'm acting again. So no tears this time. No, to answer your question, they never hurt me. Tom talked about what he called 'conditioning,'" she made air quotes with her fingers, "all the time, and that was enough to scare me."

"Moore and Porter will get their due. Run up the stairs and turn right. Are you listening?"

I saw that vague look reappear on Julia's face. She was frozen in place. I heard Hodges in my ear.

"Hodges here. Moore and Porter are on the lawn of City Hall."

"Can you run?" I asked her again.

"He's out there, isn't he?" she mumbled. "Tom, I mean. He's out there. I don't think I can make it," she said, shrinking in on herself and collapsing in my arms.

At first I thought it was all an act, another attempt to delay things. I shook her harder. No response. I carried her back to the room behind the metal door and replaced the hood over her head, but didn't tie it this time. I closed the door, leaving her there in the dark.

I heard Moore's voice in my ear, "Go down there and make sure they're ready. I'm making the call."

I ran across the floor to the far corner of the main room. Then I heard Porter's voice again.

"Look, the Smiths have everything under control. I'm going back to PCPD and get the SUV. I want to get out of here as soon as we have what we came for."

"Fine. Since we can't wait at the PCPD, we'll just wait in the car till we see her coming. Then we'll go down inside the jail ahead of her. That'll be good. Yeah, I can't wait to see her face when she sees her kid lying on the floor naked. Want to bet she caves in right then and there?"

"No, that's a sucker bet."

I heard Moore laughing as he said, "Go get the car. I'm making the call."

"Listen," I said, only slightly above a whisper, "we have a change in plan. Julia did not make it out. I repeat, Julia did not make it out."

"Copy," Valerie said. "Not to worry; the call should be coming at any moment."

I could hear the phone ringing in my earpiece. I heard Valerie answer the call in her best imitation of a freaked out mother.

"This is Valerie. Where's my baby? I have everything you want. Please don't hurt my child."

"That's good to hear, Mrs. Granger," Moore said. "I'm glad there won't be any complications. Now, if you'll bring me what I want this will all be over very soon."

"Okay, where? Where do I go?"

"Come to City Hall. Find the entrance to the old jail and take the stairs down to the door. The door is open. Your daughter is waiting for you. Hurry, Mrs. Granger. The sooner you get here, the sooner this is over."

"How do I know you won't just shoot us both once I give you what you want?"

"You don't know, but if you keep wasting my time Valerie," Moore's tone had turned cold now, where before it had sounded warm and pleasant, "I might have to hurt this pretty little thing of yours before you even get here. Now, no more stalling, Valerie. You can't trace this call. The local cops can't help you now. As a matter of fact, your family is in the police station right now raising hell. And the inept Officer Lester can't do one thing to help them. Do you know why?"

Valerie laid it on thick as she started crying now, "No, why can't they help me?"

"The locals are under my jurisdiction now. They only do what I tell them to do."

"Hodges here. Moore is at the top of the stairs."

"So bring me what I want. Bring it to me right now. No assurances, but I'll give you one guarantee."

"What's that?"

"If you aren't here handing me what I want in the next five minutes, I'll make you watch me and my boys having fun with little Leecy when you do get here."

"Oh my god. I'm on my way."

"It's Hodges. The SUV is driving over the curb and backing up to the stairs. Moore is waiting for Porter like he said. That's affirmative. Moore and Porter are now in position inside the SUV and holding."

"Okay, Ryan," Valerie said. "Now move to your secondary position at PCPD. Lester is expecting you. Hodges, keep being our eyes and ears on the SUV till Moore and Porter descend the stairs. Once those two are out of sight, you and Franks move to your secondary positions. Use their SUV as cover and take up positions along either side. Wakefield, Zach, and Leecy, hold for the all clear. Granger, are you ready?" Valerie asked.

"Yeah, we're ready."

"We?"

"You'll see."

"Okay, team; here we go. Hodges, make the call."

"Roads are clear. I've disabled the directional microphone. Moore and Porter are seated inside the SUV with the doors closed. Valerie, you're clear."

I listened to the 4-Runner come to life. I pictured Valerie driving south down the alley before turning right on First Avenue.

"Hodges, here. I've got her headlights coming right at me. She's parking on the North side of City Hall. Moore and Porter are exiting the SUV and heading down the stairs. That's my cue; I'm on the move. Franks, I'm rolling to you."

"Ryan, here. All is secure at PCPD. Be advised, Simons have lots of questions."

"Franks, here. I have Hodges and eyes on Valerie. She's crossing the lawn. We'll be in position in thirty seconds."

I watched from the corner of the old jail as Porter entered the room first, followed by Moore. Both men played flashlights across the room, and then Porter spoke in alarm.

"Where's the girl? Where's Travis and Briggs?"

The scream couldn't have arrived at a more perfect moment if it had been planned. I guess Julia had come to, and didn't like being back inside that hood. Moore and Porter were caught off guard by the scream, but didn't hesitate. They responded by running toward the sound coming from behind the metal door.

"Those little bastards couldn't wait. I'll kill them myself," Porter seethed.

"They're going to ruin everything," Moore added.

The two men never noticed Valerie standing in the open doorway, or the shadow she cast with the moonlight at her back. No, they hadn't seen her or me. I watched them as I stepped into the shaft of moonlight to greet my wife. Then Valerie and I watched Moore and Porter fling open the metal door to find Julia and the two unconscious Smith boys.

"What the fuck?" Porter asked.

"Hi, Tom," we heard Julia say. "Sorry, but don't blame me. I know this isn't what you expected."

Valerie and I were behind the two men. We heard Moore's meltdown.

"What have you done, Julia? What did you tell them? You betrayed me, you bitch! I knew I shouldn't have trusted you!" Moore screamed.

Porter played his flashlight over the bodies of the Smith boys, saying, "Who did this? How...I mean, when..." and then he stopped himself from stammering. He started again. "Tell me what..." and stopped.

The answers came to him. We watched from the shadows now as Porter turned to Moore and said, "If Julia is in here then the phone call with Valerie was all fake. They already have the daughter. We need to get out of here, Tom!"

Porter turned and saw Valerie standing behind him. She was pointing her 9mm Glock at his face.

"Hello, John." I said.

Valerie kicked the left side of Porter's face, knocking the

man to his right into Moore and the metal door. Moore fell to one knee and looked around. He saw Valerie and me standing there. Moore looked back at Julia, and we both knew immediately that he planned on using the woman as a shield.

Drawing his weapon and reaching for a frightened Julia, Moore screamed. "You fucking cunt! Come over here."

Valerie surged forward, grabbing Moore's beefy right wrist with her left hand and wrenching up and back while slamming her closed right fist into the bridge of his nose. I was swinging my baton over Valerie's head, and connected with Moore's right hand, forcing the gun to drop to the floor. I heard Moore scream from the effects of the double impacts. I watched as he and Valerie tumbled into the darkness of the room beyond the shaft of moonlight.

Porter, having recovered from the kick to the face, raced out of the shadows and slammed into me with his shoulder. I grabbed a fistful of his suit jacket and held on tight. I rolled onto my back, holding Porter close to my chest. Using his momentum against him, I rolled a complete backwards somersault, ending on top of him. Letting go of his clothing, I pushed off his chest, crashing my baton into his face. I heard him exhale and felt his body go limp as he passed into unconsciousness. I looked up to see Moore walking through the moonlight in my direction. I jumped to my feet, only to have Moore drop to his knees before collapsing on the floor next to Porter, like a curtain dropping onto a stage. There behind, where Moore once stood, was a smiling Valerie.

I could hear Wakefield in my ear. "Is everyone all right? I repeat, is everyone all right?"

I stepped over the bodies of Moore and Porter and kissed my wife. Valerie bent down and picked up a flashlight. "Julia?"

she said.

We walked back to the open metal door and found her in the same position she'd been in: laying prone and still on the floor.

I asked, "Is she alive?"

Valerie was leaning over Julia to check for vital signs when Julia asked, "Did you kill that sick bastard?"

"Moore?" Valerie confirmed.

"Yes; Tom. Is he dead?"

"No, he isn't dead. But this isn't over yet, either," Valerie said.

"Well, I wish he was dead."

"Listen up," Valerie ordered. "We don't have a lot of time. Unconsciousness doesn't last forever. I want to use the center of the main room. Face up and securely bind the arms, legs, and ankles. Make the bindings tight, but not too tight. Franks, you and Hodges are on light duty. I want the lights six inches from the face. Don't worry about head turning. With the lights that close, there is zero visibility. As soon as we see any sign of consciousness we will tape the eyelids open. Everyone remember to remain quiet. Remember your cues. Ryan, are you ready with the duct tape?"

"I've got several strips. I'm ready," Ryan said.

"Zach, are you and Julia ready?"

"Ready."

"Ron?"

"I'm ready," I said.

"Wakefield, are you ready?"

"You bet your ass."

"Okay, I see eye flutter. It's show time."

"What the fuck?" Moore bellowed.

He didn't have much time to protest. A pair of blue-gloved hands grasped him by the sides of his head and held him still while a second pair separated his eyelids and taped them open.

He was screaming now. "What are you doing? You can't do this to me! Porter! Where's Porter? Travis? Briggs? Are you there?"

"I'm here, Tom," a frantic Porter could be heard saying. "What's happening to us?"

"Don't say a word, Porter. Porter? Do you hear me, Porter? Don't say a word. And you, whoever you are," Moore yelled, "get this blasted light out of my eyes!"

"Shut up, Tom," Valerie said. "The light isn't going anywhere, and neither are you. Your friend Porter is on the floor next to you, along with Travis and Briggs, but they can't talk right now. We've taped their mouths shut. You shouldn't be worried about them, anyway. You should be worried about you, Tom."

"What is this? What's going on here? Who is that?"

"Tom, you don't recognize my voice? We were just chatting on the phone with each other; don't you remember? This is Valerie Granger. And this? Well, this is your...let's call it your reconditioning party. Now, I know it's not the party you had in mind, but trust me when I tell you this party will achieve the desired results."

"What? You? You're not behind this. Where's Wakefield? She's behind this, not some part-time housewife from Bumfuck, Georgia."

"That's been your assumption all along, Tom, and it's been wrong."

"What? That you're nothing more than a housewife and cook? Look, lady, you got me, okay. Tell Wakefield she can arrest me. Hand in the cookie jar and all that shit. But don't tell me you aren't exactly what I think you are."

"Denial? Not what I would've predicted for the behavioral analytics agent. I thought you guys were trained to unmask the truth by spotting the incongruities of speech and body language."

"For fuck's sake, lady, is now the time for a lesson? Yes, that is what we do, and it's what I did to you, your husband, and kid. Happy now? Just get on with it; whatever this is."

"So, you admit you aren't very good at your job?"

"A forty-six–year-old former CIA agent, and his forty-four-year-old wife and sixteen-year-old daughter. No threat detected."

"And yet here you are, flat on your back in the old Park City jail with your mates at your sides."

"Yeah, what of it?"

"You are in denial. I don't know about you, but if I was facing the last moments of my life, I would be very interested in how I arrived at this point. But that's me."

"I'll make it easy for you. I'm not talking. Whatever you do to me won't change that."

The sound of a man screaming filled the space, reverberating off the stone walls.

"What was that? Who was that?" Tom demanded to know.

The scream turned to a low moan, and then sobs, as Valerie answered.

"That's Travis. His knee was busted up pretty good by my over-the-hill husband, and that sound...That sound is the sound Travis makes when I stand on his knee."

"Please stop. *Stop!* I can't take anymore," Travis could be heard begging.

"Shut up, Travis. You'll pass out when you can't take anymore, and I'll wake you by pouring more water on you."

The screams filled the room again, and then they were gone.

"Travis!" Moore screamed. "Travis! Porter! Are you out there, Porter? Where's Briggs?"

"They're all here, Tom," Valerie said calmly. "Here, let me see if I can wake Briggs. He stopped responding to the water we were pouring on him, but if I stick my finger in the hole in his shoulder, that usually merits a response. You know the hole I'm talking about, right?"

"No. What hole?" Moore pleaded.

"The hole caused by my husband's knife. Here we go," Valerie said.

The scream sounded like that of a dying animal. It had a low, howling quality to it. Briggs finished with the same sad whimper as Travis.

"Tape his mouth," Valerie ordered. "Tape them all."

The hands came out of the light, and the tape was over Moore's mouth before he could protest.

"I want you to listen, Tom. I am going to tell you what I want from you. I'm going to give you one chance to give me what I want. Does that sound familiar to you? I thought I should give you the same considerations you extended to my daughter and me. So, you know the drill: if you don't give me what I want, I'll be forced to continue my little party with your friends, and eventually I'll start on you. Are we on the same page?"

Tom was frozen beneath the lights. He wasn't moving, but

I could see he was thinking. He was thinking he could talk his way out of this mess he was in.

Valerie continued. "Here's what I want to know. Tell me the name of your buyer. Give me an accurate description of the bag he seeks to exchange. I want to know how you gained access to encrypted DOD files. That's it, Tom. Tell me what I want to know and all this will be over for you. Don't tell me what I want to know, and it's safe to say we are just getting started. Remove the tape," Valerie ordered.

The room wasn't silent for long. Moore was laughing when he said, "Not a chance. I don't tell you shit until I have a deal. Can you make me a deal, sweetheart? No, I didn't think so. Get me Wakefield. I know she's around somewhere. Go get her, and make me a deal. No deal, no answers."

Valerie came up behind Moore's head and whispered in his ear. "Thank you, Tom. Thank you for making this easy for me."

"What the fuck?" Moore screamed, "You crazy bitch! Who in the hell are you, anyway?"

"Tom, I'm Valerie Simon, former agent of the Mossad. And this is how we break people in the Mossad. Maybe you should've been more worried about who I was and what I was before we came this far."

"Mossad? That's a new one. Whatever, lady. I'm not telling you a goddamned thing."

"Tom, here's a story for you. It's a true story, though most people that have heard this story believe it to be legend only. But it's not legend or myth; it's true."

There was no response from Agent Moore. He was sweating profusely and his breathing was rapid and shallow. He was getting closer to the edge. Valerie continued, and I made ready.

"There was an agent of the CIA. He was a killer. This particular agent always worked alone. He was happy that way, and the CIA liked it when he was happy, Tom. Now, stop me if you've heard this before," Valerie said.

"Of course I've heard it before, you stupid cow," Moore spewed. "Everyone at the CIA has heard this story before. It's all bullshit."

"No, I don't think so. See, Tom, I told you I knew the story was true. I know it's true because I married the agent."

"Ha! Did you forget I was in the room when your husband denied being this guy? Look, lady, I can tell when someone is lying, and your husband wasn't lying. There was no half-breed working for the CIA running around the Middle East. Your husband said it himself; it's all CIA legend. They teach a class at the Farm on this topic. If this was your best trick, you're wasting your time."

"Really, Tom? Are you sure about that? Cause that doesn't explain this," Valerie said.

The lights went out momentarily, thrusting the room into darkness. I was standing over Tom when the lights came back on. The lights were shining up into my face. The bruising on my face mimicked Indian war paint perfectly.

"What the hell is that?" Tom screamed.

I dropped to one knee and grasped Tom by the hair, lifting his head off the floor. I held my knife in front of his open eyes and said,

"*Haho hohe.*
HAHO HOHE HOKAHEY!!!
HAHO HOHE HOKAHEY KIKSUYAPI LE MAZA!!
KIKSUYAPI MI

MIEYBO OZUYE NAPA LUTE'
MIEYBO OZUYE...

The lights went out again. I stepped back into the darkness. The lights came back on, shining in Moore's face, and Valerie spoke.

"See, Tom? It's not all bullshit. And here's a little something else for you. This is just so you know it's real."

Tom was screaming and whipping his head from side to side. "What did he say? What does that mean?"

"All in due time, Tom. First, he has a gift for you."

The room filled with ear-splitting screams. Tom's head was thrashing back and forth. That is, until a wet oblong object landed on his chest.

"What's that? What is that? Get it off of me! Is that blood? What's that smell?"

"That's the scalp of Agent Travis Smith," Valerie answered.

"Get it off of me!" Tom was screaming.

But he was quieted by the high-pitched screech that filled the room. It was followed by a low moan, and then whimpering, as a second wet oblong object was dropped on Tom's chest.

"Oh my god; get it off of me!"

"That's from Agent Briggs Smith, and the next one..." Valerie was interrupted by more screaming, followed by the sounds of John Porter begging, "Help me, Tom! Help me, Tom!"

Valerie dropped the third wet mass on Tom's chest.

"That just leaves you, Tom. I must say, it's a gruesome way to die. But fitting, I suppose. After all, you planned to do horrible things to my daughter and me if I didn't cooperate with you. Oh, I almost forgot; you asked about what was said earlier. You wanted to know what it means. What my husband said was, *'Look at this.'* He wanted you to see his knife. Then he said *'Enemy. Pay attention. Remember my metal. Remember me. I am warrior Red hand. I am death.'* Kind of cool, huh? Okay, your turn. Time to die, asshole."

The lights went out, and all that could be heard was Agent Tom Moore sobbing and begging. "Please don't kill me. I'll tell you everything. Don't let that savage scalp me."

"Oh come on, Tom. You don't expect me to fall for that trick, do you? If we stop now, you waste our time by lying, and I kill you later anyway."

Tom responded by screaming, "He's got my hair! I can feel him pulling on my hair! Please, please stop! I'll talk! I'll tell the truth!" He stopped yelling and then said, "Please, no, wait..." more quietly. "I can prove what I'm saying. It's in the SUV. Look in the SUV for my computer. My laptop. The password is..."

Valerie interrupted him. "Tom, I'm sorry, but we've already checked the laptop. There wasn't anything on it that was helpful. I'm afraid you're out of options, buddy. Time to die."

"*No!* Listen to me," he begged. "The plug in the cigarette lighter in the SUV is a USB drive. The data is on the USB drive, but you have to have the password for the computer. The drive has to be inserted into the USB port before you enter the password. The password unlocks the computer and the drive at the same time."

"Okay, Tommy boy; let's have it. What's the password?"

"Look, I think I should get some consideration first," Moore said, stalling for time.

"One more chance, Tom. I've given you all the consideration you're going to get tonight. Tell me the password."

"No, it's the only bargaining chip I have."

"Okay, but what happens if I figure out the password, Tom? You'll be left with nothing, and completely at my mercy."

"No way you guess my password. All I want is assurance I won't be placed in Federal prison. I want to serve my time in one of those white-collar country club prisons. That's all I want."

"No deal, Tom. No, wait, on second thought, I'll make a deal with you. Here it is: when I figure out the password, my husband will scalp you. That's the deal you get."

"Okay, but you should know ten wrong entries wipes the USB drive clean."

"You really are stupid, Tom. I would never risk everything if I didn't already know your password. You gave Julia a pendant. You have the tattoo on your right bicep. It looks like a pretzel, but it's not. It's the command key on your computer. It's the Meta key. It's your secret key, Tom. Isn't that right, Tom? 'Secret key' is your password."

Tom Moore gave up as soon as he heard those words. I saw him lying there under the lights. I saw him give up any hope he had left. I saw it leave his body as he exhaled. He was beaten. But Valerie wasn't finished with him yet. Not by a long shot.

"New deal, Tom. You'll verify what we find on your computer. You make one mistake, then it's off with your scalp. Do you understand?"

"Deal," Tom whispered.

I looked at my watch. It was 12:45 a.m. Valerie had broken the man in less than twenty minutes. I was impressed. I saw

Zach heading for the stairs, and followed him out of the old jail. The first face I saw once I was outside was Leecy's. She ran to me and threw her arms around me.

"Well, how'd it go?"

"Just like Mom thought it would," I answered. "There's some work left to do, though." I saw Lester coming our way and said, "Give me a minute, okay sweetie?"

"Is it over?" Lester asked.

"Almost," I answered, shaking his hand. "How are the prisoners?"

Lester looked over his shoulder at the paramedic van and said, "Larry and Murphy have the one with the shoulder injury stabilized. The knife didn't hit anything major. They want to take him to the hospital for stitches, though. The other guy, the one with the hurt knee, also lost a couple of teeth. I've been told they will both be ready for transport within the hour. The black guy is in bad shape. He has a broken orbital socket and shattered jaw. He'll be with us at the county hospital till he's healthy enough to be transported. We'll keep him locked down and guarded. Can you tell Wakefield for me? Tell her we'll keep the one called John Porter unless she wants to send prisoner medical transport for him."

Lester paused as he reached for his ringing phone. "Excuse me, but Elizabeth has been calling me non-stop since I left the house. I've got to get back home."

"Sure," I said, smiling, thinking about the new baby on the way. "I'll brief Wakefield. We have it under control. Thanks for all the help on this, Lester. If you would, as you walk by, tell Larry and Murphy we'll pick up the two men and ready them for transport in about an hour."

"Will do," Lester said.

I watched Lester walk across the lawn of City Hall and drive away until his taillights were lost to the darkness. I turned to find my daughter waiting for me. I could see she had a question; it was written all over her face.

"What?" I asked.

"What about Julia?"

"What about her?"

"Is she going to be in trouble?"

"I don't know, and it's really not up to me. But more importantly, why didn't you go home with your grandparents?"

"Don't change the subject, Dad. I don't want Julia to be in trouble. Mom said she felt like Julia had been coerced. She said she'd seen the look Julia had on her face before. She thought Julia had been tortured."

"Easy, kiddo. Okay, here's what I do know. I know we couldn't have pulled this thing off without Julia's help. It was her program and her equipment that helped us fool Moore into cooperating. So I think there'll be some consideration made by Wakefield. But first, we have to verify the information on Moore's laptop. After we do that, whatever happens to Julia is up to Wakefield. Good enough?"

"I guess so."

"Now, take your uncle's car and go to your grandparents' house right now," I said. I hugged her so tight that I thought she might break. "I love you. I'm so glad you're safe."

"I love you, too, Dad. See you at Reuben's."

"See you at Reuben's."

I saw Zach was still in the front seat of Moore's SUV and walked over to see what he'd found on the USB drive. He saw me coming and said rather formally, "Mr. Granger, hey."

"What did you find, Mr. Zach?"

"Everything, if this is indeed real. We got it all. How did your wife know his password? That was pretty amazing."

"She made an educated guess and then read his face. She watched his reactions. When she said 'secret key,' she knew she had it."

"Really?"

"Now, if you've got everything, let's get to it."

"After you, sir," he said, and then asked somewhat awkwardly, "Mr. Granger, can I ask you something?"

"Sure, Zach; what's on your mind?"

"That stuff you said down there... was that real Indian stuff or did you make it all up?"

"The words are all real, Zach, but the act was just an act. No different from one of your computer programs. You turn on a program, and it performs a specific function to achieve a desired result."

"So you were acting in a made-up role. Playing a part in your wife's production."

"To some extent, yes. Just remember that all the good lies have an element of truth to them, Zach."

CHAPTER
TEN

"Tom, Tom," I could hear Valerie saying as I re-entered the old jail with Zach in tow. "Stop your crying. You need to verify your laptop data, and then you'll be free."

I could see Tom was trying to identify the three wet masses on his chest, but he couldn't raise his head high enough. He finally gave up, accepting they were what he'd been told they were, and exhaled. His body went limp again.

"Fine. Where do you want to start?" Tom asked.

Taking the computer from Zach, Val said, "Let's start at the beginning. I have a file here named DOD. Tell me about it. I'll read along while you explain."

There was little doubt Tom was a beaten man. I listened to his monotone telling of the story. I thought Julia's computer-generated voices had more life than his voice had now.

"I got bored with my life and work, and I needed more money. I knew the CIA had some million-dollar DOD contracts. Now, I'm good with the computer, but I don't have the skills to hack into the DOD. I needed help. This was where Julia came into the picture. Julia and I had been seeing each other for a few months, but I knew she was a straight arrow. She wasn't going to do anything illegal unless she did so out of fear. I had to create an environment where Julia felt threatened, but not so threatened that she'd leave. Julia was withdrawn from her coworkers, overly shy, a loner type that made poor eye contact when she talked to people. She used her work as the excuse to never be available.

"That vulnerability is what drew me to her in the first place, and in the end, what I used to manipulate her. I started talking about my time with the task force. I told her the human trafficking stories. I introduced her to my old Army buddies, and would talk about the gang rapes with those guys while she was in the room."

Moore began to wiggle side to side as if he was making himself more comfortable in his restraints. He was beginning to relax. Not only that, but his tone changed. I could see Val standing on the edge of the darkness. Her face was cast in the soft glow of the flashlights. I was about to motion her to stop the interrogation when I saw her left hand was waving me off. She knew Moore was feeling emboldened. The more he talked about his control over Julia, the stronger he'd become. She wanted him to feel that way. I wanted to know why.

Moore started again. "It didn't take too long, about a month, I'd say, before Julia was begging me to stop talking about the human trafficking conditions, and to stop bringing my old Army buddies around so much. I had her right where I wanted her. All I had to do was tell her that my old buddies thought she was real pretty and that they couldn't stop talking about her. I told her they were into the swinger lifestyle and had asked me to bring her along for some fun."

Moore was smiling now.

"That was all bullshit, but she bought every word. She said she'd do anything for me if I promised to keep them away from her. That was it. She was hooked. After that, all I had to do was periodically reinforce the threat by having one of the guys come over to the apartment, or if I really wanted to scare her, leave one of them alone with her. One time, I even had Travis and Briggs bump into her while she was out shopping. It was so easy. I'd given her a version of the pendant by that time, and that one had a tracking device built into it. I assume you found the transmitter and recorder inside the one she was wearing today. Anyway, she was hooked and under my thumb, as the song goes."

That was it. Moore was all the way back. His original swaggering arrogance had returned. He tested the parameters his regained confidence gave him by asking, "Is that how you got onto us? The pendant?"

"Not how this works, Tom. You verify the information first. Then we can answer your questions," Valerie said.

"Could you at least allow me to blink my eyes?"

"Remove the tape," Valerie ordered.

Ryan appeared out of the shadows and removed the tape from Moore's eyelids. Why was Valerie giving into a demand? I would never have given an inch until I had all that I wanted from him, but Valerie was working another angle. Was she setting Moore up for something else?

"Okay, where was I?" Moore asked, and then remembered his place, "Right, with Julia hooked, I started looking for a way to target in on a big military contract. We spent a couple of months searching the DOD database for anything with a huge price tag. Breaching the security on the DOD system wasn't easy by any stretch of the imagination, but I have to admit, Julia made it look easy. I don't know how she got in or how she covered her tracks, so don't ask me, ask her. All I know is it took her about eight hours one Sunday, and we were in. It wasn't long after that I got onto this blimp deal. Yeah, that's right. The DOD had contracted for a blimp to be produced for aerial surveillance in Afghanistan. The damn thing was longer than a football field. I was about to jump on this blimp project, because the DOD was paying $30 million for it, but before I could act, the DOD pulled the plug. They sold the damn thing back to the company that made it for $300,000. I was livid. The waste of taxpayer money was enough to upset anyone, but the fact that I'd missed a golden opportunity to make a fortune was what really incensed me. I went back to the drawing board.

"And then I found it. I remember it was a Sunday afternoon last June. I literally stumbled across this little family business in Georgia. I read the DOD file on INESCO and thought it was too good to be true. I mean, INESCO is just a mom and pop outfit with fifty employees. I showed Julia what I'd found. We got so excited that we called in sick the next few days so we could research INESCO. When we discovered INESCO had a relationship with NASA, we hacked NASA to find out what you'd done for them. But that relationship was so long ago that it was dead end.

"So, we kept on searching through countless files. I was ready to give up. Honestly, I was, and then we found it. We found DOD code 97CLK after opening hundreds of files and reading hundreds of dead ends. File 97CLK was the jackpot. The DOD classified the project as next generation stealth and a threat to national security. Project 97CLK was the closest thing to cloaking an object the DOD had ever seen. The DOD was excited, but their internal memorandum urged cau-

tion and asked to proceed with the typical approval and pro-
curement process so as not to draw unwanted attention to the
project. Idiots, I thought at the time, because the normal approval process could take up to ten months or a year. I didn't
want to wait that long to get paid. That's when I changed my
plan. I decided to steal the project and sell it to the highest
bidder."

"So far, so good, Tom. Tell me about the buyer."

"No, I want you to hear it all. I want you to know everything. You see, I called Porter, Travis, and Briggs. I brought
them up to speed and sent them down here to Georgia. They
started their recon a year ago. None of you dopes knew it was
happening. They worked night and day for a couple of weeks,
looking for a way to steal the technology. When they determined they couldn't steal it, they zeroed in on Anderson. The
head of R&D for INESCO was the most likely candidate. We
decided to make him steal it for us. We ran our little scam on
him. We scared the shit out of the guy. He'd have done anything we asked him to do, but I have to admit, I believed him
when he said he couldn't steal it. We put eyes and ears on
him just in case he ran to the cops. We soon realized there
was only one person that could give us what we wanted, and
that person was you, Valerie. So the recon started all over
again. We kept watching Rod and his family, but you and your
family were the targets. Porter was primary. He was tasked
with gathering information on family Granger. I used my CIA
clearance to run background checks on you three and your
extended family. Everything was proceeding just as planned.
Rod had told us you, and you alone, could identify the project
file. Porter had determined that your kid was your one weak
spot. The background checks came back clean on you and the

kid, but we had the red flag on Granger. I asked around. I made discreet inquiries and came up empty on the guy, so we didn't worry about him."

"The buyer. Who's the buyer?"

Moore wasn't having any of it. He was back in control of his emotions and the situation. "Look, if I'm spending the rest of my life in some deep dark CIA hole, then I'm telling this story my way. And another thing: you're answering my questions when I'm finished. I want to know how you got onto us. You don't like it? Kill me."

The silence lay heavy in the air. No one spoke. I knew enough to know Valerie wasn't thinking about how to respond. She'd led Moore to this point for a reason. The lights went out, but Moore didn't scream this time. When the flashlights came back on, Ryan was holding two of them and shining them on Moore. Hodges and Franks could be seen cutting the bindings away from Moore, sitting him up and turning him around with his back now to the entrance of the old jail and me. Moore was now facing Valerie, Wakefield, Zach, and Julia, but I don't think he could see them. The flashlights were placed on the floor in such a manner as to make the beams of light cross each other a few feet in front of Moore's face. Moore was sitting on the floor rubbing his arms and legs, now free of their restraints.

"Porter came up with the kidnapping plan," Moore said, "but I liked the idea. I know we made a mistake not taking Ron's CIA past more seriously," he added before pausing. He looked up at the group standing in front of him, and then down at his chest.

"What in the hell is this?"

"Those are damp paper towels smeared with a fake blood

product called Truclot, by LUNA Corporation. The military uses Truclot to train field medics. The product resembles human blood in every way, especially smell."

He peeled the fake bloody towels off his shirt and tossed them on the floor. Moore looked from side to side, and then behind. If he noticed me near the open cast iron door of the old jail, he didn't show it.

"It was all an act?" he asked.

"The buyer, Tom. Tell me about the buyer," Valerie repeated.

"But how?" he asked, and then, answering his own question, "Julia! You're in here, Julia, aren't you? You ran that little program on your little box and fooled me," he said. He cupped his hands over his eyes and searched the group until he found her. "My other mistake was you. I should've taken it to the next step with you."

"You'll have plenty of time to enumerate your mistakes later. Right now, I want to know about the buyer," Valerie demanded.

"I'm getting to it. Ease up. Tell me something; did Julia crack and spill it all for you?"

Valerie walked out of the shadows and squatted down so she was face to face with Tom.

"No, you self-righteous pig." She dropped an earpiece on his lap before she walked away. "Julia remained loyal to you till the end. Unlike you, she never said a word. The buyer. I want to know about the buyer."

"What is this?" he asked, holding the earpiece in the light. "It's an earpiece. So what?"

"You wanted to know how we got onto you. That's how.

That earpiece was in my daughter's ear you dumbass. Now, tell me about the buyer."

Seemingly unfazed Moore asked, "Don't you want to know the rest?"

"Fine. Go ahead. I can see you have a deep desire to hear yourself talk. So go ahead and talk, Tom."

"Everything was in place. The plan was flawless. We take the kid and then you exchange the project associated with DOD file 97CLK for your daughter's safe return. But the DOD screwed it all up. They moved up the approval date. They decided to fast-track the project. We had to scramble. That's why we hired the local boys to kidnap Leecy, and not real pros. Another mistake, I admit, but in the end we accomplished the goal. We had the girl, and then I got greedy. I lost sight of the original plan. I wanted to make you, Valerie, work for me, and that clouded my judgment."

Valerie's laughter filled the room.

"You egomaniac. You actually believe that if not for a few mistakes, this colossal cluster-fuck of a plan of your design would've worked? Are you really that arrogant? Look where you are right now. Hodges and Franks have their firearms trained on you. It took me twenty minutes to get you to break. You picked an emotionally compromised woman to try and recondition. She wasn't under your spell, Tom; she was reliving a past event. But you, with your superior behavioral analytic skill, missed it. You thought she was responding to you. She wasn't. I saw what Julia was going through. How do you miss a thing like that? She was only looking for a way out. I gave her one. You underestimated Granger, and didn't even uncover one thing about my past. The shot I made in the dark from twenty-five feet away should've been enough to tip you to something, but it didn't. No, and now we have your laptop. The identity of the buyer and the specifics about his bag and payment are in your notes. We know who he is. Julia's already tracked his passport. We have his flight information. I just want you to confirm what we have, but at this point it doesn't really matter. You've confirmed enough of what's in your files for us to know the rest is accurate.

"Zach was right about you. You're so convinced that you are the smartest person in the room that you fail to give anyone else any credit for being intelligent. That's what screwed you, Tom, not Julia, or the mistakes you made. Because if you were as smart as you thought you were, those mistakes could've been overcome. But you're not. Your exaggerated sense of self was your undoing. It was your own hubris."

The sound of footsteps on the stone floor replaced Valerie's words. One by one, the room began to empty. First to leave the old jail were Franks, Hodges, and Ryan. Julia and Wakefield followed them out of the room. Zach was bringing up the rear when it happened.

Moore sprang to his feet, grabbing the young MIT grad around the neck with his left arm and holding a gun to Zach's head with his right hand.

"My hubris? What about yours?" he screamed at Valerie. "Who doesn't disarm a prisoner? Now, I'm walking out of here. I'm driving away in one of the SUVs, or I'll shoot him. Do you understand me?"

Wakefield spoke for the first time.

"Thanks Tom," she said. "I wanted this to end cleanly, with no loose ends."

Her words had a chilling effect on Moore. I could see him piecing the puzzle together in his mind; he was an extremely smart person, after all. The problem was: he wasn't the smartest person in the room.

Valerie pulled her weapon and fired. The shot struck Moore between the eyes.

Valerie said, "We just needed you to give us a reason."

Zach could be heard repeating, "Holy shit. Holy shit!"

"You're fine, Zach," Valerie assured him. "Why don't you head on up the stairs so Ryan and Hodges can remove the body?"

Hodges and Ryan hustled down the stairs and loaded the body into a black body bag Valerie had asked Lester to procure for her earlier. I watched them double time it back up the stairs with Moore heavy in the bag. I was about to ask Valerie a question when a long shadow appeared on the floor. It was Wakefield.

"I'm impressed," she said. "The Mossad trains their people well. I'd heard about their interrogation techniques, but tonight was a first for me. The way you twisted him up and spun him out was impressive. But tell me, how'd you know he'd make a play at the end?"

"His ego was too massive to sustain a hit like the one he took when he was broken. The only reason I asked him to play a role in confirming the data on the computer was to repair the damage to his ego. Once he became combative again with me, insisting he be allowed to say what he wanted to say, I knew he was ready. All I needed to do at that time was tear him down again. Humiliate him one more time. It was only a matter of when, not if, he'd act, to prove to himself he was the smarter person."

"And the gun?" Wakefield asked.

"What about it?"

"Was it loaded?"

"Does it matter?"

Wakefield didn't respond right away. She turned toward the stairs before speaking.

"So, even before we made contact with Leecy, you decided not to give Moore what he wanted. I suppose we could play the what if game and speculate how this could've ended, but I've never been one to second guess." Pausing briefly on the stairs, Wakefield turned to face us.

"I'm grateful to you both. We'll pick up the other bad guys on our way out of town. They'll be debriefed, and then dealt with accordingly. I've already forwarded the information about the buyer to the FBI. They'll pick him up when he lands in Atlanta." She turned again and walked up the stairs, stopping to say, "Tell Leecy that Julia won't face prosecution. I'll personally see to it that she gets the help she needs. I don't think we could've pulled this off tonight without her."

"Lester said to tell you that Porter's injuries prevent him from being transported tonight," I said.

"No, I'm sure Lester is mistaken. We'll pick up Porter as planned."

"We could've pulled it off without Julia, you know, but it would've been a lot bloodier," Valerie said.

Wakefield laughed, and then she was gone.

I hugged and kissed Val before taking her by the hand, and we walked up the narrow staircase of the old jail together. We stepped onto the lawn of City Hall, only to realize Wakefield, Hodges, Franks, Ryan, Julia, Zach, the SUVs, the ambulance, and the other vehicles had all been driven away.

"How did they do that so fast?" I asked. "Looks like we're

walking."

"No, we're not. Look over there," Valerie said as she pointed toward the restaurant.

I could see the parking lights of the Honda Civic as the car drove toward us.

"I told her to go to her grandparents," I said.

"Yeah, I know you did, but she's smarter than you, and knew we'd need a ride home."

I held Valerie's hand as we crossed the lawn of City Hall. I stopped in front of the Historical Marker and said, "Wait, I want to read this."

"'December 10th, 1890. The citizens of Parkland, Georgia were slaughtered on this spot by a neighboring tribe of Cherokee Indians. The fifty citizens lost their lives in what is considered the most deadly attack by Indians on settlers living on Georgia soil,'" I finished reading.

"What do you make of this, Mr. Wild Indian Man?" Valerie asked with a smile.

"It's all bullshit. My great uncle told me about this when I was a kid. His version was very different."

I heard Leecy calling us from the car. "Come on. Let's go home."

"Well, what did he tell you?" Val asked.

When I didn't respond right away, she pressed.

"Are you going to tell me what your uncle told you?"

"Was the gun loaded?" I countered.

Val smiled again and said, "Get in the car, Granger. Let's go home."

"What are you two talking about?" Leecy asked.

"Your father is keeping secrets, Leecy," Valerie said as she buckled her seatbelt.

Leecy reversed out of the parking space, saying, "No secrets, Dad. You know the rule."

"Mom's keeping secrets, too, Leecy," I said in my best child-like voice.

Leecy was speeding away from City Hall, lecturing, "It's been a long couple of days. I haven't showered since I can't remember when, and I wanna sleep in my own bed. So spill, you two."

"He won't tell me the true story behind the historical marker," Valerie informed Leecy.

"She won't tell me if the gun that was left on Moore's person was loaded or not," I said.

"Easy, the gun was loaded. Even a nut job like Moore would've noticed the weight difference between an empty gun and a loaded gun. As far as that bogus Historical Marker is concerned, I Googled that last year after the topic came up in history class. People did die there, but only after the citizens of Parkland, as Park City was known back then, kidnapped some of the Indian women and children that were passing through the area. The white citizens wanted to force the Indians to leave the area and thought they could achieve that goal by taking hostages. The Indians were preparing to meet the demands of the settlers and break camp. The Indian Chief sent a scout to the white settlement, which was located on the land where City Hall now stands, to make sure the Indian women and children were being treated well. That's not what the scout witnessed. No, instead he witnessed the white men taking advantage of the women and some of the older children. The scout reported back to the Chief and the rest is history, literally."

"Interesting that kidnapping and sexual assault almost happened again in the same place. I wonder if Moore knew about the true story and picked that spot on purpose," I said.

"No, the spot was chosen because of its proximity to the police station," Leecy said.

"And now we know the answer to the other question," I said.

"What question?" Leecy asked.

"The question of who's the smartest person in the room." Valerie answered.

EPILOGUE

December 23, 2013

Holiday travel was in full swing, as Christmas was two days away. The Atlanta Hartsfield-Jackson International airport was as busy as I'd ever seen it. Valerie and I were flying to New York, renting a car, and driving to New Haven, Connecticut, to visit Leecy for the holidays.

Leecy had left for Yale in late August, and we hadn't seen her since. She was taking a double load of classes in pursuit of her degree, so there was no time for family visits even during scheduled school breaks. She would call us occasionally and we'd Facetime with her, but that just wasn't the same as seeing her in person. We missed her, and decided to do something about it.

"Have you ever?" Valerie asked as we slogged through the main concourse after checking our luggage at curbside check-in.

"No, this is ridiculous, and we haven't even made it to the line for security yet."

"Maybe the crowds will thin out once we get to our gate," she said, and then asked, "Did you drop off all the gifts? Did you see Lester and Elizabeth?"

"Yes. All gifts were delivered. I did see the new Chief of

Police and his wife this morning. You should've come with me, because I got to see baby Winston."

"You did? Is he as precious as his pictures? How's Liz?"

"Yes, and yes he is, and she's doing great. They're all just great. Liz said to tell you she'd miss you. She said Park City won't be the same without Valerie Granger living there."

Valerie turned toward me in the security line, and in one of her rare moments of self-doubt, said, "We're doing the right thing?"

Not really a question, but more of a statement seeking confirmation. I wrapped my arms around her and kissed the top of her head.

"Doing? We've done it. No time for second guessing now. We've sold our home. Our belongings. Our cars. We resigned our positions at INESCO. It's all done, sweetheart. We're unencumbered."

She leaned her back against me again and watched the faces of the people in the crowd. The security line wasn't moving very fast. We had plenty of time to watch the people in the crowded airport as we inched forward at a snail's pace. We were content to be there and just be.

"David called again," Val said suddenly, "while you were out this morning. He asked me to reconsider."

"Really? I thought he was happy with the decision."

"Mom and Dad are sorry to see us move away, and are struggling with why I didn't bring them into my confidence sooner, but they'll get over it. They just need a little time."

"What'd you say?"

"I just told them all I loved them, and we'd come back to visit regularly. But I made it clear we wanted to move out of the area and be closer to wherever Leecy wound up. They'll be okay. Change is hard on everyone."

"INESCO is in good hands. They'll be fine. Your family will come around."

We'd reached the ID and ticket check portion of the TSA line and presented ourselves for inspection. Once through, we entered the body scanner. That was that. We were through security. We slipped on our shoes and headed for the down escalator, the plane train, and eventually our destination at Concourse C.

The crowd of people waiting for the plane train resembled a New York subway platform at rush hour. We had to elbow our way through the large mass of bodies to get to the moving sidewalks. I preferred the moving sidewalks to the train, anyway. The walking gave me a chance to stretch everything out in preparation for sitting on the plane. We walked around a family standing in the middle of the floor staring up at the arrival and departure screens.

That's when I saw a familiar face.

"Your two o'clock," I said to Val.

She looked to her left before turning her head to the right. She saw the person in question and looked down at the floor.

"Yes, I see. Don't forget, Leecy is making dinner for us in her apartment tonight. Do you think we'll make it by 10:00 p.m.?"

I looked up and slightly to the left before responding. Another familiar face.

"Yes, I see that'll be tough to do. I thought we were surprising her tonight."

"We were going to surprise her, but I called and warned her we were coming. She's very excited to see us. She said she had lots to tell."

Val stepped off the moving sidewalk and veered toward the escalator for Concourse C, and I followed her lead. We snaked our way through the crowd and found a spot in line and waited our turn on the escalator. I checked my watch. It was 3:15 p.m. Our flight left in an hour. We had plenty of time and no reason to rush.

At the top of the escalator, we turned right with the crowd. We moved like cattle through a short corridor. When the crowd reached the main hall of Concourse C, we broke to the right toward Gate 13. The gate was crowded. It appeared everyone in Atlanta was flying to New York City. I looked around for a place to sit down but found nothing. Valerie pulled me by the arm.

"Come on," she urged, "Gate 10 is empty. We can sit down over there."

I looked in the direction she was pulling to see she was right. Gate 10 was deserted, and for good reason. There was a cleaning crew assembled outside the adjacent restroom. They were busy roping off the area, and everyone was giving them a wide berth.

We found a couple of seats on the far end of the gate area, facing the window. We sat down with our backs to the crowds and watched the dance of people with orange-tipped flashlights, luggage movers, fuel trucks and planes. We were the only people in the gate area. That is, until I saw the figures approaching us in the reflection of the window. Then I saw their faces as they sat down in the seats behind us.

"I take it you orchestrated the bathroom scene for our benefit. Or are you guys flying commercial, now?" I asked.

"Yes, those are my people, Ron," Wakefield said. "I needed to talk to you and Valerie before you left for New York, and I never fly commercial. I do like to come here and people watch, though."

"Yeah, we spotted your team as we made our way through the airport," Valerie said.

"Ryan was at our two o'clock when we first entered the underground walkway," I said.

"We picked up Franks at our ten o'clock," Valerie added.

"Hodges was coming down the C Concourse escalator as we were going up. That one was blatant. I knew we'd be seeing you next," I finished.

"Like I said, I needed to talk. You two headed north to see the kid?" Wakefield asked, and then not waiting for a response she added, "Let me tell you, she's doing exceptionally well, which is no surprise to anyone at the Farm. She's at the top of her class."

Valerie said, "That's good to know, but we're more concerned with how she's doing academically."

"She's top of that class, too," Wakefield said.

"Get to it, then. Our flight boards in five minutes."

"Yes, I am fully apprised of your travel schedule. I have news from this summer."

"We're listening," I said.

"The Smith boys, Travis and Briggs. Well, it turns out they are brothers. Both of them dishonorably discharged from the Army before ever becoming actual Rangers. They'll be spending the rest of their lives in Leavenworth Penitentiary. Porter is in a Federal prison in upstate New York. His real name is

Carl Reeves. He had several outstanding warrants in the New York area, and the state was happy to prosecute him. Porter was not Army. He was a friend of Moore from Moore's college days."

"Sounds like those guys are where they need to be. What about Julia?"

"Julia and Zach are heading a new division in charge of updating and protecting the Federal payment systems. Julia showed us how Moore wiped the system clean of Travis and Porter and changed Briggs Smith's file information. She told us that Moore planned to erase all of them from the system once they had their big payday. Julia is a very bright girl, and I've also been making sure she gets the therapy she needs. Turns out she was abused by her stepfather. That explains the PTSD-like reaction to Moore's tactics."

"What about the buyer?" Val asked.

"The FBI picked him up when he landed. I don't know his exact location at the moment, but I'm sure it's unpleasant."

"Thank you for the update. I'm happy Julia is going to be okay. I know Leecy will be glad to hear the news," Valerie said.

"Leecy already knows," Wakefield said, "which brings me to my real reason for being here. You two are without a home, your child is away at college, and you don't have anything tying you down. I was curious what you are planning to do with this new footloose lifestyle."

"We haven't given it that much consideration," Valerie said.

"Here's something to consider, then," Wakefield said. "You two make an excellent team. You know what each other's thinking, like ESP. I could sure use it on my team. I want you two to come work for me. Freelance, of course. Freelance pay is really good. More than enough to supplement your new lifestyle."

Valerie looked at me and said, "I take it freelance work still means what it used to mean?"

"It does. I have something on the books that a family of three would be a perfect cover for."

"Sounds interesting. When would we start?" Val asked.

"As soon as possible."

The gate attendant's voice came over the loudspeaker. She was announcing the First Class boarding of Flight 2217 for New York. That was our flight. I stood up, ready to leave, but Valerie lingered a bit longer in her seat before standing and taking my hand.

"We can't speak for Leecy," I said to Wakefield, "and I wouldn't dare insert myself into her business."

"Here," Wakefield said, handing Val an envelope, "you should read this. I think it'll help you make your decision."

"Goodbye, Tammy, and happy holidays," I said, as Valerie and I walked to our gate. I presented our boarding passes and headed down the jetway. We found our seats in row three. We sat and watched the people filing past us in search of their seats. The First Class attendant made the rounds, taking drink orders, which Val and I both declined. The Captain's voice was soon heard over the speakers, announcing our place in line for takeoff, the weather conditions in New York City, and flying time to our destination.

The plane was moving slowly over the tarmac when Valerie turned in her seat to face me. I looked at her fully. She was holding the envelope in her lap. She opened the unsealed flap and we read the note together.

Dear Mom and Dad,

If you're reading this, then you've talked to Wakefield, and you know there's a mission. What you don't know is I'm now part of Wakefield's team. I'm not waiting for you at my apartment. I'm sorry, but you both know how this job can be. I want you two to join me, just as Wakefield does.

There's a private jet waiting for you at Teterboro Airport to bring you to me, and car and driver waiting at LaGuardia to take you to the jet. I hope to see you soon.

All my love, respect, and admiration,

Leecy

"You in?" Val asked.
"I'm in."

ABOUT THE AUTHOR

John J. Davis is the author of the *Granger Spy Novel* series, including most recently *Blood Line* and *Bloody Truth*, available Spring 2015. He lives in the southeastern US with his wife, daughter and two dogs.

Author Website
www.johnjdavis.com